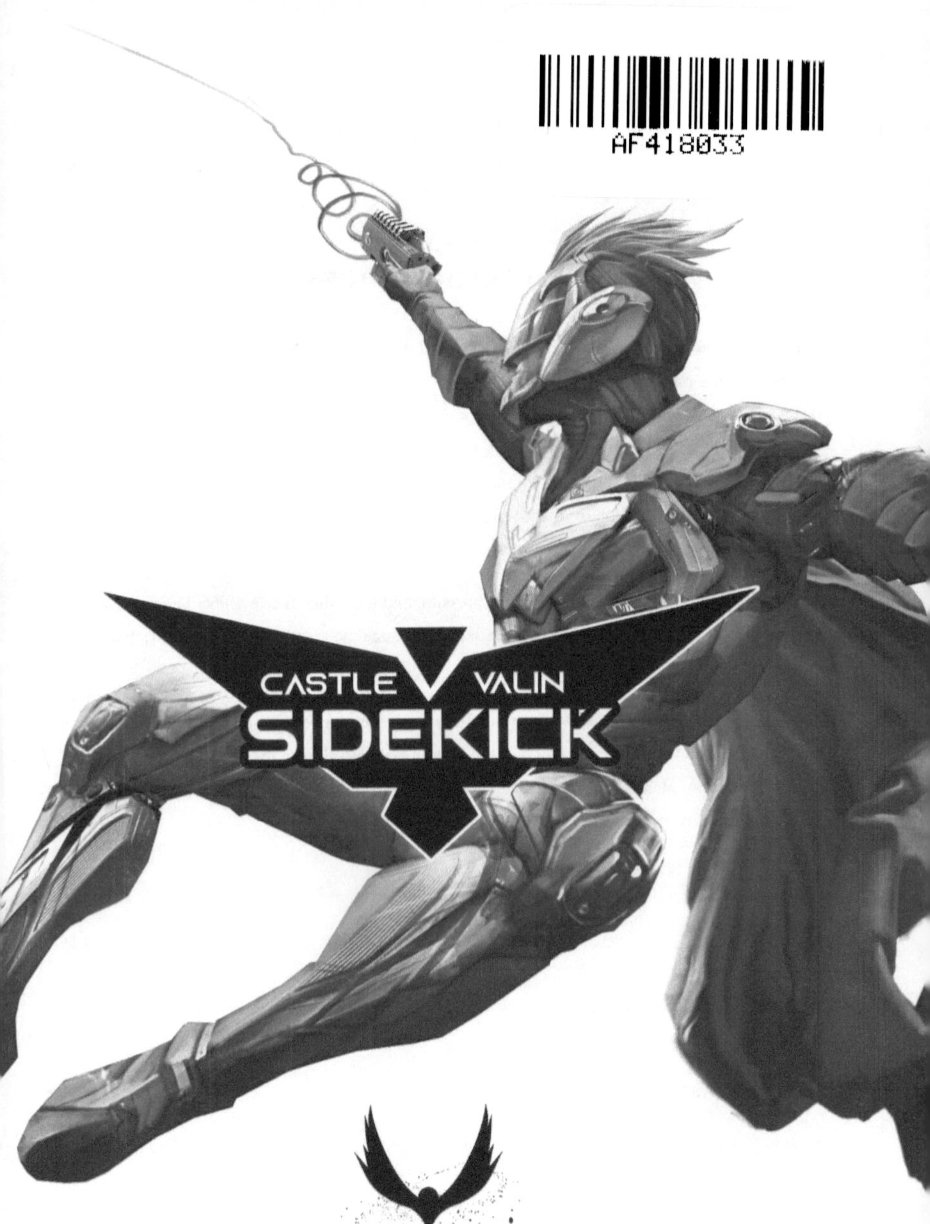
AF418033
CASTLE VALIN
SIDEKICK
aethonbooks.com
jaimecastle.com | christophervalin.com

***To both my little Sidekicks
and their furry counterparts:***
Oliver, Juneau, Sora, and Luna
—J.C.

To my dad, who always believed in me.
—CJV

ALSO IN SERIES

SIDEKICK
SUPERTEAM
SCIONS

ONE

It actually sounds pretty stupid when you say it out loud. Is it one word or two? Hyphenated maybe? Not sure. Most of us masked crime fighters don't use the term.

It also suggests someone has superpowers. Me, not so much. I have a really useful ability, but I wouldn't call it a superpower. It's kind of like an eidetic memory, only better. Most people would say it's a photographic memory, but that's wrong. I not only remember things, I can copy them. Perfectly.

Because of this, I can learn things really fast. Like martial arts skills.

Don't get me wrong; I've trained hard. Really, really hard. Enough to be a black belt in a bunch of different disciplines. But I basically just have to watch a Jackie Chan or Bruce Lee movie—or, better yet, an MMA or UFC match—and I can mimic every move perfectly.

Right now, I'm out on my nightly patrol after having

spent the afternoon watching my favorite parkour channel on YouTube. I swear, every week these guys come up with something I've never even thought of.

From up here, the city looks beautiful. Before you judge me, New York is way different from above than it is at street level. From the rooftops, leaping from building to building, it's like the Fourth of July with all the lights. Call me weird, but I love the place. It's my city.

Bleep.

Groan...

"Go ahead," I say as I plant my hands on a low wall and dash vault to the building ten feet below.

"Sawyer, I'm receiving reports of some dirty boys three blocks north of your position."

That's Amber. She's an artificial intelligence built into my helmet. And yes, she always talks like that. It's really sort of off-putting if I'm honest. You see, my partner Frank—better known to the world as the Black Harrier—has a bit of a... vice? I guess that's what you'd call it. My mom would call it womanizing—and she wouldn't be wrong.

This might be a good time to mention that my mom doesn't know I work with Frank. Actually, she doesn't even know him—no more than anyone else who watches TMZ or reads the viral gossip blogs everyone posts to social media.

Amber used to belong to him. He's since upgraded to Tiffany. I guess he likes the idea of a sexy woman in his ear all the time, and for some reason, he thought it was appropriate to hand this one down to a fifteen-year-old boy.

"Thanks, Amber," I say before taking a sharp turn and hopping to the next rooftop.

I'm about four stories up on an apartment building's fire escape. Down below, I can see at least a dozen gangbangers and one scared-looking thirty-something-year-old woman.

Silent as a jungle cat, a series of rail flows over and under the emergency ladder housings has my feet on asphalt. Three or four of the thugs notice me immediately.

"What, you've never seen a kid in a costume in October?" I ask.

Harrier hates the word costume—like it's a curse word. He calls it a uniform. Some of us would rather be honest about it. Sure, it's got technology built-in that most of the world can't even imagine, but it's still just a costume.

Now all twelve—make that thirteen, I just noticed the one sneaking up behind me—of them are staring at me. The good news is, their victim has recovered her purse and is now running away, leaving behind her high heels. They're expensive-looking. Like, what-is-she-doing-on-the-lower-east-side expensive-looking. I don't know, maybe I just still haven't gotten used to the new nightlife around this part of town.

"You screwed up, kid."

"Oh, without a doubt. For one, I forgot to turn off my old Xbox, and you know how hot those things get."

The jerks don't even give me a chance to finish my quip before they're attacking me. At least the real villains in the Big Apple like some good banter, but these guys? Ridiculous.

The first thug attacks me. I think I'll call him Bowl Cut.

Remember how I said I can replicate an MMA fight after watching it once? As I sidestep, I put that into practice, grabbing Bowl Cut's wrist with my right hand and then jabbing the heel of my left palm into his shoulder. I feel a satisfying *pop,* and I'm positive he won't be a problem anymore.

They're all a little scared now, I can tell. Though to their credit, the fight's on in full force. However, they're making the usual mistake of trying to take me on one or two at a time.

As usual, I'm kicking all their butts.

"Behind you," Amber says.

She can see things I can't, with cameras built into the helmet. That's why I'm able to elbow the guy sneaking up on me in the eye without even looking. You think eyes are off-limits? Did you miss the part where I said I was fighting thirteen guys?

And reminder... I'm only fifteen. For six and a half more minutes, anyway. At 10:34 p.m., I'll officially hit the big one-six. Yay. *Happy birthday to me.*

You'd think these losers would get the hint after I defeat five or six of them, no problem. I mean, the girl they were trying to assault is long gone now. But no, they keep coming at me, one after another. And even when they do land a punch, the armored parts of my costume—including the helmet housing Amber—make it so they hurt their hands more than they do me.

I can never understand what these guys are thinking. *I know he just took out five of my buddies without breaking a sweat, but I'm the one who's gonna beat him down.*

I have to admit that one of my favorite things to do is really petty. I find way too much joy in dodging and letting my attackers assault their buddies. Which is exactly what I just did.

Pock Mark—that's as good a name as any, I guess—is

hunched over, trying to keep the blood in his nose with two cupped hands after... I don't know... Knock-Off Nikes walloped him in the face with said bo-bo brand shoe.

As I take these guys on, I do start to wonder why this seems to be happening so much more lately. Of course, there's always crime in the city—it's freaking New York—but the past couple of weeks, it's starting to get out of control. And not just a little bit. It didn't even build up over time. Just all of a sudden, my job was ten times harder than usual.

Well, not really that hard. It just takes me ten times as long to take care of it.

Punch to the solar plexus. Kick to the jaw. Knock-Off Nikes and another one goes down, but they keep on coming. Then the part that always seems to happen in these situations: the biggest, toughest guy they have steps up and the rest back away. I'm not sure why he's been hanging back, but I have a feeling he wanted the rest to wear me down so he can take me out easier and boost his reputation as a badass.

I'm gonna show him just how wrong he is.

Big Guns runs at me with a roar, and his fist pulled back above his head like he's about to bring down a sledgehammer he isn't holding. This guy obviously never had to learn to fight because he's so big and strong. I barely have to move to step out of his way and watch him plow into the wall behind me.

"*That was hot,*" Amber says.

"Not now," I growl, sounding a bit too much like Black Harrier for my own tastes.

Big Guns says some words reserved for shows with M ratings on Netflix and spins toward me. He's really pissed off.

And pretty dazed. After shaking his head like a dog just out of the water, he tries to grab me.

"*Watch out for the ground and pound,*" Amber says.

I ignore her, but she's right. He probably wants to take me down to the pavement so I can't dodge him. I give him a knee to the junk—nope, that's not off-limits either. In fact, there's only one rule: *No killing*.

Every guy has felt that, but not many have experienced graphene armor to the groin. He slumps to his knees, holding his crotch, then falls over on his puckered face like a tree being cut down.

"Timber!" I shout, then step over his body.

The three baddies who are still conscious look at each other and try to escape.

"Nope!" I say while grabbing the two closest to me and slamming their heads together. Both fall unceremoniously to the ground. It's a little *Three Stooges*, but it works.

The third tries to limp away, and even though I'm barely breathing hard, I don't feel like chasing him. I toss my boomerang and tag him at the base of his skull, which may not have knocked him out. But when his face hits the corner of a dumpster on his way down, I'm pretty sure he's done with.

That's when I hear *him*.

"Not bad." That was a legit voice changer. In the middle of an empty alley at, like, 10 p.m. I hate it. So much. He does it when he's in costume. I've told him how lame it sounds, but he still insists on it, even when nobody's around to hear it except me.

"Not bad? I thought it was pretty damn good."

"*Mmmm, me too*," Amber purrs in my ear.

You might have noticed the little *bleep* earlier before she started talking. It's a feature I added. Truth? She used to scare the hell out of me. I'd be leaping around the city, and suddenly some sultry voice starts whispering in my ear? God... she nearly got me killed more than once.

Now, that little *bleep* lets me know she has something to tell me. I call it an Amber Alert, and yes, I know how insensitive that probably sounds. It's set up kind of like my phone's screensaver. After three minutes of silence between us, she needs to alert me that she'd like to speak. Don't look at me like that. She's a machine. She's not real—no matter how insanely hot she might sound.

"Enough, Amber," I say.

She'll know that's an order for her to go back in her box. If she wants to talk again, she'll need to alert me.

The Black Harrier steps out of the shadows, where he's apparently been standing, watching me. With the almost all-black costume, it really isn't that hard for him to do. Unlike me, with my bright red *uniform* and blond hair.

"Language."

So ridiculous. He has no problem taking me into situations where I'm more likely than not to get killed or maimed, but I'm not supposed to swear around him.

"Yeah, sorry," I say. "How long were you standing there?"

"Long enough."

I'm serious, he sounds like Darth Vader or something. I almost want to laugh sometimes.

"And you didn't think it might be a good idea to, I don't know, give me a hand?"

"You didn't need any help."

Wow. From the Black Harrier, that's pretty much the highest compliment you can get. Then, in typical fashion, he has to knock me down a peg.

"But there are still some things we need to work on to increase your efficiency."

I nod and decide not to ask him where he was all night, even though it's the fifth time in a couple of weeks I've had to patrol alone.

"Is tomorrow okay?" I always have to confirm things with him. Never assume.

"Tomorrow."

"Okay, then." I stand there awkwardly a bit longer, waiting for him to say something else. After a more-than-uncomfortable amount of time staring at one another, I say, "Well, I think I'm pretty much done here. Sounds like the cops are on the way. I need to get home to finish my home-work and check on my mom."

He grunts. He always gets extra-broody when I bring up my mom. I swear, sometimes he's such a tool that I almost don't want to be his partner anymore. I shoot my grappling hook at the top of the building next to me and prepare to go up.

"Kite."

I hate the way he says my code name. In fact, I hate that code name.

"It's 'Raptor' now," I remind him. "'Red Raptor.'"

"Right. I keep forgetting."

Yeah, sure you do. More like you're so mad I changed it without your permission that you refuse to accept it.

"But until it gets approved by—"

"...by the Guild, it's not 'official.' Yeah, so you keep reminding me."

The Guild... *guuuh.*

Basically, a hundred years ago or something, all the world's best supes decided it would be smart to inflict everyone with a bunch of laws and rules. Now, anyone who wants to fight crime has to go through them. It's like the worst kind of union imaginable, but Harrier is one of the guys in charge, so he's a real hardass about it.

He tosses me a package wrapped in newspaper. The guy's a billionaire, and he can't splurge on some gift wrap?

"Happy birthday," he says.

Dude, something strange is going on for sure. And who gets the newspaper anymore?

"Uh, thanks." This is so weird, I'm not even sure how to respond. I just stare again, waiting for something else. As usual, he just stands there, being all tough and silent.

I thumb my grappler button and rise up toward the rooftops. I cat vault upward and land on the retainer wall. I can't process the fact that I'm holding a birthday present from Harrier. I know you don't know him, but one time, a villain named Doctor Evo manipulated the genes of a Sea World–sized aquarium filled with bull sharks, and they grew legs, then proceeded to terrorize the city, somehow being able to breathe on land. This... this is way weirder than that.

As I turn around, I see Harrier pull something from his utility belt and examine it in the moonlight...

"Amber, zoom in?"

"*Anything you want, honey,*" she says.

Huh. It's some kind of business card and something scrawled on it in red ink. Even with Amber's magnification on my face mask, Harrier's moving it too much for me to read anything. I pause and watch while something changes in his demeanor. Yeah, he's wearing a mask, but I know him, and I can just tell. Whatever is written on there, it's for sure bothering Harrier.

Between his unusual absences, which have forced me to patrol alone, and giving me a birthday present—not to even mention this, something is wrong. And I can't shake the feeling in my gut that whatever has him acting so weird has gotta be really, really bad.

TWO

I didn't go home.

I needed some more time to process everything, so I decided to stay out a bit. Besides, with the growing crime throughout the city, I figure her streets need me more than usual—especially since Harrier wasn't doing much lately.

"Amber," I say, knowing I'm giving her the opportunity to gab my ear off.

"Yes, Master Vincent?"

That's my last name. Sawyer William Vincent. Lots of first names, really. She never calls me that, but she loves being sarcastic too.

I ignore the comment and ask, "What do you think that was? The card, I mean."

Amber hesitates, as if thinking. I know that's stupid, since she's just a machine, but Frank really gave her a personality and sometimes it's hard to differentiate between fact and fiction, you know?

"I don't know. Maybe an escort service?" she asks.

I roll my eyes and slide to a stop on a Chattahoochee stone rooftop.

"What in the world would he do that for?"

"Oh, sweet innocent Sawyer—"

"Okay, shut up. I know what an escort service is for. I just mean... he's freaking rich. And famous. He can get any woman in the city without even trying."

"Sometimes, it's nice to not have any... emotional attachments."

"What would you know about emotions?" I say as I start off again and clear a sizable gap.

"That's hurtful," Amber says.

"I just get the feeling it was important. That look on his face..."

I let the thought hang in the ether for a bit, and my mind is so distracted, I almost don't notice a figure standing on the rooftop as I sprint by.

Actually, I don't notice at all until Amber says, *"Proximity alert."*

It's another one of her features. She doesn't tell me when someone is nearby on street level because, well, she'd never shut up. But up here, high above the city, there are very few reasons for me to run into anyone, especially this late at night.

I stop and duck behind an HVAC system. Peering around the corner, I catch a glint of light coming off what looks to be white armor. There's definitely a figure standing in the shadows, obviously female, hard to tell her age. I see a blonde ponytail coming from under the back of her helmet, and I get a strange tingle in my stomach. What's that all about? I can barely even see the bottom of her face.

"Amber," I whisper, "see if you can tell me who that is..."

"*Analyzing.*"

I swear, as soon as I'm in charge, I'm changing the voice to some kind of butler with a British accent. It's *way* too distracting, even when she's saying words like "analyzing."

When I was reprogramming her for various new tasks, I tried to change the voice, but of course, Harrier has it locked with some encryption not even I could break through. What a hill to die on, Frank.

My helmet's heads-up-display bursts to life with over-lying green text. Some info about a new heroine known as "Osprey," but there's almost zero about her. It's really nothing more than some tweets from a guy called @byrdwotcher—and yes, based on the stuff he's saying, it's definitely a guy.

I decide that there's enough to prove she's on the good team. I have the sense enough to leave Harrier's present to me tucked between two of the dark green AC units. My hands are already up palms out, slightly raised, to show I'm not a threat as I step out from my hiding place. I don't even make it one step, saying, "Hello—" before she's jumping toward me with a flying kick that I'm barely able to block with my bracer.

"Whoa!" I gasp. I don't even know how she got to me so quickly.

The next thing I know, she's leaping off the roof and onto the one across the alley. It was super graceful, like a dancer or something. I don't know why she'd run away like that unless she has something to hide, so I take off after her.

"Wait!" I realize I probably won't be able to catch her because she's at least as fast as I am, so I pause long enough to devise a plan. It'll be hard for her to lose me with her white armor at night unless she has some tricks up her sleeve.

As if on cue, trick number one comes my way.

She turns and tosses a throwing star at me. There really isn't any danger of it hurting me through my graphene plate armor, but on pure reflex, I jump to the side. I successfully avoid it, but that gives her an even bigger lead.

I've got tricks too, you know, I think as I toss a bola at her to slow her down. I aim for her torso. I don't want her to trip and fall off the edge of the building. As if she knows it's coming, she goes into a slide and almost succeeds, but it still catches the top of her helmet and wraps around it in a weird, tangled way. Frustrated, she yanks her helmet off and tosses it at my head, forcing me to duck.

"*Wow, she's hot*," Amber says.

"Not now!" I shout, sending her into quiet mode.

While I'm distracted, both by the flying helmet and my sexy ear-partner, my quarry-turned-assailant dives off the other side of the building toward the street, which freaks me out. Can she fly?

I don't know the answer to that, but I know for sure that I can't.

Without a choice, I leap off after her and immediately shoot my grappler toward the building across the street. That's when I realize she's right in front of me, her strange, wing-like cape acting almost like a parachute. I catch a quick glimpse of her face, but she wears a white domino mask just like Harrier and me, only ours are black. Her fist is cocked back and—

POW! She punches me as my momentum takes me forward, and I start to fall until my grappler connects and starts to pull me toward the building across the street.

When I reprogrammed Amber, I included an emergency bypass in the programming. Still, the hardest part was figuring out how a machine could decipher a situation well enough to know when something really was an emergency.

Luckily, this time she's right.

"Alert. Colliding with pavement at this velocity will most likely lead to—"

"Yeah! I get it! I'd be dead."

The side of the building comes at me like a subway train. I barely have time to brace myself before slamming into it a lot harder than I want to. Despite my armor, the jarring motion alone has me feeling like I'm gonna pass out. Then I feel the line pulling me up. I get the sensation in my shoulder like a tiger just wrapped its jaws around my arm and wanted it for a toy.

Using as much effort as I have left, I throw myself over the lip of the rooftop. Hey, at least I'm not a puddle on the sidewalk below. When I turn around, I can barely see my opponent sprinting back on the other roof and grabbing her helmet.

I'm not positive, but I'm pretty sure she gives me a little wave before taking off in the other direction.

I change on the roof of my crappy apartment building as usual and take the stairs down to our little cracker box on the top floor. Looks like they painted the walls again in a sorry attempt to cover the graffiti. Never works. You can still see everything through the coat of cheap paint. And they don't even try to patch up the holes anymore.

The fight with Osprey bothers me, but I can worry about that later. That feeling I had earlier about Harrier is still nagging me a lot more. What was it about Frank that was so off tonight? That he was so nice to me, for once? And that business card. Maybe I'm paranoid. Everyone hands out business cards in New York. It was probably some shady electronics dealer who gets his merchandise when it "falls off a truck."

I haven't been home all day. I have an excuse ready to go, but then I realize it won't be necessary as soon as I walk in the door. Mom's asleep on the couch, red hair a tangled mess over her face. No big deal at eleven at night, right? Maybe she was waiting up for me.

Yeah, right.

The only reason the bottle of vodka she has nestled against her chest hasn't spilled is that it's just about empty. And the only reason the cigarette in her other hand didn't burn our building down is that the ashes fell onto a plate sitting on the floor.

I start to think she's forgotten my birthday again until I notice what's on the plate: a cupcake covered in wax from the melted candle planted in the center of it. Guess I should've stopped by after school before going out on patrol.

I grab the cigarette and the vodka and toss them, then

take a frayed blanket off the back of our ratty couch and cover Mom up. I haven't eaten since lunch in the cafeteria, so I decide to try a taste of the cupcake. The paper comes off stiff, the burned portions sticking to it. Peeling off a chunk of the bottom, I take a bite that isn't covered in wax.

Then I gag. Maybe the wax would be an improvement. Well, at least she tried this year. I'll give her that.

As usual, it's up to me to clean up the mess in the kitchen even though I didn't cause any of it. The dirty dishes have been sitting here so long that they've become science experiments, and I just can't take the smell anymore. Maybe I'll discover the next wonder drug if I test some of this stuff on the rats that live in our walls.

I grab her coffee mug that's, no doubt, been there since this morning and the cupcake plate. Lifting it reveals a home-made birthday card with a balloon drawn on a regular piece of paper folded in half. "To Sawyer, Love, Mom." Hmm. It's not much. Just four words, but it's more than I usually get from her. That's almost as strange as Harrier giving me a present.

I swear loudly. I forgot about Harrier's gift after everything that happened with Osprey.

"Sawyer?" Mom says.

My chin falls to my chest, and I let out a heavy sigh.

"Oh, hey, Mom."

I assume she's gonna berate me for being late and missing her "special" birthday celebration, but she just smiles sleepily and says, "Happy Birthday, honey."

She sits up and reaches for the TV remote.

"Thanks," I say. "Why don't you, uh—you should go to bed."

What I really need is for her to go to bed so I can go get Harrier's present, and there's no way I'm gonna be able to sneak out now that she knows I'm here.

"What? No. It's early."

"You were asleep, though," I say, desperate.

"I was just resting my eyes. But you... you have school tomorrow." I start to turn when she says, "And Sawyer. Tomorrow we'll talk about you not coming home."

I don't respond, but I'm not really too worried. Her words are slurred enough that I know she won't even remember this in the morning.

Seven steps take me to my sanctuary: a ten-by-ten bedroom with a twin bed mattress on the floor and a desk made from cinderblocks and plywood. I flip open my laptop —the one I told Mom everyone at school got thanks to a new government program—and type in my password: redR@ptor15. That's a name I can live with. Being called "The Red Kite" made me feel like I'd never be taken seriously. I mean, nobody even knows it's a bird. I do need to change the number to sixteen before I forget, though.

I'll give Mom twenty minutes before she's out cold on the couch again, and I'll be able to go retrieve the gift, but until then, I'll check for anything I can find on Osprey. It's clear that, like me, she's patterned herself after the Black Harrier in her look and style. Unlike me, however, she isn't directly connected to Harrier. If I know him, which I do, he'll freak out when he finds out some girl is out there copying him without his permission.

No major articles or blog posts, just a poorly-made 1.0 style website called The Unofficial Osprey Fan Club.

I scroll through a bunch of nonsense and speculation until I find something that causes me to stop. Somebody managed to get a shot of her with his phone. It's not all that clear, but I can still make out the bottom half of her face under that white mask of hers. Man, she looks good in that costume. I'm pretty glad I don't have my helmet on. There's no chance I wouldn't be enduring ridicule by Amber right now.

I leave a couple of comments on the message boards, fishing for some info on where I can find her. It probably won't work, but you never know when something might be helpful.

Yeah, I know it all sounds kind of stalkerish, but what am I supposed to do? It's not like there's some clubhouse where teenage costumed heroes hang out. One way or another, I need to find her and figure out why she reacted like a crazy person upon seeing me. Absentmindedly, I rub my shoulder, which still hurts.

Careful to exit out of all open browser tabs and clear my history, I slap the laptop shut. Then, I sneak out to the short hallway that connects my room and bathroom to the living room where I hope to find my mom asleep again.

Bingo. Out like a light.

THREE

RELIEVED.

It's a little after midnight, and I'm back on the rooftop where I'd first met Osprey. Luckily, she hadn't found my newspaper-wrapped birthday gift.

I feel embarrassingly excited about what might be inside, so I waste no time tearing off the paper. I can see right away that it's a new cape.

Black. What a surprise.

But as I unravel it, I realize something is different. The edges turn rigid when they're snapped out. A glance into the box, and to my further surprise, there's something else. A new utility belt? Equipped with... jets?

Okay, I totally have to check this out. Now.

It takes a little while to figure out how to attach the cape. I was thinking too hard. The cape grabbed hold of the armor like a magnet, only that definitely wasn't what it was. Graphene isn't magnetic—which is good when you consider one of Harrier's enemies controls metal through magnetism.

Frank's company—oh, right... the Black Harrier, or Franklin Douglas III, is the CEO of Douglas Industries. Honestly, I don't even know half of what they do. They're one of those companies who has their hand in every pot but makes an insane amount of money.

So, they have a crazy-awesome R&D team led by a dude named Mr. Chen. He's always coming up with crazy stuff that Harrier and I get to use on the field. Being a bit of a tech-head myself, I can't wait to probe him over what the material is.

It looks like the cape extends into a sort of glider and attaches to my gloves just like the neck does. And the jet canisters are pretty small, so I don't think they're intended for long flight, just enough for short bursts to keep me high up while gliding.

Let's give it a shot.

I start out slow and jump off the AC unit. As the edges go rigid, I'm able to float down. After a couple more tries, I start to get the hang of it. Harrier and I have used gliders before, but those were big, bulky rigs. It's a lot different when it's my actual cape. More like those wing-suit things that lets you skydive without a parachute.

Standing on the edge of the roof, I look out over New York. Nine million people going about their lives, most of them never giving a thought to people like Black Harrier and me, out there protecting them every night. I find myself scouring for Osprey, like somehow I'm gonna see her again. Like she hung around, waiting for me.

Bleep.

"Yeah?" I say, opening up the channel for Amber.

"*Is everything okay? Your heart rate has increased expo-nentially.*"

"You try jumping off a building," I say, totally lying. "Switch to silent."

I've jumped from rooftops more times than I can remember. My heart's going nuts because I'm thinking about Osprey. Damn teenage hormones. I physically shake my head in an attempt to clear my thoughts and look down at the street below.

Most people would probably hesitate at this point, but I didn't become a masked crime fighter because I was afraid of trying things. So I drop my helmet visor and leap. For a moment, I feel weightless. Then, as I start my descent, I extend the cape.

I'm able to stay in flight long enough to reach the building across the street, then I press the palm control for the jets to push me higher.

Nice. I could get used to this. Let's see how high I can go.

Getting a running start this time, I jump, straighten like an arrow, spin, and then *poof*, I let my cape snap out into rigid wings.

"Wooo!" I scream, and it gets buried in the sound of wind whipping past my head.

I cut a hard turn toward the nearest skyscraper and circle up to the top. It's an older building, probably built in the 1930s, and has those convenient ledges that Harrier likes to perch on like he's a stone gargoyle. Fits his personality.

I stop on one to take a short break, then take a dive off the edge, a good fifty stories above the street. I blast the jets again and straighten out. At this height, I could probably glide across half the city.

A red kite, believe it or not, is a bird in the Accipitridae family, which also includes other raptors like eagles, hawks, buzzards, and, of course, harriers. If people knew that, I wouldn't need to change my name. But right now, soaring like this? I feel more like my bird of prey namesake than I ever have before.

Bleep.

Guuuh. Not now.

I close my eyes and feel the air blowing against my face, and I realize I've never felt more free in my life. No mom, no school, no Black Harrier, no worries. Just flying through the night sky above the city lights. If I start getting around this way, I might miss the fun of leaping across the city parkour-style, but I think it'd be worth it.

I stay at a decent height to practice some more, figuring I'll circle down to my apartment building when I get close.

Bleep.

Another Amber Alert comes in as I'm coming up on another skyscraper closer to my neighborhood.

"What is it?!" I say at the exact moment I realize I'm not gonna clear the huge building, so I tap the palm control again.

"*You're out of fuel,*" she says. "*Bone dry.*"

She's absolutely right, but it's too late.

I try a sharp turn to get past the building, and it looks like I just might make it, but a gust of wind pushes me back at the last second, and I smack hard into the corner.

Ow! That effing hurt. Knocked the wind out of me, too.

"*Sawyer, you're heading—*"

"I know!"

Now I'm in free-fall. And it feels like I'm about to pass—

Wham! Something collides with me, and for a split second, I think I'm hitting the ground sooner than I expected. Or maybe the side of the building again. But instead of being, like, *dead*, I'm heading back up somehow.

Realization hits me about as hard as the pavement would have. Harrier was spying on me. Watching. He probably gave me this birthday gift as some kind of sick test to see how I'd behave in such a dire situation. That jerk. I can't believe it. I mean, yeah, he probably saved my life, but—

"Hold on. We're almost on the roof."

Wait. No robotic voice-changer. That wasn't Harrier. That wasn't even close to Harrier. It's a woman for sure, but not Amber.

As soon I feel myself lying on a rooftop, I retract my visor and do what anyone would after an experience like that. I throw up.

A lot.

At the absolute worst time possible, too. Because when I look up at my savior, I immediately realize that I'm finally face to face with the woman I love.

Well, technically, we just barely met. But still, I think I love her. Especially now.

"What happened?" I ask Osprey as she stands above me, closed fist on one cocked hip. So. Freaking. Beautiful. "How did you..." My voice is hoarse and sore from puking. I sound almost as ridiculous as Harrier.

"I thought I made it clear for you to stay out of my business," she says.

Whoa, whoa...

I think for a second she's gonna kick me or something. I toss up two placating hands and say, "I wasn't—I didn't—"

Real smooth, Sawyer.

"*Look at those curves*," Amber says.

"Shut up!" I shout, slapping my helmet.

"*Excuse* me?" Osprey says.

My face goes as red as my costume, and I try to stand. It's not graceful, but I make it to my feet.

"Not you..." I say.

"There someone else up here?"

"I—uh..."

"It doesn't matter. I'm only going to tell you this one time. Whatever this is... it stops now."

What the actual eff is going on here? This is the second time tonight that she happens to be where I am, and she's acting like I was what—spying on her? Stalking her? I think about saying something, but she turns to walk away. Her costume is so much like Harrier's and mine, only... tighter.

"Hey!"

She stops but doesn't turn to face me.

"I... Thanks. Thanks a lot."

Then, she does something that makes my stomach flop around like a fish. She smiles at me. I can't believe she looks so good when she's not beating me up.

"Yeah," she says. "Just be more careful with your new toys next time."

"How did you know—"

My next words bounce around in my mouth, my tongue

battling with my teeth like I'd never talked before. She's walking back toward me.

"Mind if I...?" She gestures at the new gear.

"Uh... yeah... for sure! Go ahead."

Osprey looks at the edges of my new cape, then checks out the small jets on the belt. She leans in close, and all I can think about is my breath.

Is my breath okay?

I just freaking threw up. Of course my breath isn't okay.

Omigod, I had that chili dog for dinner tonight. Better hold my breath. I need a mint. Why don't I have any mints? I need to add a mint compartment to my utility belt.

"Pretty sweet, but not much capacity for fuel. Which I'm sure you realized a few minutes ago as you were plummeting toward the asphalt." She laughs, and it's literally the most beautiful sound I've ever heard.

"Uh, yeah. Makes sense, really. It would be way too heavy otherwise."

As she stands, done examining my belt, she tucks a lock of blonde hair behind her ear. "Harrier's a smart guy. He's got it all figured out."

Why do I feel so jealous? Of course she worships him. Judging by her costume, she's practically *his* stalker.

But obviously, she's been keeping an eye on me also. I smile, just thinking about it. Then I hope she didn't notice me smiling as I return my face to normal. Crap. What's my normal face look like? I purse my lips a few times, trying to act natural.

"You okay?" she says.

"Yeah. Fine." My throat's still hoarse. Probably will be

until I drink some water. I decide to take advantage of her sudden shift in demeanor. "So. You, uh, patrol around here much?"

"Just recently. I've been going around to different areas. Getting to know the city better."

"Oh. That's cool."

That's cool?

I'm a badass freaking crime-fighter, why do I sound like such a dork? Get it together, Sawyer. You're gonna blow this. "So, earlier..."

She looks down and seems a little embarrassed. "Yeah. I know. I'm sorry."

Sorry? I don't expect that at all.

She continues. "I was sort of following you, and when you caught me, I didn't know what to do. I... guess I got a little carried away."

"You were following me?" I say, hoping it doesn't sound too much like an accusation because I'm more than a little flattered.

I shrug. "Oh, yeah, I get it. Well, I guess you more than made up for it. By saving my life, I mean."

When she doesn't respond, I try to think of what to say next. And nothing comes to mind. Absolutely *nada*. The awkward silence feels like it lasts for days. I realize I'm staring at her like an idiot, and I probably still have vomity drool all over my chin.

Finally, she breaks the silence.

"Well, you take care of yourself. Next time, I might not be around when you get into trouble." She grins at me and shoots her grappler across the street. It looks like the same design Harrier and I use, attached to the bracers on our forearm.

"Wait!" Geez, could I sound any more desperate? "Do you think sometime we could… I don't know… patrol together or something? Maybe tomorrow night?" Smooth, d-bag. Real smooth.

She thinks for a couple of seconds. Then, to my utter amazement, says, "Sure, why not? But what would the Black Harrier have to say about it?"

I make a way-too-exaggerated wave of dismissal, along with a lame sound like air leaking out of a tire. Apparently, I'm just so bad at this. "It's not like he's my dad or anything."

"I wondered about that," she says. Before I can respond, she says, "Okay, it's a date. I'll meet you here at eight." She thumbs the button on her grappler and disappears into the night.

I almost can't move, stunned at hearing the word "date." Then I remember I have vomit all over my costume.

And my breath.

FOUR

School.

Much worse than fighting crazy villains.

People assume the really evil guys like Doctor Delay or the Magnetist come from insane asylums or high-security prisons. I think they come from my high school.

Like my mom, the teachers have no idea who I am. No one does. They also don't know my special talent. Because of that, I purposely play dumb with them, so they don't expect too much out of me. I can live with Bs. And I don't need my guidance counselor trying to stick me in some AP class because she found out how smart I really am.

That's not me being arrogant. Things like complex math problems and spelling come as easy to me as fighting or parkour. If I see the solution once, I'll know it forever. Same with athletics. Nobody knows how good I am at sports, especially gymnastics and wrestling. Otherwise, I'd be spending all my free time after school practicing with a team.

There is one thing I'm not afraid to excel at in school, and that's technology. Between my computer class and robotics club, I get to use school hours to play around with things I'm working on without drawing any attention to myself. I've been able to make some pretty cool modifications to my costume and old utility belt. I even came up with the prototype for the retractable grapplers we use to get around the city, although Harrier was able to create much cooler ones based on my original idea.

Money makes everything easier, in case you didn't know.

Even there, though, I don't really fit in, because the tech geeks see me as just some skater dude who listens to loud music. But the skaters think I'm a poser. And the popular kids... don't get me started. They don't even notice me.

I'm pretty much invisible to just about everyone here. And that's just the way I like it. Who needs a bunch of friends always calling up, seeing if I want to go hang out at... I don't know, like, the mall or whatever? Not me.

And, it's not like I'd have the time or the money to take any girls out on dates. That's why I don't bother asking anyone out.

Yeah, *that's* the reason.

For example, here comes the hottest girl in school—the captain of the cheerleading squad, Fabiola. All the girls trailing behind her in her entourage are almost as hot as she is, too. They're walking by me when my skateboard falls out of my locker and rolls right in front of them. They step right over it and keep going without even looking in my direction.

See? That's me. I just show up in my plain T-shirt and jeans, no popular bands or brand names plastered all over my clothes, nothing to draw attention to myself. I keep a low profile and blend in with the crowd. It almost always works.

Almost.

Unfortunately, there's always some Neanderthal whose hobby is to spot invisible people like me and make us his next victim. My personal caveman's name is Logan, and I'm pretty sure his parents actually named him after the guy with the claws from the comics and movies. Except this guy only has the bad attitude without the Bushido code and dry wit to go with it.

He's also a lot taller than the Logan in the comic books. In fact, he's the tallest kid in school. He plays center on the basketball team and fullback on the football team. Not to mention a bunch of other stuff. But I'm not here to read his triumphal entry. He's pretty much everything that school-version of Sawyer William Vincent is not.

With all those things, he doesn't have a lot of time for stuff like homework, but it doesn't seem to bother anyone else or hurt his grades. Not even the teachers or administrators.

As long as he can manage to juggle his various sports schedules, what difference does it make if he actually learns anything?

I think I showed up on his radar a few weeks ago when he was picking on a kid smaller than me, and I decided to get in the way. He was tormenting this poor guy, and everyone was either too indifferent or too scared to do anything about it. Even though I made it look like an accident, my interference still drew Logan's attention enough that he abandoned the other kid and made me his new "buddy." Obviously, I could pretty much destroy him in two seconds, but like I said, I try to stay incognito.

So, I let him think he's pushing me around, and just make sure he never really connects with a punch or shoves me too hard into a locker. I've watched enough stuntmen in action films to know how to make it look real to everyone else, including Logan.

Meanwhile, the smaller kid I saved, Javier, has attached himself to me in kind of an annoying way. We definitely don't hang out after school or anything, but he tries to sit with me at lunch and stuff. And he isn't much of a conversationalist. I try not to be mean, but a lot of times, I find myself trying to lose him or make an excuse to get away.

Today, he sneaks up on me in the hall like a little ninja as I'm putting my skateboard back in my locker.

"Hey!" His voice is high-pitched, like it's perpetually in the process of changing but never quite gets there.

"Hey, Javi." I hope I don't sound as annoyed as I feel when I greet him.

His unibrow creases as he searches for something to say. I can tell he wants to talk to me really badly but has no idea what topic to bring up.

"Um... did you... do your math homework?"

I toss the books I'll need for my next couple of classes into my backpack and pull out the ones I'm done with. "Yeah."

"Me too! How about history?"

"Yeah," I say again as I slam my locker and double-check the lock.

"Cool. I did it, too. What about—"

"I did all my homework. No need to go down the checklist." I try walking away without being too obvious that I'm trying to ditch him.

He follows behind me. *Come, little doggie.*

"Yeah, I finally finished it all, too. I was up until almost nine-thirty working on it. I thought my mom was gonna kill me for being up so late."

"Well, I'm glad to see you survived." Ugh. Why did I do that? I'm just encouraging him.

"I was wondering if you wanted to hang out after school sometime. Are you into collectible card games?"

"Uh... not really. I can't afford them." I try speeding up. Almost to class, then I'm home free.

"Yeah, I have to save my allowance for weeks to get a single pack. Um... I don't have a skateboard, but I could watch you do your tricks. I don't mind."

"I don't know if that would be very fun for you. I'm sure we can figure something out one day. When I'm not too busy." I'm *always* busy. That's my secret loophole without lying to him.

He starts to sound desperate. He must be able to tell he's losing me. "Maybe we could—"

Suddenly, Javier freezes like a rabbit who just spotted a wolf. His eyes widen as he stares past me and starts to get this weird twitch. He makes a strange, high-pitched squeaking sound.

I turn around and spot Logan coming toward us, and mentally prepare myself for the idiocy. Javier scurries off in the opposite direction like the rodent he resembles. One of Logan's minions tries to trip him, but he manages to hop over the guy's leg and get away. Wow, that kid can really hop, too.

The bell rings, and I use the excuse to follow after Javi. I try to play it cool since I'm not actually afraid of the muscle-for-brains bully, but I also don't want him to know I'm not afraid.

It's really a delicate game I play, and it sometimes gets tiring. There've been more than a few times I almost clocked the dude.

I'm not gonna get far, anyway, since Logan and Javi are both in my history class, and so is...

Fabiola.

I take my seat one row behind and a seat diagonal to her. Logan plops down directly behind me and shoves his desk into my shoulder blades.

A few giggles issue from his equally brainless cronies, but Mr. Peel appears in the doorway just in time to shut everyone up.

"Mr. Andrews," he says to Logan. "Why don't you come sit in the 'special' seat?"

He motions to a spot at the front where no one likes to sit because the ceiling tends to leak on rainy days. I snicker a little. It's raining. In the olden days, he'd probably be wearing a "dunce" cap.

"I'll get you later, loser," he grunts in my ear as he shoves by. Then to Mr. Peel, he says, "Thank you, sir. I love sitting this close to your desk."

"Mmm-hmm. Turn to page three hundred and ninety-four."

I absentmindedly turn to a page bearing a picture of Ulysses S. Grant, while watching Fabiola flip her long, straight, black hair over her shoulder. The smell of fresh lilacs wafts toward me.

Then, I can't breathe when she turns and stares at me. Her eyes are so green, especially when contrasted with her chestnut skin tone. I smile awkwardly, but she definitely doesn't smile back. She, instead, makes a little face like I'm a clump of dog poo on the bottom of her sandal.

It's about that time that I realize *everyone* is staring at me. Then I hear my name.

"Mr. Vincent... Sawyer... are you listening?"

I snap out of it and realize Mr. Peel is talking to me. I look at him.

"If you're done gawking," he says.

The whole class starts laughing, as if that's what I need.

"I was... I..." I've got nothing, so I shut up.

"Right," he says. "So, can you tell me anything about Ulysses S. Grant?"

What I didn't say is: *Actually, I can tell you everything about Ulysses S. Grant. I know way more than you do about our eighteenth president who was supposed to be with Lincoln the night Abe was assassinated, who won the first battle for the Union in the Civil War, hated wearing uniforms, and whose real name is Hiram, by the way.*

Instead, I say, "Looks like he was in some kind of war."

The class laughs again, only at me this time.

Mr. Peel turns around to write on the whiteboard, and I feel something wet hit the back of my neck. I reach up and pull down a spit-soaked ball of paper. I turn to see one of Logan's lackeys laughing and prodding his friends.

Two seconds. It's all I need, and they'd never walk again.

The rest of class goes pretty much as usual, and I try to keep my head down and get to lunch.

When the bell finally dismisses us, Mr. Peel yells something about homework, but I don't hear him as I shove past Logan's goons and rush back to my locker. I was hoping to make it to the cafeteria before Logan can catch up, but a voice behind me says I had my hopes too high.

"Guess what day it is today, loser?" Logan invades my personal space as he towers over me. I act as casual as possible under the circumstances. He makes absolutely sure he's loud enough for everyone in the hallway to hear. They do, and now, they're all staring in our direction. Everyone.

I should just stay quiet and play dumb. But I don't. I recently read that some expert somewhere says we have like eighty emotions in addition to the ones we already recognize. Right now, I'm feeling all of them coursing through me. Probably more than I can even identify. From worry over Harrier and what might have been on that business card to concern that my mother might actually remember how late I was out last night and try to ground me when I get home. Then, there's anger toward Logan, and excitement over meeting Osprey tonight to patrol together.

So, no. I should stay quiet, but I don't.

"I'm pretty sure your mom said it was her birthday when I was with her last night."

Logan is slightly infuriated at this. No, that's not true. He's pissed. Especially when everyone else, including his friends, laugh so hard at my answer. They start egging him on, asking if he's gonna take this crap from some "little pleb" like me. He responds in the only way someone as dumb as he knows how. He grabs the front of my shirt in his huge hand and tries to be more clever. He fails for sure, but hey, it's the effort that matters, right?

"Wrong. It's the day you finally get your ass beat." His face is red. Like, redder-than-my-costume red. He shoves me into my locker.

Don't say it, don't say it, don't say it... I'm gonna say it. "What's the matter? Did I wake you up when I was sneaking out of her bedroom?"

He swings. I move. He ends up punching a fist-sized impression into the locker.

Enraged and in pain, Logan screams. The string of obscenities would be seriously impressive if it wasn't aimed at me. Harrier would have a stroke if he heard me talk that way.

The crowd scatters as campus security rushes over. My first instinct is to disappear into the crowd, but that's the crimefighter me, not the high school student me. Sure, I might be able to get away, but there are too many witnesses around, so I'm gonna get busted anyway.

So much for my "powers of invisibility."

A few minutes later, Logan and I are sitting across from Principal Blanchard. If I'd ever felt okay with using the term jarhead, it would be about Mr. Blanchard. He used to be in the Marines before he became a P.E. teacher and, eventually, a principal. He still acts like he's in the military—and looks like it, too. I wouldn't be surprised if he really did eat crayons.

I have a lot of respect for veterans. Harrier saw combat in Afghanistan himself. But this guy? He's a real putz.

I look around his office at all the sports memorabilia, trophies, pennants, and I can't help but wonder, does this guy actually give a damn about education?

"Logan, your parents are on their way to pick you up and take you to the emergency room. The school nurse thinks your hand may be broken."

My eyes can't physically roll back any farther, and I think Mr. Blanchard notices because he gives me a little look like he thinks I should be doing pushups or something.

On the other hand, he looks very sympathetic toward Logan even though he knows he regularly bullies kids smaller than him. I know he knows, and he knows that I know he knows. But he still doesn't do crap about it.

Logan just nods. I think he's trying really hard not to cry from the pain, and he's afraid his voice might crack. *Aww, poor widdle bully.*

"Sawyer, we can't seem to be able to get a hold of your mom." He pauses for me to respond. I don't. "We just have the one home phone. Is there another number where we may be able to contact her, such as a cell phone?"

Did you try Reilly's Pub?

"No, sir. I'm not sure where she is."

I try not to look at Logan, who's holding his bandaged hand and staring me down like a pit bull on a leash. Whenever the principal isn't looking at him, it's like he's ready to rip my throat out with his teeth.

"A work number, perhaps?"

If she had a work number, it would be on the freaking

student information card that took me an hour to fill out at the beginning of the year.

"No, sir. She, uh... she's between jobs right now."

I see the side of Logan's mouth go up in that combination sneer-grin he does so well. A short fantasy of me taking Blanchard's giant football-shaped trophy and bashing Logan repeatedly in his stupid skull plays through my mind. I try not to smile at the thought.

"I see. Then we'll just have to hold you in the office until after school. We can't have either of you walking around campus after such a display, since it would give the appearance that you did nothing wrong and that there were no repercussions for actions like this."

"Like what?" I say before I can stop myself. "What *did* I do wrong?" Then I add, "If you don't mind me asking."

Mr. Blanchard looks confused as to how I could ask such a question. "Mr. Vincent, Logan's injury could cause him to miss a significant part of the season. Surely, even you could understand how serious that is."

Even me? Wow.

"Yeah, he punched a locker because I ducked. How exactly is that my fault?"

Mr. Blanchard stands and rounds the desk. He looks down at me, hands behind his back, drill sergeant style.

"Several witnesses—trustworthy students, I might add—"

In other words, Logan's popular friends...

"—heard you making inappropriate comments to purposely anger Logan. Obviously, and understandably, he was unable to control his emotions."

"So you're saying that my witty retorts to his threats were

somehow just as serious as him trying to take my head off with that meat hook of his?" I'm sure my incredulous expression is just getting me into even more trouble.

Mr. Blanchard draws a straight line with his lips but is saved from whatever nonsense justification he was about to spew by a knock at the door.

"Logan's parents are here to pick him up," his secretary says. She shakes her head and looks sympathetically at Logan's hand, then shoots me the stink eye.

"Tell them to come right in."

When I see the worried look on Logan's mom's face, I almost feel bad. Then I remember the sociopath she raised, and any remorseful feelings vanish. She immediately starts to dote on him, helping him out of his chair, and hugging him. He's gonna milk this thing as long as he possibly can. He starts now by playing it up for his mom. He's all hunched over, holding his hand, and she totally buys into it.

His dad seems to kind of know better. Surprisingly, he looks pretty angry at Logan. Then I realize he's as big a douche as his son is when he says, "I hope this doesn't affect your scholarship chances, son."

Logan's mom gives his dad the *shut up, or you're cut off for a long time* look.

Mr. Andrews turns to the principal. "Thank you. We'll be back tomorrow for the meeting."

"I'll see you folks then." Mr. Blanchard looks worried, too.

Again, I know I should keep my mouth shut. And again, I can't help myself. "It was nice seeing you again, Mrs. Andrews."

Logan's mom gives me a confused look, which totally makes sense since we've never seen one another before in our lives.

Logan turns back, and his look tells me I'm a dead man once his hand is better.

But it was worth it. Totally worth it.

FIVE

EXHAUSTED.

That's what I am by the time the third death bot comes at me. It's not the most original name, I know, but it's really, really accurate.

Humanoid—that is, it has two arms, two legs, and a head—it lunges at me. Its movements are slow but superfluid, almost exactly like a man its size would move. And the only man I know of its size is that old basketball player, Shaquille O'Neal.

That can't be his real name, right?

I dodge left, barely avoiding a circular saw blade attached to its right arm. It had come down vertically. Anyone knows that's the most ineffective way to attack. It covers the least amount of ground. Now, if I'd have programmed this thing...

I swear as it does exactly what I was gonna say. Its second blade spins toward me in a horizontal swipe, while the first comes back three feet below that one in the exact opposite direction.

There's a taxi directly behind me, so I'm forced to crouch and jump. While tucked into a little ball, I spread out flat, still in the air, then push off the taxi with my feet, kind of like an Olympic swimmer, and spear the robot where the solar plexus of a human would have been. Had this been a human, the sheer force of it would've driven the wind from his lungs, and I'd have been able to finish him with a kick to the side of the head.

But this isn't human. Not one bit. My shoulder feels like it cracked in half, the same one I hurt when fighting Osprey in midair above 9th Street.

Even so, I manage to roll clear of its reach and wall run to safer ground.

Its head spins to follow me. The movement is hella creepy since it's now walking in reverse with just one single eye fixated on me. Legs and arms technically still backward, it raises an arm, and I immediately know what it's planning.

On cue, one of those spinning blades soars through the air, intent upon taking off my head. I dive and slide over the hood of a '73 El Camino. Cool car. I land in a crouch just behind the vehicle and scan my surroundings, looking for anything that might save my hide.

It's dark... really dark. The streetlights are all dead. That was my fault. I thought maybe I could shut down the robots with an EMP grenade. Apparently not. Whatever was powering the bots was completely impervious.

It's not like we've never seen stuff like that. Before I was his partner, Harrier and the first Red Kite—I'm actually the third—had to deal with a literal alien invasion. It all got covered up, but Frank's still got CCTV footage from several places, as well as satellite imagery his company was able to procure.

For whatever reason, the creatures—the Tuldarians—haven't returned. Or maybe they have, and I'm part of the masses not privy to it.

I mentally shrug away the thought since I currently have far more pressing matters to deal with.

At the end of the street, another death bot ambles toward me. I have one advantage: they're as slow and lumbering as hundred-year-old tractors.

I check my utility belt but find nothing of real use. Boomerangs and bolas aren't gonna do much against these metal monstrosities. But I have to come up with something because they are now closing in on me from both sides. I'm just lucky the new one wasn't desperate enough yet to expend one of its blades by shooting it my way.

I stand and break into a run toward the newcomer, and just as I'm about to strike, Harrier appears in front of me.

"Kite," he says, voice muffled and airy through his device.

I skid to a stop.

When I say he appears in front of me, I mean precisely that. He walks right through the death bot like it doesn't even exist, which, since this is a simulation, I guess it doesn't.

Out of breath, I say, "What is it?"

He stands there looking at me, while everything else on the fake New York City street stands still as a frozen lake.

"Hello?"

"I know about her."

An eighty-pound sledgehammer to my chest couldn't have been more jarring.

"You... what?" I ask. But I know exactly what he's gonna say...

"The girl. I know about her. You're done seeing her."

I often wonder if he's capable of forming sentences with more than five syllables until I remember that he's also the incredibly articulate CEO, philanthropist, billionaire playboy Franklin Douglas III.

I take one more look around at the simulation I've been working my ass off to complete for well over an hour now. "Isn't there a better time for this?"

"No."

With that, he turns and walks away, and within seconds, the sim ramps back up again, and the death bot's sawblade slices into my chest.

Everything goes red, and the illusion disappears.

It didn't hurt. I didn't even feel it, but that wasn't the point. I take my training seriously, especially when I was so damn close that time.

Stepping out of the practice room, my teeth are grinding, and my heart is pounding. Who the hell does he think he is, anyway? He can't just tell me what to do.

But he can. He absolutely can. He may not be my father or anything like that, but everything I currently know is because of him. I would just be some lame kid living with his mom in the slums. Sure, I'd still have my awesome ability to maintain and recall anything I ever see, but I wouldn't have the training to control it. That was Frank. He taught me to own it, so it didn't own me. You wouldn't believe how overwhelming it is to remember everything.

At that thought, my ire wanes... sort of. I'm still shaken over what he said about Osprey.

Things with Harrier weren't always like this. When I first became his partner, I was in awe of him. Before the Black Harrier existed, this city was like a war zone with all the criminals and gangs terrorizing everyone. He brought order and justice and did it almost single-handedly.

Problem is, Harrier put down all the mob bosses and crime lords, but then the "supervillains" started rising up.

During the day, he went around town like a carefree celebrity, but that was—and still is—a load of crap. He's hiding the fact that he's never gotten over his dad's death. His mom had died giving birth to him, and his dad raised him alone until he was killed by a gang of criminals when Frank was a teenager. Frank was reckless when he was younger, out of control, even after his dad died. But something made him turn his life around and dedicate himself to fighting crime.

I still don't know what that was.

I met him by accident. It was just after my thirteenth birthday, and I was skateboarding home from school. Some bangers in my neighborhood whose crew I'd refused to join jumped me and pulled me into an alley. They were gonna give me a serious beating. Maybe even kill me.

I was surrounded. They'd smashed my board in half. Then, like hyenas, laughing and everything, their circle started moving in, and they were shoving me between them. No matter how much danger I've been in since then, it's never approached the fear I'd felt at that moment. I was sure I was dead.

Suddenly, Harrier appeared out of nowhere, which was

strange because he's very rarely out in the daylight. He told me to run, and I almost did. But then something happened. As I watched him fight, I suddenly felt like I could do the same thing. After half a minute, I'd seen enough of his moves that I decided to try some.

The next thing I knew, I was bending a guy's leg backward with a kick to the knee, then breaking the jaw of another guy with a palm to the face. There I was, fighting back-to-back with my hero. It was amazing. Exhilarating. I'd never felt anything quite like it.

I'd always found it really easy to learn tricks on my board if I saw someone else do it or watched a video. But it still felt like I was learning it on my own. But there, in that alley, watching Harrier, it was like something on the inside of me unlocked. Okay, that's cheesy, but there's no other way to explain it.

Maybe it was the surge of adrenaline or the feeling that I'd become powerful enough to take on those guys, but this was something on a whole different level.

Harrier noticed, and I thought for sure he was gonna yell at me to run again. Instead, he stood there and watched me take out the last two guys by myself.

Even with his visor retracted into his helmet, I couldn't see his eyes behind those tinted lenses on his mask. However, it was obvious that he was doing some serious thinking. He walked over and stared at me for a long time. But it wasn't like he does now. Now, he just broods. Then? It was like he was assessing my worthiness or something. For the next five minutes, he questioned me about everything: me, my mom, school—just... life. I had no idea what was going on, but I wasn't about to lie to him or keep quiet. He'd just saved me.

Finally, he asked me if I'd like him to train me to defend myself. It didn't even take a second for me to respond. Was he kidding? Of course I wanted the best fighter in the world to train me.

The rest is history.

The memory helps wash away the rest of my anger just in time. A large metal door swishes open like we're on the bridge of the Starship *Enterprise*.

The Aerie.

That's literally what Harrier calls it. As if the whole bird of prey theme isn't stupid enough already, he uses a name for a place that practically nobody else knows about except for me. And he couldn't keep it simple and call it "The Nest" either. It had to be a fancy name for it. I've never had the heart—or the guts—to tell him that actual black harriers have their nests on the ground.

Not that I normally mind being here. Harrier's penthouse is nice enough, sitting on top of one of the tallest buildings in the city. Douglas Tower has the best restaurant in town on the ground floor, along with a few high-end shops. The next several levels are offices, including Douglas Industries. And then the upper section is reserved for the most expensive condos in the city, with the top few floors belonging to Harrier himself.

But the secret level above the penthouse, that's a whole different thing. The fastest computers I've ever seen, a helipad that lifts when the ceiling opens, and more high-tech gadgets than an E3 convention. The entrance from the outside allows me to come and go without people wondering what a teenager is doing here all the time and Harrier to enter and exit while in costume.

There are also several training facilities, including the simulation room I was just so rudely interrupted in, and the one where Harrier trained me three years ago. I almost hate to admit it, but everything he shows me does make me better. It's been that way all along. No matter how good I feel like I am, he's always able to help me improve.

In my opinion, though, the coolest things here are the various Black Harrier costumes lined up in their plexiglass lockers. One for every occasion; fighting, detective work, base jumping, scuba diving, even skulking around in the sewers. Some are lightweight for stealth, others are heavily armored, but they're all mostly black with some gray or silver thrown in. And they all have the white on the underside of the cape, like an actual black harrier, only to be seen when he's swooping down from above.

The only thing I don't like about the Aerie—other than the name—is the shrine to the two previous Red Kites. I'm not even sure how he gets those costumes to stand up like that... almost like they're on invisible mannequins, or even freakier, like someone is still inside of them. They simultaneously make me feel like a poser and make me worry about what's in store for me.

"I hope I was clear about how I felt regarding that girl." Harrier doesn't even bother to look up from his supercomputer when we have these talks, as if I'm simply a distraction he's trying not to pay too much attention to. I mean, okay, so he's probably doing something super important. Still, he could at least act like we're having a conversation. And—so annoying—he's *clacking* away at a keyboard from, like, the '90s or something. He can *so* afford the latest in touch screen and even holographic technology, too. But, of course, he prefers the "old-fashioned" way.

"I wouldn't exactly call her a girl."

He actually stops typing for a second.

"What would you call her then?"

Him and me. All alone. Voice-changer still on.

Even so, he's got me there.

Woman? Chick? Smokin' hot superheroine?

"Why can't you give her a chance?"

He's back to typing again. "She's unsanctioned."

"By who?"

Uh oh, here it comes.

"*Whom.* By me. By the law. And, most importantly, by the Guild."

"Yeah, yeah. Definitely don't want to be stopping crime and saving people without your union membership card, right?"

Clack, clack, clackity, clack, clack.

"Stay away from her."

And we're back to five syllables.

"Okay! I got it." I turn and hit a practice dummy extra hard since I can't take it out on Harrier. I'm sure he notices.

Another pause in the *clacking*. "I need your help tonight."

Another hit to the dummy. "I'm busy. I have a project due at school tomorrow."

"The project can wait. This can't."

"It's gonna have to," I say. "I'm already missing some assignments in science class, and if I don't turn this in, I'm gonna be failing."

"And?"

"*And* I don't want to fail science."

"Fine. I'll handle it by myself."

Sometimes I'd prefer it if he'd just yell at me. These stone-cold statements followed by icy silence are almost unbearable.

It's almost eight, and I'm meeting Osprey whether he likes it or not, but I can't help feeling like a total jerk. Especially after he'd just given me a birthday present. Barely ten seconds go by before I feel too guilty to stay quiet.

"Look, maybe I can help out for a couple of hours, then—"

"I'll be fine."

Geez, I thought only women pulled this passive-aggressive crap. My mom's an expert at it.

I start walking toward him, but I don't really know why. It's not like I'm gonna reassuringly place my hand upon his shoulder or anything.

When I'm a few feet away, I say, "Are you sure? I—"

In a swift movement, Harrier swipes something off the desk and shoves it into his lap without moving any other part of his body, then goes right back to typing. I'm pretty sure it was the same business card from last night.

I curse internally.

Why didn't I notice that before? I could've put this whole mystery to rest if I'd just seen it. However, just because I didn't get to see what it says, doesn't mean I don't now know without a doubt that it's something he doesn't want me to know about.

"In fact," he says, "maybe you should go now. Get a head start on finishing your... *science project*."

Now's my chance. *Take it. Take it. Take it.*

"If you say so." I turn to leave the Aerie.

Just as I'm about to reach for the exit hatch, he says, "Say hello to Osprey for me."

I freeze in my tracks and swallow hard. He knows. *Of course* he knows. And he knows her name? Who is this guy? Sometimes, it's easy to forget he's the greatest hero alive.

I'm too ashamed to even apologize. I spin toward him and for the first time, notice what he's working on. Up on the screen is a photo and intel on his former arch-enemy, Chef Maléfique. Stupid name for a supervillain, I know. Apparently, it's French for "Evil Chef." And, no, I have no idea why he called himself that. Any time I bring him up, I get shut down.

But why would he be looking him up? Chef Maléfique blew himself up before I even started working with Harrier, so I can't think of any reason he'd be working on this.

I almost say something, but I swallow the words as it hits me again—the nagging feeling that something is wrong, and this time it comes on like a panic attack. I clench my teeth and try to insist I'll go with him, but the words just won't come out. I stand there for about thirty seconds, trying to do the right thing.

Instead, I open the hatch and glide out into the evening sky without even looking back.

SIX

Weird.

Not sure what it is lately, but I'm used to my mom being gone or passed out, and again, there she is, wide awake and watching some stupid reality show. Instead of putting on my costume and sneaking through my window, I have to change on the roof and stash my clothes somewhere.

I sling my backpack over my shoulder and try to cross the room as quickly and quietly as possible.

Mom turns down the volume on the whiny voice of some so-called reality star. "Where are you off to?"

"Library. Science project."

"I need to talk to you about—"

"Sorry. Gotta go." I close the door before she can get out another syllable and rush up the stairs before she can follow me. I'm pretty confident she's heard all about my little scuffle with Logan by now, and the meeting she's supposed to have with Principal Blanchard tomorrow.

Before I don my costume, I sniff it to make sure it doesn't

still smell like puke. The bleachy smell from the cleaner I used last night isn't much better, but it'll have to do.

I always wonder, when I'm changing like this, if someone in one of the nearby buildings ever spots me and is curious about what I'm doing. Not that New Yorkers care much about what other people do—especially this close to Halloween—but it would definitely be weird if they did.

As I'm putting on my new cape, my mind wanders to Harrier. What's he doing tonight that he would need my help? He's never asked me like that before. Does it have something to do with why I've been patrolling on my own so often lately? I'm sure he'll be okay.

After making sure my costume's in order, I glide to the building where Osprey and I met. The butterflies in my stomach and weakness in my limbs make me second-guess the idea of patrolling with her. What if I'm not focused enough? I could actually get killed out there.

But as soon as I see her waiting for me—and she sees me—I know there's no way I could ditch her. I don't want to either. The way she looks, the way she stands, the way her costume...

Bleep.

"Heart rate?" I ask.

"*Not even a hello? I've missed you,*" Amber says.

"Yeah, it's just the new cape. Still getting used to it."

"*Mmmm-hmmm.*"

"Silent mode," I say, then retract my face shield. My domino mask still covers my eyes and the top half of my face, but I figure it's a bit weird to show up to a "date" with my face covered.

Osprey doesn't seem upset that I'm a little late thanks to Mom, so that's good.

"Kite," she says as I touch down on the rooftop. When she says my old codename, I don't mind it as much.

"Hey, Osprey." Did my voice just crack? Dammit. Stay cool. Stay. *Cool.* "I actually go by Raptor now. Red Raptor."

"What was wrong with Red Kite? I kind of liked it."

And I kind of like you.

"Nothing, as long as someone knows it's a pretty awesome hawk. But most people think of a toy that flies in the air."

Osprey laughs. "I have to admit, I did think that when I was a kid. But I guess that must've been a different Kite back then."

"Yeah."

As expected, she knows her Black Harrier lore.

"When did you take over?"

"I'm actually the third. I've only been his si—partner for a few years."

I almost said sidekick. I *never* say sidekick. This girl has me off my game like no one ever does.

"I never realized that," she says.

I can't blame her. Most people don't know there were three of us. Harrier and Frank, since sometimes they seem like totally different people, rarely talk about the previous Kite. Not even I know what happened, just that one day he was gone and I was him.

"What happened to the other two?"

I knew that question was coming.

"I wish I knew. He won't talk about it." And I've asked. I've asked a *lot*.

"That doesn't sound good."

She pushes a strand of hair behind her ear, and just like it had the first time, the action makes me weak. What the hell is wrong with me? I'm the freaking Black Harrier's partner!

"Yeah. Tell me about it. That's the other reason I wanted to change my name. I don't like having to live up to what those other guys did." It feels good to tell somebody this. I certainly can't tell Harrier.

A bit of his paranoia washes over me, and I can hear his voice in the back of my head. *The girl. I know about her. You're done seeing her.*

Maybe he's right? Maybe he knows something I don't. Why am I trusting her so much? I really have no idea who she is or what her real agenda might be.

"How'd you come up with the new name?" she asks before I have the chance to worry any more.

"I don't know. It just kind of came to me."

Liar.

I spent hours trying to find something that wasn't either already taken by a real crimefighter or trademarked by some comic book company or movie studio. But it makes the most sense. Harriers and Kites are raptors. And fun fact: so are Ospreys. Though she probably knows that.

"Red Raptor. I like that too. But now you have a similar problem to the one you had with Kite."

"What's that?"

"Everyone might think you were named after a dinosaur instead of a bird of prey."

"Yeah, I guess. But it's a lot better than a diamond-shaped toy on a string."

"I suppose I can't argue there," she says. Then, "So... where should we start?"

Every time she smiles at me like that, my chest constricts. What is up with that? I clear my throat to make sure it doesn't crack again.

"Ummm..."

Grab some dinner? See a movie? Followed by some serious making out?

I continue to try to appear as nonchalant as possible. "Whatever, I guess. Where do you usually go?"

"Well, I have my earpiece tuned in to the police scanner. When I hear something's going on, I try to beat the cops there."

Wow. That's smart. I mean, I have Amber to tell me of anything strange happening in the city, but I can't expect someone without Harrier's resources to be able to afford a super-smart A.I.

"Yeah. That sounds pretty good." I do my best shrug. I wish I could see her eyes, but she has those same reflective lenses in her mask that Harrier uses. I bet they're blue. Or green. Or brown... like caramel. Hazel maybe?

"Until then, we can just... patrol."

"Right. Cool."

I need to get a book with things to say to girls that won't make me sound like a total dork.

Patrolling with Osprey for the first time takes me back to when I first started with Harrier. I had no idea what I was doing, and he had me stay off to the side and observe for a long time before he allowed me to get in on the action. I was still in my regular clothes then, so nobody suspected I was with him.

Meanwhile, he was training me at the Aerie and showing me all the moves he knew. Since I picked up everything so quickly, it was just a matter of going through all the different styles of fighting and then practicing them for a week or so. His style is a combination of a bunch of various martial arts and fighting techniques, but he wanted me to learn everything from the easy beginner moves up to the most complex combinations for each discipline.

Within a few months, I had so many choices every time I made a move that it was kind of overwhelming. But soon, I narrowed down the hundreds of options to certain ones that I liked and were the most effective for me. My style isn't even the same as Harrier's. I use a lot of kicks while he prefers punching most of the time. I think it's part of his anger management program.

He drilled it into me to "Never fight angry." He was preaching to himself, so to speak. We always most easily see our own sin in others.

It wasn't all just training me to fight, though. Harrier also became my mentor. I didn't have a dad around growing up, and even though he isn't much of a father figure, he's still a strong role model for me. He's helped me to learn a ton of things about life that I just haven't gotten growing up with a single mom.

Plus, he bought me practically anything I wanted or needed. The only problem was that most of the time I couldn't bring it home.

Eventually, he gave me my Red Kite costume and made it official. It was pretty close to the others' costumes, but there were some mods and improvements. I've made some changes of my own over the past three years, too—even changing the symbol. Which, like the name change, Harrier didn't embrace easily.

But across all three Kites, one thing that's always consistent is the red, black, and white coloring.

There's a popular joke among crimefighters that the heroes like to dress their sidekicks in bright colors, so they make better targets and keep the heat off of them. But I don't think that's true, at least in Harrier's case. I think the red is so I always stand out no matter how many people are around, so he can keep an eye on me and make sure I'm safe.

Plus, I'm not his sidekick. I'm his partner.

At least, that's what I always tell myself.

"You see that?" Osprey says, pulling me back into the present.

In New York, you never have to patrol long before spotting a crime of some sort. Most times, it's a mugging or a robbery. It almost always involves some loser with a fake gun.

This time, it's a little different—but I can still see the old "there's a gun in my pocket" thing going on.

Below, a dude is arguing with an old man to get out of his car. From the roof, we can't hear the words, but I've heard it all before. The old man has his hands up in surrender, and he's moving slow to get out of the car while the young guy motions frantically with his pocket-gun hand.

"You go behind him," I tell Osprey. "I'll take the front. If he runs, take him down?"

She nods.

Using our capes, we glide down. I snap mine shut just above the car hood and land with a loud metal *thud*.

"Nice night for a carjack!" I say.

The guy with the fake gun turns on me, a wild look in his eye. This guy is whacked out on something strong for sure.

Crouched, I spin and sweep the man's hidden weapon aside, then lash out with my other boot to his face. He staggers backward and into Osprey, who finishes him off with a gut punch.

When the criminal is moaning on the ground, I zip tie his wrists together.

"Call it in, Amber," I say.

"*Your desire is my duty*," Amber says.

"Yeah. Silence mode, please."

The last thing I need is Amber's sexual innuendos while I'm patrolling with Osprey.

I stand and clap my hands together, turning to face the victim. I have a huge smile on my face, and I expect him to as well. Instead, his scowl almost says as much as his words.

"You motherbucker!" The guy says, except that isn't what he says.

"Whoa, whoa!" I say, backing away.

"Look at my car!" He stabs a finger at the hood where there's a distinct impression of my booted footprints.

Behind him, Osprey is giggling at me.

"I'm sorry," I say. "I was just trying to help."

"Help do what, you idiot? That guy had no weapon, and I got insurance. Now... now, what do I do? Tell them it was foot-sized hail?"

"I'm... I'm sorry?" I say. It comes out as a question. I've literally never experienced anything like this with Harrier. People are usually thrilled to be saved and even more thrilled to meet Harrier.

"Buck you!" he doesn't say. "Get the hell out of here."

I cross the pavement to where Osprey stands, hand to her mouth, covering a smile, and leave the guy to his bucking.

"Wow," I say once we are back on the rooftops. "Can you believe that?"

"It's New York. Of course I can believe that."

I shake my head as we start to parkour across the city once again. For the most part, Osprey keeps up, which is impressive. Granted, I'm going pretty easy on the moves. Doing my best to show her some cool stuff, but not look like I'm showing off. I think it works.

Bleep.

At the same time I receive my Amber Alert, Osprey says, "Hold on a sec." She puts a finger to her ear and listens for a moment.

"Yeah?" I whisper to Amber, not sure I'm ready for Osprey to know I have a sex demon talking in my ear.

"Okay, got something," Osprey says.

Then together, she and Amber both say, "Corner of First and Houston."

Before I can respond, she leaps off the roof. Sure enough, she's already copied the design of my new cape, and she's gliding toward First Street faster than I can keep up. I don't see any jets, though. If she figured out the cape in one day, that'll probably only take, like, another week or so for her to tackle.

I leap off the rooftop after her and realize I still need to practice this some more. I'm used to jumping around on rooftops and swinging from my grappler line. Gliding through the air is totally new to me, and since I haven't seen someone else really do it, I have nothing to imitate. It's definitely fun, though.

"What's going on, Amber?"

"*A group of naughty robbers at J. Jewelers.*"

"How many?"

I'm moving too fast to see the looks on the faces of the people below, but I can see them looking up and pointing at us. Some of them are recording us on their phones. I bet we make the papers tomorrow.

Too bad nobody reads the papers anymore. Maybe we'll be all over social media. Not that I have time for that sort of thing. I'm a little busy with the whole crimefighting and, you know, generally saving the world thing.

"*Her butt looks amazing in those tights,*" Amber says, her voice slathered with sex.

"Amber, please, focus." What I really mean is that I can't lose *my* focus. "How many robbers?"

I swear whenever I speak to the AI that way, there's a slight pause like she's mad. That's gotta be in my head, right?

"*Only nine.*"

Only.

"Thanks, Amber. Silent mode, please."

As I follow Osprey, I start to fantasize about her being my partner instead of Harrier. We could be together all day and hang out, then patrol at night. Then we could go home and

—*whoa*! I need to pay attention. I almost hit that power line and fried myself. Definitely need to focus.

But what would happen to Harrier? Would he just go on alone? Find a fourth Red Kite? Why do I really care? Most of the time, he just acts like I'm a pain in the ass anyway. Except today... when I abandoned him for Osprey.

The guilt runs deep, but I'm gonna have to deal with it at another time.

Osprey swoops down, and I follow. We arrive on the scene, but I have no idea what to expect. Amber was right—it's J. Jewelers, a chain of high-end diamond dealers here in the city. All I see is a building with its alarm going off and broken glass everywhere. When Harrier and I work together, we always have a plan. Osprey apparently just jumps in and improvises.

As we close in, I can see that it looks like a typical jewelry store robbery. Bust through the window, get in, grab what they can, get out fast.

Unless Harrier and I happen to get lucky, we don't usually come across this kind of action. So why did Amber pick it up this time?

I start to ask her, but Osprey lands outside the store's entrance just as the first masked robber exits with his bag full of goodies. She smashes him in the face with a roundhouse kick before he even notices she's there.

Okay, I guess we really are just going in with no plan at all. No time to worry about it now.

Another advantage of the new glider cape is that I'm moving pretty fast when I slam feet first into the next guy out the door. He flies backward into another, and they are both out cold with no more fuss. Osprey gives me a big smile, which unfortunately means I'm not paying attention when a fourth guy starts taking potshots at me with his pistol.

Bleep.

Yeah, that doesn't do me a lot of good after the bullet leaves the gun. I'm really gonna have to tinker with her emergency programming.

Luckily, the thug's aim sucks, and the bullet whizzes by without touching me. It seems whatever the cape is made of is at least as strong as my graphene armor. The bullet stops dead and falls harmlessly to the sidewalk.

The guy looks at me, stunned. I toss one of the throwing stars from my belt at his gun, and it lodges in the end of the barrel, just like it's supposed to. As I leap forward and knock him down with a foot to the face, I recognize the mask he and his buddies are wearing. From afar, it looked like a typical bank robber type setup, but up close, I see the multi-colored, spandex-looking things...

No. This is *not* good. They're the henchmen of—

"La Cucaracha!" Osprey calls him out like we're in a cartoon or something. It's the first thing she's ever done that I didn't totally love. Taunting one of New York's most dangerous?

Now I know why Amber picked up on this.

Why the hell didn't you tell me? I think, but I don't dare say to her. The last thing I need is her voice in my ear, further distracting me.

Right now, my instinct is to run. To call Harrier for help. But I don't want to look weak in front of Osprey.

"I don't believe we've had the pleasure, *Mija*."

Like any good boss, La Cucaracha stands inside the jewelry store, watching his men get pummeled.

I'm not sure the guy is even Latino, but he always throws in some Spanish words to keep up his shtick. Why someone so huge would name himself after an insect never made any sense to me. And for anyone to adopt the moniker The Cockroach? Blech.

But I'm pretty sure super-intelligence isn't one of his powers. I mean, Spanish isn't my best subject, but shouldn't it be 'El Cucaracho' or something? He's all strength and looks like one of those Photoshopped bodybuilder guys who are too huge to be real.

From what I've heard, he's actually sort of an outlaw hero back in Mexico, like some kind of Robin Hood or something. I guess he robs wealthy Americans and sends it all back there. I'd almost applaud him... but the problem is, he isn't just stealing, he's also hurting a lot of people along the way.

"It's Osprey," she says, flicking her wrist and producing a stick that extends on both ends into a five-foot staff. "And trust me, jerkwad, we've met."

He tilts his head like a dog.

"Oh, well, I'm sure it was a pleasure," he says. "Now if you'll *perdóneme*. We have work to do."

"I promise this is going to be one of the *least* pleasurable experiences you've ever had."

Witty banter. I like that. Usually, Harrier just grunts and barks orders. But it's also kind of stupid. Like I already said, La Cucaracha is huge, and she darts into the store and leaps straight at him. I can't see his face because of that half-green-half-yellow *luchador* mask he wears. But I can imagine he's smiling. He's also stronger than any bodybuilder out there with his exoskeleton that gives him super-strength—and, hey, it does make him look sort of like a cockroach now that I think about it.

She doesn't stand much of a chance against him on her own. She's fighting out of what seems like anger, and like I said... Black Harrier has always taught me, that's the worst place you can be. That's when you make mistakes.

It's a good thing I'm here with her.

She swings her collapsible staff at him, and he grabs it away from her with no effort whatsoever. Then, he bites down on the middle of it, pulls down on the ends, and snaps it into three pieces with his mouth. The guy's a brute even when the exoskeleton isn't enhancing his strength.

As La Cucaracha swats Osprey away, she crashes through the storefront glass and slides to a stop by my boots. Luckily, her armor seems as sturdy as mine, so she wouldn't have been hurt too badly.

"What are you doing?" I ask.

"I hate bugs," she says.

Oh, okay, the banter continues even when the villain can't hear. Wonderful.

"Well, he's gonna kill you," I say as I throw one of my smoke bombs at him.

While he stomps around in confusion, I help Osprey up. She starts rushing toward him again, and I yank her back. She practically snarls at me and holds her arm like it's injured. I don't think she has any experience fighting actual supervillains, and she's probably embarrassed by how easily he took her down. I get the impression that, up until now, this has been some kind of game to her.

"Come out, *parajito*, and face me." He flexes, and his muscles bulge so much that I think I can hear them.

"We need a plan," I say, keeping my voice low even though he probably wouldn't hear me over his own bellowing. "Get ready to slam into him from the back. I'm gonna come in low and sweep his legs."

Osprey nods, if a bit reluctantly, and I watch as she uses the cover of smoke to duck behind the U-shaped cases filled with priceless gems and metals. She disappears into the smoke and moves around behind La Cucaracha. I give her a few more seconds to get into place, then I run straight at him. As the smoke starts to clear, he sees me and reaches forward like he's gonna grab me. This also forces his momentum to follow. At the last second, I turn sideways and roll the last few feet into his shins. Osprey hits him in the back just at the right time, and he falls forward like a bowling pin. The exoskeleton may make him stronger, but it also impedes his movement.

His face slams into one of the display cases, and it smashes to pieces under his weight. We jump out of the way as glass shatters all over the place.

Any average person would be lucky to be alive after that. I'm pretty sure we just pissed him off. He struggles to get up and screams with rage, blood covering his now-shredded mask.

"He's too strong. We need to disconnect his power source. I'm gonna distract him. You try to grab onto those cables and yank them out." I make sure Osprey nods her understanding, and then rush the big bug again.

I try to land a kick to his chest, but he grabs my leg while I'm in the air. I know people talk about someone's grip being like a vice all the time, but his really is. There's no way I can break it. He swings me around in a move like we're fighting a Hell in the Cell match or something and tosses me through the *other* front window of the store. Despite my disorientation, I manage to wrap myself in my cape before I skid across the sidewalk and back onto the street.

One of the first things Harrier taught me was how to land without getting hurt, so I'm in pretty good shape as I try to figure out my next move. I just hope Osprey—

No. He must have caught her as she tried to pull out the cables that deliver power from the large battery in the middle of his back. La Cucaracha holds her up with one hand around her neck, The Undertaker style. But I get the distinct impression he's not about to smash her down with a chokeslam. With that grip, she doesn't have long.

Since his back is to me, I should have one chance to do this.

One deep breath. It's all I have time for. Then I run and flip through the gap in the storefront window, landing just behind him. I pull a cyclone blade from my belt and slice the cables.

He immediately screams and drops Osprey. Smoke rises from his back as his technology seizes up on him, and sparks fly from the cables. He falls headlong to the ground, and broken glass falls free from half a dozen display cases and both windows.

I hear the sirens, and the street is filled with blue and red flashes as the cops finally show up. I'm really not in the mood to give a report right now, and some police officers really don't appreciate us doing their jobs for them. I quickly help Osprey to her feet, then we take off out the back door.

SEVEN

"WHAT THE HELL WAS THAT?" I ASK, AND I CAN BARELY believe I'm talking to Osprey like this. The girl I've been pining over. Who'd consumed most of my thoughts for the last twenty-four hours. And I'm yelling at her. But she deserves it, right? I mean who does that? That was freaking La Cucaracha.

We are now safely above the city again, watching from a distance as the police do their job and toss the robbers into their squad cars. It would have been pretty romantic if I wasn't so pissed. As they drive away, I'm surprised and a little frightened by the absence of La Cucaracha in the walk of shame. Has he gotten away?

"What was what?" she has the audacity to ask.

Bleep.

"Not now!" I scream.

"What?" Osprey says.

"Nothing."

"What is your problem?" Osprey asks.

Me? What's *my* problem. Are you kidding me? That was amateur hour back there, and we both almost died.

To her, I simplify it. "That was stupid."

"You're stupid," she says in what could be the most immature response I've ever heard.

"Wow," I say. It's all I can even come up with.

I bailed on Harrier for this. To gallivant around the city with someone I, apparently, barely know, diving headfirst into supervillain battles.

He was right. He's always right. I should have stayed far away.

I shake my head. "You know what? I gotta get home. I'll see you later, maybe."

"You're acting like I did something wrong," she says to my back. I turn to her, and she's standing with her arms crossed in a totally defensive posture.

"You *did* do something wrong!" I want to leave, but for some reason, I can't let this go. "You don't just leap into a situation with one of the world's most dangerous criminals without even discussing a plan. You could have—*we* could have been killed."

"Don't you do this, like, for a living, or whatever?" she argues.

"Yeah, and I'm approved by the Guild to do so." And there it is. I am actually Harrier now. All I need is the stupid voice-changer.

She looks to the side like she's disgusted. "Whatever. If you're afraid of a little bug, maybe you shouldn't be doing this."

"Enough with the 'little bug' stuff. That guy is massive,

and he could have been the one squashing us like bugs. What were you thinking?"

That question seems to give her pause. She turns her back to me and takes a few steps. I consider following, but I give her space and wait.

Maybe she's right. Who am I to question her? I agreed to go along with her, didn't I?

That's when it hits me. Like a two-by-four to the face.

"You knew about the robbery, didn't you? You were using me."

I don't even need a response. I know it's true. Good thing too, because she's silent as a ghost.

"You went from attacking me and almost killing me, to what—us out on a 'patrol date?'"

How stupid am I? I can't believe I fell for this. What an idiot. *Hi, I'm Sawyer and I become a complete doofus the moment a pretty girl smiles at me.* Well, not anymore. I'm nobody's fool.

"Unless you've got an answer for me, I'm out of here."

It looks like she's about to say something when I hear the sound of stone cracking and little rocks bouncing like a tiny, little avalanche. Her eyes go wide, fixated behind me, and I spin to see a green and yellow head appear just above the low wall of the rooftop. True to his name, the freaking cockroach is using his exo-suit to crawl up the side of the building.

"That was *no muy bueno*," he says.

"Look, I'm sorry," Osprey says to me. "Just please don't leave me here alone with him?"

I worry that I'm falling for it again. She's using me again, like twenty minutes later. But there's more than just desperation in her voice. It's like she's begging. What am I, heartless? Harrier wouldn't leave her. If I did, I'd be breaking the only rule, killing her by not helping.

I take a deep breath and turn to face La Cucaracha. "How did you get out of there?" I ask. I'm sure he'll answer. Let's have a seat, maybe a spot of tea, Mr. Skuzzy Bug.

To my surprise, he does just that.

"Do you think I'm *estúpido?*" The Spanish thing is becoming incredibly annoying and more than a little bit racist. "Backup battery."

By now, he's standing fully on the roof, towering over us and looking even more imposing, silhouetted in the light of a giant full moon. With Halloween coming up, why not bring out all the crazies?

I look to Osprey, who doesn't even have her staff now, and she looks scared. I don't blame her. I'm terrified. The only thing going for us is that there aren't eight more of his men waiting to take our heads off. Problem is, he's probably enough all by himself.

I nod, and we both rush in.

Unlike ignorant back alley thugs, we don't attack one at a time. She and I engage him with a flurry of blows, and all of them connect. He, however, doesn't even flinch. It's like we're hitting steel with Q-tips.

He grunts and says, "My turn." Then, with a roar that barely sounds human, he punches forward with both closed fists. They connect and send us both soaring across the roof. I hit my head hard on something, but I'm too woozy to care what it is. Even with my helmet on, it rattles me.

I look to the side and see Osprey stand and disappear out of sight before my world goes black.

I come to confused. Really, really confused.

I'm still on the rooftop, staring up through my visor at a starless sky. Harrier says that the movies and TV shows are all wrong, that if you're knocked out for more than a minute, you risk brain damage. Since my brain feels fine, I'm guessing I wasn't out very long.

Then I remember La Cucaracha and Osprey. I bolt upward, and my head becomes a swivel.

Nothing.

No one.

"Amber," I say.

"*It's about time,*" she says. "*I was getting lonely.*"

"Yeah, yeah. Where's Osprey?"

A slight pause?

"*Always a bridesmaid, never a bride.*"

You know, it's one thing for my artificial intelligence to have a voice like a high-end stripper, but add a measure of snark to it, and it's difficult to get anything done.

"Amber, where is she? This is important." I can't believe I'm doing my best to keep the frustration out of my voice, so I don't upset the computer voice in my helmet.

"*How do you expect me to know the answer to that, Sawyer?*"

I have been dreading this moment and hoping it wouldn't

come. I rub the back of my neck. "I... uh... sort of slapped a tracker on her."

Amber is silent and judgmental. Not really, she's just a computer. Maybe it's my own embarrassment.

Shameful, perhaps, but now I'm glad I did it. When I helped her up during the first fight with La Cucaracha, I'd grabbed her hand with my right hand, and when bracing her back, I tagged her.

She'll be mad at me for all of two seconds once she realizes that's the only way I can help her if La Cucaracha has her.

"*I see a restraining order in your future,*" Amber says.

"It's not like that, and you know it. I didn't know if I could trust her. I needed to be able to find her, no matter what."

Wait a second. Why in the name of everything holy am I explaining myself to Amber?

"You know what? Just find her, would you?"

"*Triangulating.*"

Damn right, she is. I'm the boss.

Just then, I hear a scream, and I know it's Osprey. I speed for the ledge, and without even looking first, I push off, and I'm Eaglestar, flying through the air. Snapping my cape, it becomes rigid, and I glide swiftly toward the sound.

"*Osprey is one block east,*" Amber says.

"Thanks. Keep me posted on her movements."

"*Oh, you'd like that, wouldn't you?*" Amber says.

Then I see her, ground level. She's giving La Cucaracha hell, but I think he's toying with her. I break into a dive, gaining crazy speed. Just as I'm about to hit him face-first, I flip around and nail him with two stiff legs right in the back of his head. If he saw me coming, he sure didn't do anything about it.

Using his head like a springboard, I shove off toward Osprey. Without even thinking, I wrap an arm around her, extend my other one with my grappling hook tight in hand, and fire toward the nearest building. Together, we rise above the city streets.

"What are you doing!" she shouts. "I had him!"

"You absolutely didn't have him," I say. "He was playing with you."

We land on a nearby rooftop.

She looks at me like I've stolen her milk money.

"You could say thank you," I say, really tired of the games.

The expression on her face is not what I expected. She looks... impressed.

"We can talk about this later. For now, are you okay? Can you run?"

"Yeah. I think so."

"Good, follow me."

She does her best to keep up as I parkour from roof to roof until we are a respectable distance from La Cucaracha, and I'm satisfied that he won't be sneaking up on us again.

"I'm not helpless, you know," she says, seeming pretty sore as we cross another rooftop.

I stretch a hand out for us to stop. "Look, I know you're mad about what I said, but La Cucaracha isn't someone to take lightly."

"You think I don't know that?" she says. She spins away and kicks at the rooftop stones. They clatter in silence.

Unchartered territory here, Sawyer, I tell myself.

I, of course, was right. I don't know what to say, so I just shut up.

A few minutes later, I'm rewarded for my patience.

"You were right," she says.

I was?

"I'm sorry."

You are?

"That's why I had to draw him away from you. I couldn't live with myself if I got you hurt, or worse."

Is this another manipulation tactic? Is she just trying to cover up for her dumb mistakes? I don't know, but I have to give her the benefit of the doubt.

Now my own bout of silence lingers on.

"Can you say something?" she asks, her voice meek.

I clear my throat a couple of times. "I... I've fought the guy so many times with Harrier. He's dangerous. Really dangerous. A lot of villains want to play games and pull elaborate stunts. Not him. La Cucaracha will tear your limbs off for the fun of it."

"I know. Really. I'm sorry."

"It's okay," I tell her. "From now on, you stick with me, no matter what. Okay?"

"From now on? So you forgive me?" She almost sounds like Amber. Definitely at least some minor manipulation there.

"Yeah," I say. "I guess."

"*Awwwww,*" Amber says. "*Not tell her about the tra—*"

"Silent mode," I say, unable to believe everything we'd

done had happened within the three-minute period I allot Amber before an alert is required.

"What does that mean?" Osprey asks.

I explain to her about Amber, and she says, "Whoa!" I left the part out about her sounding like a super horny streetwalker.

"It sounds cooler than it is," I tell her.

"I doubt that. I didn't even know tech like that existed. Can I talk to her?"

The thought of Amber talking to the girl I like is even more horrifying than introducing Osprey to my mom.

"I'd rather you not," I say. "Not yet, at least."

She looks a bit dejected but seems to accept my response.

"What's it like?" she says. "Being his—"

"Sidekick?" If I haven't mentioned it, I *hate* that word.

"I was going to say 'partner.'"

"Oh. Sorry. Little sensitive about that, I guess."

"Why?"

Do you have a few days to talk about it?

"It isn't easy living in the shadow of someone like the Black Harrier."

"I'd give *anything* to be his partner."

Not sure what to say to that. But I remember feeling the same way once.

"Yeah. It's kind of one of those, 'Be careful what you wish for' type of things, you know? When I first started working with him, I was in awe. But just like everything else, it wears off."

"I guess I really don't know what it's like for you, but I

can't imagine ever getting sick of it. He must teach you so much."

Now I'm feeling guilty. What *is* my real problem with Harrier? Is he really that bad, or is it me? Am I being an ungrateful little brat? A typical rebellious teenager? Or maybe just a grade-A jerk?

"Um, yeah. I guess he does. Now it's my turn."

"For?" she says, skepticism oozing off her.

"What happened between you and La Cucaracha?"

The look on her face makes me wonder if I'd accidentally killed her puppy.

She takes a deep, shuddering breath.

"About a year ago, I fought him."

"A year? You've been doing this for a year?"

"No, I was out of it for a while after that fight. He... he put me in the hospital. Almost killed me."

I can't even form words. I think I say, "Wow," or something similarly inappropriate.

"I told my parents I got hit by a speeding taxi while I was walking down the street. Luckily, I didn't have a costume back then, so when I showed up to the hospital, bloody and broken, they didn't suspect anything—or at least if they did, they never said anything.

"Even after I recovered, I didn't really recover, if you know what I mean."

I do. I guess that's the reason Harrier is so adamant about heroes being licensed.

"So why go after him again?" I ask.

"What would you do?" Her tone is slightly accusatory, but I guess the question makes sense.

She isn't wrong, either. If I were her, I'd have an arch-nemesis for life. Actually, it's kind of cool that she has one, even if he had no clue what he'd done. Oh. Ouch.

As if she read my thoughts, she says, "Crapface didn't even remember me."

"I'm sorry," I say, and I know it's not enough.

"Yeah, thanks."

Heh. Superhero problems.

We arrive back at our meeting place, too battered to do any more patrolling. Osprey walks up close to me and reaches out, then wipes some blood off of my face.

"Thanks for showing me a good time, hero."

Omigod omigod omigod, is this really gonna happen? Is it? She leans in close, and I close my eyes. Then she kisses me.

On the cheek.

I open my eyes, and she's already backed away. Osprey holds out her hand.

"Hey, before you go, I have something for you."

That smile. God, I love that smile.

"Really?"

She tosses me a small tin box. I look at the front. Not just mints—the really strong mints. I'm not sure whether to be insulted or hopeful.

"You might want to keep them in your utility belt." She shoots her grappler at a nearby rooftop and zips away into the night.

EIGHT

I'm so up from my night with Osprey, I don't even notice the light beneath my bedroom door.

But when I open it, and Mom's there, sitting on my bed, arms crossed, cigarette in hand, blowing smoke out of her nose like a dragon? I know there's gonna be a long discussion. At least there's no bottle this time.

She doesn't even wait before she starts laying into me, fiery hot as her hair.

"Where the hell have you been?"

She lowers her voice on the word "hell" like God was gonna hear her and smite her. For Mom, that was a curse word as bad as any.

"I was out," I say, nonchalantly entering and lowering my stuff to the floor.

"Out where?" She stabs the cigarette into a paper plate, which I can't imagine is a smart idea, and drops the butt into an empty diet soda can.

"Just out. With a girl."

Since when do you care?

She rolls her eyes. "I hope you used protection. The last thing you need is to be paying child support for the next eighteen years."

"Mom, it's not like that."

But I sure wish it was.

She stands and gets in my face. "You think I'm stupid?"

"Well, you did manage to get knocked up when you weren't much older than me, didn't you?"

Oh, man, that was dumb.

She slaps me across the face. Not in a child abuse sort of way. More like an old-timey, black-and-white movie sort of way.

I just fought Arnold Schwarzenegger on crack, and it still hurts, though.

"I shouldn't have said—"

"And where'd you get this?" she asks, pulling out my older, spare costume. She shoves it at me, and I couldn't be more shocked. I'm sure it shows on my face. My heart pounds like it's holding a sledgehammer, and it's trying to break out of my chest cavity with it.

"That... that..." I almost can't get any words out because I can't breathe.

"Must have cost a fortune. Just for some stupid costume party, or... or comic book convention?"

The relief is so overwhelming that I almost collapse into a puddle of goo. I'm such an idiot. Why would someone assume I'm some kind of crimefighter just because I look like a cosplayer?

"But—"

She strikes up another cigarette and waves the smoke away with her hand like my whole room doesn't already smell like an ashtray.

"I called the school today to check the time of our meeting tomorrow about you beating up that kid."

"Oh my God, Mom, I didn't beat anyone up."

"That's not the story they tell. You are out of control, young man."

Young man. Is there any more derogatory term to be called by your parents? I don't think I've ever seen her this angry.

"While I was on the phone, I had a little hunch, and I asked about your computer. You know what they told me? They said there's no government program, and they don't know where you got it from. And this..." She tosses something at me, and I almost don't catch it in time. "This... i-thing—"

"Tablet."

Damn, I thought I'd hidden that pretty well.

"Whatever it is, it's even more expensive than the laptop. I think it's pretty obvious what's going on here."

"It is?" *Wait.* So did she figure it out or not?

"You're selling drugs."

I can't help it. I bust out laughing. It's like one part humor and a hundred parts relief. I really need to learn some self-control.

"What's so funny?"

"You think I'm... I'm..." I laugh some more. It's just so stupid. A drug dealer? I literally took down a drug dealer two nights ago. Oh, man. I sigh. That's rich.

What I don't think about is how disrespectful this must sound to her.

"You stay out until all hours. You come home with bruises and cuts that you can't explain. Like this one. And this... What the heck happened to you tonight? Jesus. And you buy all these expensive things when we don't have any money. What else can it be?"

Hmmm. Good question. What else could it be?

She blows out a puff of smoke, filling my room like a nasty biker bar. "Things are going to change. I'm getting my act together, and so are you." This causes her to think twice about her cigarette. She looks at it, then smashes it out.

"What?" That took a turn. I don't think I could have expected that in a million years. No, a billion. I can't believe where this is going. How did things turn so crappy so fast?

"Yes, you heard me. Things are going to change."

"I can't wait," I say, and plop down on my bed with my head in my hands.

Life just keeps getting better and better.

"I like to think of my students as delicate flowers," Mr. Blanchard says from the other side of his desk.

Ho-lee sh—

"And, Ms. Vincent, I'm afraid your son is wilting."

"Wilting?" my mom says. Her hand reaches for her mouth, her words almost a whisper like she's in shock.

"Mmm-hmm. And I fear it's partially my fault." He shakes his head dramatically.

I can't believe the level of garbage going on here.

"Oh, gosh, no. Mr. Blanchard. Don't even think that."

I'm sitting here in a metal folding chair that Hector the custodian brought in for my mom and me, stunned that this conversation is even being conducted, while Logan and his mom sit in the plush chairs.

Apparently, Logan's dad was too busy at work, selling used cars, to be bothered to show up.

"I should've seen the signs," Blanchard says. "Mr. Treasure, the overseer of our Robotics Club says your son has been working on 'questionable projects.'"

My mom looks at me, and I just continue sitting there in shock.

"Mr. Peel, our esteemed history teacher, says that Sawyer here is a constant distraction and never pays attention."

Logan smiles, then quickly wipes it off his face when Mr. Blanchard looks to him. With those acting skills, he should be auditioning for the school play.

"And poor Logan here. Even worse, his mother. The things Sawyer said can't even be repeated in the presence of you two lovely ladies."

"Well, I think I've heard enough," Mom says. "Mrs. Andrews, I am so sorry for my son's behavior."

"Mom!" I protest.

She turns and shoots daggers at me with her eyes.

"Mom," I say softer. "You're not really buying all this crap, are you?"

"Sawyer, have some respect," she says. Then she does that silent "I'm sorry" thing that adults do to Mr. Blanchard.

You know, the one where you mouth the word and gesticulate with your hands?

"Mom, he hit *me*."

"Then why is he the only one injured?" she asks.

"Because I ducked, and he hit my locker! The dent is still there. Geez. I'll show it to you."

"That won't be necessary," Mom says.

"Or possible," Blanchard adds. "Mr. Hector takes good care of our school, and he didn't notice any dents, new or old."

"Unreal," I say, shaking my head.

"You've got to understand, Mrs. Vincent, Logan is our star athlete. He's going to be on the bench, nursing that broken hand for quite some time. This could affect his entire future. We have to make an example of your son. Otherwise, we're going to have a school full of students who think they can just pick fights whenever it strikes their fancy."

"This is bullshit," I say under my breath.

"Sawyer!" Mom says.

"Mr. Vincent!" Mr. Blanchard says at the same time.

"My word," Mrs. Andrews whispers.

After everyone has recovered from what they act like was the first time any of them had heard a swear word, my mom says, "I understand, Principal Blanchard."

Aaaand, why wouldn't she? After all, she was head cheerleader in high school before she got pregnant at only eighteen during her senior year.

"Again, Mrs. Andrews, I'm so sorry," she says to Logan's mom.

"At least it's good to know he comes from good stock," Mrs. Andrews says.

Good stock? What is this, the medieval times? God, kill me. Just end it now.

After Logan and his mom leave, the meeting changes focus to my "Underachievement." Apparently, my aptitude scores were off the charts, so the only way I could be doing this badly in school is laziness.

Me. Lazy. Right.

When the new semester starts next week, I'm gonna be placed in honors and AP classes, and I'll be expected to work extra hard to catch up. I'll also be placed in a special program for "at-risk" kids, where I get free tutoring after school and for a few hours every Saturday. And, to top it off, my mom is gonna start dragging me to church on Sundays, followed by Bible study.

I'm totally screwed.

P.E. class.

Hate it. I ditch it, figuring I can't get into any more trouble than I'm already in. Not only is Coach Carmichael my least favorite teacher, but it's right before lunch. This is the only chance I'll have to tell Harrier I won't be around for a while, since my mom found my phone and took it away, assuming it was part of my dark, shadowy secret life slinging drugs.

Can't help but snigger at the thought.

Calling Harrier from a landline won't be possible because

I have no idea what his number is. It was pre-programmed into the cell phone he gave me, and there was some kind of app on there that masked the number. Besides, who has a landline anymore?

So, I head to the Aerie as quickly as I can. Without my costume, new cape, especially, the trek is a bit longer than it could've been. But in New York, no one even looks twice at a kid my age leaping and vaulting up and down walls. Hopefully, I can be back before lunch ends after P.E., so I don't have to miss history class also since I now know that Mr. Peel thinks I'm some kind of a trouble-student.

But when I get to the Aerie, Harrier isn't around. I check everywhere and even go down to the penthouse in case he's still asleep after a long night. It would've had to have been a night of debauchery since I know for sure he wasn't patrolling. No luck. And his bed doesn't look like it's been slept in—or *not* slept in, for that matter.

I guess he could be at some kind of board meeting or something downstairs at Douglas Industries, but he rarely shows up for those kinds of things. He always lets Mr. Chen —the one other person he trusts besides me—take care of all the business stuff.

Then again, maybe he just got lucky and stayed in a hotel or... *gasp*... at her house. I did see him on TV a couple of days ago, out on a date with that one actress. I can't think of her name, but you'd know her if you saw her. She's been in a bunch of stuff.

He pretends the billionaire player thing is just an act, but I know him well enough to see that it's the one thing he legitimately enjoys about being a handsome, rich guy. Franklin

Douglas III usually crests any "most eligible bachelor" list, leaving even the most popular movie stars and athletes in the dust. As a matter of fact, he even beats out Black Harrier, since nobody knows they're the same person.

I teased him about it once, but after the harsh overreaction I got, I never brought it up again. The way he acted, you would've thought I'd made a joke about his dad being murdered or something.

Back in the Aerie, I look around the place, and I consider Osprey's words. How she'd give anything to be Black Harrier's partner. Now that I'm grounded for the next millennium, I feel like I should've enjoyed the place more when I'd had the chance. It has everything, and I've just taken it for granted. Why do people always do that?

It's seriously weird, him not being here. He's always here, and if he's not, Frank Douglas is on the news. I haven't really thought about that business card, I've been so preoccupied with Osprey, but I look around for it with no luck.

I promise myself that if this blows over and things go back to "normal"—I can't help but smile at that word—then I'm gonna appreciate being here a lot more. And I'll appreciate him a lot more, too.

I leave Harrier a message on the desktop of his giant computer screen to make sure he doesn't miss it. The heavy clack of the keyboard under my fingers feels surprisingly satisfying, and I might actually understand why he likes it so much. I tell him I'm not sure when I'll be able to go back to crime-fighting, or when I'll even be able to contact him.

I leave out the fact that I'm starting to feel like I may never see him again.

NINE

GROAN.

The next couple of weeks are the worst ever. It's all about going to school, improving my grades, and being punished for stuff I never even did. Plus, Logan's always mad-dogging me and making sure I know he's my stalker now, even though he's waiting to get his revenge. Oh, and to round out the pile of dung? His hand wasn't even broken, and it's getting better fast. Now he just has to wait for the right time.

And it turns out I did get into even more trouble for ditching P.E. Now I'm the towel boy for the wrestling team on top of everything else. And three guesses who the star of the wrestling team is.

Actually, I bet you can get it in one.

Meanwhile, I don't see Harrier, I don't see Osprey, and I don't get to do any crimefighting. In fact, without my tablet, my phone, and my laptop, I feel like I'm living in the Stone Age. I even had to hide my costume really well on the roof of our building, since my mom regularly ransacks my room now.

One day after wrestling practice is over, I'm getting ready to put away the mats when I hear someone approach me from behind. From the heaviness of the footsteps, I correctly assume it's Logan.

Everyone else has already hit the locker room, and Coach Carmichael is in his office. Logan's had the bandage off for a couple of days now, so I know what's coming. The difference is, this time, he can't have any witnesses because of what happened last time.

"Hey, loser." I can hear the sneer in his voice.

I try to ignore him, knowing that it isn't gonna work.

"Hey, I'm freakin talking to you, butt nugget."

Oh, butt nugget. That's a good one. Bullies, dumb as dirt, every time.

"Turn around," he commands me.

Figuring I have to play the part of helpless nerd, I turn around slowly and face him. As much as you can face someone who's more than a foot taller than you, anyway. He looks down at me, his lip curled into a snarl. He even looks like he's shaking like a crazy person. If he only knew I've squared off with La Cucaracha.

"My hand is better."

"Bet you missed it at night."

"Yeah, funny. Won't be laughing long, though." He makes a fist and punches his own palm to illustrate his point.

"You don't want to do this, Logan."

"What the eff are you talking about?" He looks at me suspiciously.

"I don't want to hurt you again."

He laughs. "You didn't hurt me, loser. I hurt myself. But this time, there's no locker, and I'm not gonna miss."

He swings, and I easily step out of the way. But as he loses his balance, he decides to barrel into me with his shoulder, a move so stupid that I wasn't prepared for it at all.

We both fall to the mat, and he tries to get on top of me. He's actually a really good wrestler, but I'm... well, you know. I turn him around and grab his arm, twisting it behind his back. With my other hand, I tap a pressure point—the brachial plexus—that paralyzes him.

"Had enough?"

I guess he hasn't. "You better freakin kill me, 'cause I *will* get you for this."

How do you even deal with a psycho like this? Obviously, I can't kill him. What am I supposed to do?

"Gentlemen!" Coach Carmichael really knows how to yell. "What's going on here?"

I look up, and he's standing in front of the entire wrestling team, most of which have looks of utter disbelief etched on their faces.

"Did you see that?" one says.

"What a freak," whispers another.

"Daaaayum, Logan got owned."

I let go of his arm and jump up. Logan collapses onto the mat, and I hear a quiet groan leak out of him.

"Uh... Logan was just teaching me some wrestling moves, Coach."

"Well, he must be quite a teacher. I've never seen anyone pin someone who outweighed them by so much like that."

The shock is as apparent in his voice as it is visible on his face.

Dammit, Sawyer. This is not how you stay invisible.

"I, uh... I'll just finish with the mats and the towels, sir."

"Forget the towels! You're an official member of the team now."

The other wrestlers look at one another in shock, and I look down at Logan, who's struggling to get up.

When is this hell gonna end?

At home, Mom has been staying sober and going to AA meetings. I never thought I'd be mad that she got her act together —okay, reality? I never thought she'd get her act together at all —but it's the worst time ever for me. Suddenly, she thinks she's super-mom just because she makes me some toast in the morning before school and isn't passed out drunk when I get home.

She also doesn't currently have any boyfriends, something which has definitely been an underrated joy in my life. Don't misunderstand. Most of the guys she's dated were complete losers who made her look like a great catch, and the ones that weren't were obviously only after one thing—and that thing isn't something a kid wants to think about when it comes to his mom. But at least they kept her attention off of me.

I'm not sure where she got her inferiority complex because it's painfully obvious that most men like her—a lot. And yet she always ends up with the worst guys possible.

More than half the time they're married or have serious girlfriends, which has led to endless fights between my mom and other women. Some of them have even shown up to our apartment at all hours, demanding to know where their men are.

To make matters worse, we live in a one-bedroom, so when she does have a guy over, they're either in the middle of the living room or—grossest of all—in my bed.

A few of them have even tried to hit me, but once I learned to fight, that came to an abrupt and bloody end. They never tried it in front of my mom, so that left me free to break some wrists, noses, and ribs before these ass-hats knew what hit them.

To top it all off, she's making a little extra money now by watching the neighbors' little kid while they're at work, which is a lot. In fact, I think they pretend they're at work quite a bit more than they actually are to get a longer break from him. So, in addition to not having any privacy, I have the little monster running around the house when I get home. And the shows he watches... with those songs that get stuck in your head... I literally feel like I'm going insane.

Between my mom's reality shows, trailer-trash talk shows, and the little asswipe's cartoons and annoying sing-song crap, I can't even watch the news.

I'm totally out of touch.

I walk in our front door, and Mom is making dinner. It appears to be an attempt at spaghetti, only the sauce looks like ketchup, and there are cut up hot dogs in it instead of meatballs. I know I shouldn't be so picky, but Harrier usually gets us takeout from the best restaurants in town, many of which he owns, which are not only healthy but delicious. I'm gonna have a hard time keeping this stuff down.

The brat she babysits, Aiden—even his name bothers me—doesn't seem to have a problem with it, though. He's scarfing it down like he hasn't eaten in days, and it's all over his face. When he opens his mouth to show me what's in there, I gag.

"Have a seat. I'll get you some." Mom's proud of this crap?

I sit on one of our rickety, mismatched wooden chairs, and the rug rat stares at me from across the tiny table, still chewing with his mouth open. All of a sudden, he stops eating and closes his eyes. The next thing I know, he sneezes right at me, spraying me with greenish snot and red and white bits of food.

Totally disgusting.

"Gross!" I shout, and Aiden laughs like the little imp he is.

My mom, of course, doesn't even notice it's all over me.

"Bless you!" she says, tussling Aiden's black mop. "Sawyer, you might not want to get too close, he's pretty sick."

I do my best to wipe everything off me. "Yeah. Thanks for the warning."

Mom dumps some of her pasta-ish stuff into a plastic bowl and sets it down in front of me. For the first time in my life, I wish we had a dog just so I could feed it under the table.

Except that might be cruelty to animals.

"Sawyer, there's something I've been meaning to talk to you about."

Uh-oh. I don't respond. I just look up from my food.

"I know I haven't set the best example for you. When I said things are going to change, I meant it. We're going to make something of ourselves."

Mom is full of staggering sentiments lately, this one ranking high on the list.

"I—uh, okay?"

She smiles and says, "How was school today?" She looks at her watch. "You're home late. You're still grounded. You know that, right?"

"Yeah. I..."

I decide to tell her since she's gonna find out soon enough anyway. "Coach, um, made me part of the team."

"What?" She really could've turned down the shock a little bit to spare my feelings.

"The wrestling team. I'm on it now." As much as I hate the situation, I have to admit I enjoy telling her now that I see how low her expectations are for me.

"That's... amazing. How did it happen?"

Okay, Mom, you can pick your jaw up off the floor already.

"I just tried a couple of holds with some of the guys after practice, and the coach said I was pretty good."

Can't tell her the truth, that's for sure.

"Huh. Well, I certainly wasn't expecting that to happen. But good for you. I'm glad you finally found something you're good at."

Ouch. Not that I'd know from personal experience, but moms aren't supposed to talk to their kids this way, are they?

I take a drink of the watered-down grape Kool-Aid she gave me to wash down the bad taste in my mouth. From the food *and* her comments. It doesn't help.

"That's not true. I'm good at... at..." *What?* Go ahead and tell her: Krav Maga, Kung fu, Karate, Tae Kwon Do, Judo, Jiu-Jitsu, Muay Thai, kickboxing, nunchakus, acrobatics, computers, detective work, parkour, swinging from rooftops, *freaking flying...*

She raises her eyebrows, waiting for an answer. The kid is staring at me, too, snot running down over his lip, dangerously close to his mouth.

"I don't know. *Stuff.*" I stand up and set my bowl in the sink, then stomp off to my room like a three-year-old.

Busy feeding Aiden, who now has spaghetti on the top of his head, Mom doesn't even look at me.

Why am I so upset? I've spent years covering up the fact that I'm so good at everything. Apparently, I'm really good at making believe I'm not good at *anything*. Is it really unreasonable that people believe it?

As I'm passing the TV, which mom must've left on, I spot Harrier in the little box above the news anchor's right shoulder. I stop and turn up the volume since the brat is singing some song from one of his shows at the top of his lungs back in the kitchen.

"Where is the Black Harrier?" The anchor is a pretty woman with blonde hair. Kinda reminds me of Osprey. "With our favorite night-time avenger absent, the city is experiencing a noticeable uptick in crime. From robberies, carjackings, and muggings to rapes and murders. Has New York stepped into a new era overnight?"

That's not good. If other people are noticing Harrier being gone, that means I'm not being paranoid. Of course, Harrier has done this before when he's had missions in other countries or went deep undercover, but I decide I should probably look into it anyway.

"Notorious supervillains have been spotted all over the city. Sources tell us, La Cucaracha's gang has hit more than twelve jewelry stores in just the past week. So, I ask again, where is Black Harrier?"

If anyone knows where he is, I'm guessing it'd be Mr. Chen. I guess a trip to Douglas Industries is in order. Good thing tomorrow's Saturday.

Since my mom doesn't have a regular job, she sleeps a lot during the day and stays up most of the night to make sure I'm in bed. She probably won't even notice I'm gone.

SNACKS.

Everyone needs them. While skating on the way to meet with Chen, I stop at the Mini-Mart on the corner for some junk food. Luckily, Mom still hasn't found the debit card Harrier gave me for things like this. I grab a bag of my favorite spicy chips and an energy drink and head for the checkout, but I notice something's wrong.

The guy behind the counter has his hands in the air, and there are five guys a little older than me grabbing the money out of the register and anything else they can carry. I look up at the security mirror and see that three of them have guns pointed at the guy. Unlike that carjacker from the other night, these guns look real. Two Sigs and a Glock. Not exactly cheap either.

I swear under my breath and duck behind a rack of gummy snacks. They haven't noticed me yet, so I decide to take them out as quickly and quietly as possible. I crouch and silently approach them from behind. But the clerk blows it by looking directly at me as I'm about to attack, and the bad guys immediately turn and point their weapons at me.

Now it'll probably get messy.

I jump on my board and throw my energy drink at the one farthest one from me. It explodes all over his face as it cracks him in the nose. I hear a gun fire, but I don't feel anything. Scared shooters rarely hit their targets. The problem is, that means someone else might have been hit, included anyone who happened to be walking by. I take solace in the fact that I heard no glass shatter, and in a split second, I'm right on top of them.

Now that I'm closer, I grab the gun arm of the guy closest to me and spin him around so that he's in front of me. Luckily, I'm right in thinking that his friend isn't gonna shoot him to get to me. But he does try to shoot over his friend's shoulder and hit me in the face with the bullet—except he fires wide and it smashes the glass on the refrigerated display nearby, busting a forty-ouncer, which sprays all over the place.

The destroyed fridge upsets the clerk so much that he starts yelling at the shooter, which is about as stupid as stupid gets. The only good thing about it is that the guy turns to point his gun at him instead of me, which will give me a chance to make a move.

I karate chop a pressure point on the neck of the guy I'm holding, and he drops. Then with a swoop of my legs, I have Trigger Happy down on the ground. A quick blow to the face, and he's out cold, leaving only two more to handle.

Leftover Punk Number One goes to shoot me, so I kick my skateboard up into my hands and swing it at him. It knocks the gun free, which allows me to take him down with a combo move that ends with my knee against his temple. Four down, one to go.

Number Five is too scared to shoot. He drops his weapon and just looks at me, which is a reaction I get a lot from someone who's seen me take down several of his friends. I start to smile, but then I realize I don't have my mask on.

And then, I recognize this kid from my history class. I think his name is Benji... yeah, dumb name. We stare each other down for a few seconds. Then, as if an unspoken agreement has taken place, he nods at me and runs out of the store. That's when I notice there's someone else in the store with us.

I turn and look down one of the aisles, and Javier is standing there so still, with his mouth so wide, he could catch flies. Bowling balls pop out of his eye sockets, and he drops the chocolate milk and mini-donuts he's holding.

Crap.

He looks like he's afraid of me, and he takes off running out of the store. Before I can go after him, the clerk starts berating me in a language I don't understand, as if stopping a robbery and possibly saving his life isn't enough.

He's mad that I messed up his store and let one get away.

So now, not only am I stuck on the wrestling team, but some kids from my school know I'm not what I appear to be. I wonder if any of them have the brains to put together that one of their classmates can take down criminals the same way as the famous teenage sidekick who operates in the same neighborhood. I doubt those goons are very bright, but Javier could be a problem.

So what happens to me if everyone finds out I'm Red Ki —er, Raptor, anyway? Do they lock me up for assaulting so many people, even though they all deserved it? Do they give me a medal for helping to put so many criminals behind bars? Do the police throw me into an interrogation room and question me until I give up the identity of the Black Harrier?

I have no idea.

While other kids my age are worried about having a sweet pair of kicks or getting rid of that zit on the end of their nose before their date Saturday night, these are the things I have to think about. Hiding my secret identity. Pretending to be a loser who sucks at everything in life. Oh yeah, and trying not to get murdered by one of a dozen supervillains.

It's strange rolling up to Douglas Industries on the ground floor. I can probably count on one hand the number I've times I've entered the building this way, and have fingers left over. All of those times, it's been to eat at the restaurant. I stop and check myself in the blue-tinted reflection.

Am I a mess after kicking those dudes' asses? I've canvased my body ten times in case of blood or anything else that would get security suspicious, but I guess it was a pretty clean fight, all in all.

I kick my board up into my hands and sling it to my backpack. I look up at the impossibly tall building in the middle of Manhattan and stride toward the doors.

The doorman looks down his nose at me as I approach the lobby entry.

"Can I help you with something?" His voice is dripping with condescension.

Dude, if you only knew who I was and how many times I've hung out in the penthouse. You open a freaking door for a living. "Oh, sure, you can leave that package with me... Ma'am, I believe you just dragged poop in on your shoe... Let me get that for you."

"Nah, I'm okay," I say as I reach for the door handle myself, not expecting him to do it for me.

He puts his foot in front of it, and the door shudders, making our reflections ripple. "I'm sorry, do you have business here in the building?"

I hate to say this, but I may have to get this guy fired. Assuming I ever talk to Frank again, that is. Does he even know how his employee treats people down here? Probably not. I mean, it's not like he's gonna act this way in front of the owner of the building.

"Yeah, as a matter of fact, I do. I'm meeting with Mr. Chen." That's a lie. He has no idea I'm coming.

The doorman gives me a disbelieving look. "At Douglas Industries?"

"Bingo, that's the Mr. Chen I'm talking about. Now, can I...?" I try pulling on the door handle again. His foot remains planted.

"Look, kid. I can't let in every teenager with a story. You got some sort of... proof?"

Okay, he's got a point. Maybe I won't get him fired. In fact, he should probably get a raise. I didn't even think I'd need proof. I don't even know what proof would look like.

Damn him for actually making some sense. Now how am I supposed to hate his guts?

"Is it common practice to not let people into a public building?"

The guy pretends to pick some lint off his sleeve. "As a matter of fact, this building is private. Do you have any proof of your meeting with Mr. Chen?"

I shake my head. "No, I don't have a note from him saying I'm allowed to enter the building if that's what you're implying. I don't get it, is there a problem here? Why are you giving me such a hard time?"

Just then, a couple of guys in two-thousand-dollar suits walk up to the door, and the doorman puts his hand on my chest to hold me back as he opens the door, smiles, and nods at them. He closes the door immediately.

Yeah... okay... back to firing.

I really wish I could break his wrist as he removes his hand from my chest. Remember, Sawyer, you're one of the good guys.

"How come you didn't ask those guys if they have any business here?"

Frustrated, he suddenly drops what he probably thought was a super-professional demeanor. "Because they *look* like they belong here, and because I see them every day. You think you're the first kid trying to get in who doesn't work or live here and isn't visiting someone who does?"

"I just told you, I *am* visiting someone who works here. Mr. Chen?"

"Luis Chen is a very public personality. Everyone knows

he works here. Anyone could say they are visiting him. My job is to obtain proof before letting in riffraff."

"Oh, I'm riffraff, now?" I say.

He looks me up and down, then shrugs.

"What if I just wanted to go to *Le Meilleur Plat?*"

Best French food in the whole city. Super expensive. Super delish. My mouth starts salivating at the thought.

"Dressed like that?"

Riiiight.

"Come on, kid. You're wasting my time. Unless you can show me that you really have a meeting with Mr. Chen, then I can't let you in. My job's at stake."

I go to pull out my phone to try to dial up to Mr. Chen to let me in, then realize I don't have it. It's only about the zillionth time I've done that since Mom took it away. I'm such an idiot. I should've figured out a way to make an appointment to see him. I mean, it's Saturday. He might not even be here.

"I don't know what to tell you. I'm supposed to meet with him about doing some community service for the Douglas Foundation, but he didn't give me anything to get me in the door."

He looks me up and down again, but this time it seems like he's softening a little. "Charity, huh?"

I try to do my best puppy dog eyes. I have no idea if it's decent or totally ridiculous. "He visited my school last week. Found out I was a... a trouble-student. 'At-risk,' they said." A good lie has a bit of the truth, right? "But then my robotics teacher showed him some of my gadgets, and he offered to show me around his lab. He offered to take me under his wing."

He still doesn't appear convinced, but I'm wearing him down.

"Please, Mister. This is my last shot before I end up in juvie. Or, at least, that's what my mom said. If I go home without paperwork from Mr. Chen saying I can start this internship, I'm screwed."

The doorman looks up to the sky for a second and lets out a breath. I think he's about to give in, but instead, he goes into a long story about this being his first break. He shows me gang ink on his wrist and tells me how Mr. Douglas gave him this opportunity. He tries to give me his phone number in case I need some accountability or something. I think he actually cries.

"If it wasn't for this place," he says, lovingly tapping the door, "I'd be doing hard time. I know it."

"Uh. Yeah." I rub my neck. "So, can I go in?"

"Okay. Fine. I'm a sucker for a redemption story."

"Really?"

"Yeah. You go get 'em, kid. Just don't get me into any trouble for this."

"Thanks! I really appreciate it." I rush through the door before he changes his mind.

From behind me, he makes that sound you do to a dog when you want it to stop whatever it's doing, and I turn.

"Board stays here," he says.

"Yeah. Okay. Sure," I say.

"You know what? Just leave the bag, too. Can't be too careful."

I groan as I remove the backpack, skateboard still attached, and place it behind a podium by the door.

"Nothing better be missing when I get back," I say.

The doorman juts his chin out and lets the doors slam shut.

"A-hole," I say under my breath.

Douglas Tower is easily one of the most lavish places in the city. The lobby looks like something straight out of a science fiction film starring Tom Cruise. Glass and metal everywhere. No crystal chandeliers like the other snobby places. Instead, these huge LED discs hover about twenty feet above me, varying in sizes, but many of them are up to a couple dozen feet in diameter. It's all unbelievably impressive and lights the room in a soft, white glow.

Four glass elevators rise up from the center of the lobby and break through a ceiling—also made of glass—about four floors up. They'll continue out in the openness of the outside air another, like, fifty stories.

Currently, one set of elevator doors is about to close, so I sprint over and jam my foot in just in time to stop them. They open up to an already-crowded elevator full of business executives and wealthy residents. Every one of them looks pissed at me as I squeeze in amongst them and reach over to press the button for the main office of Douglas Industries.

The doorman wasn't wrong. I feel really out of place in my T-shirt, jeans, and hoodie with them all dressed in expensive suits and dresses. At first, the only sound in the elevator is the muzak they play over the speakers—really horrible stuff. Then, two of the business bros start a conversation about TPS reports that makes me wish for the muzak by comparison.

The elevator is so crowded that when it stops at a floor, half of us have to step off momentarily to allow others to exit.

Then, it starts up again, and we "burst" through the glass above us—I mean, not really, it doesn't break, but it looks like you're heading right for a ceiling, and then you're looking at the city. Best view there is other than Frank's penthouse.

After what feels like an eternity, we finally get to my floor, and I feel the exhilaration of a prisoner being set free from years in the slammer.

There are no fake greens, no magazines in waiting rooms, no TVs playing silly advertisements for products. Just like Black Harrier—all work. Really, it's Mr. Chen's influence, though. He runs the place.

I approach the reception desk as Douglas employees rush around in all directions, in and out of the many glass doors leading to various offices and conference rooms. The giant DI logo looms above the head receptionist, who sits in the middle of a long, round desk surrounded by four other people answering the phone lines.

A gorgeous redhead with lips the color of ripe plums stares and is genuinely surprised to see someone like me walking in. Makes me wonder if hiring receptionists is one job Frank does himself around here. "Can I help you?"

For a second, I'm speechless. Now, *she* is what I would expect from Frank Douglas.

"I'm, uh, here to see Mr. Chen."

She's taken aback by the statement. I'm sure the only

thing that would have shocked her more would be if I'd asked to see Frank. "Do you have an appointment?"

"No, I didn't really think about it. I guess I really should've called ahead."

Somehow, she gives the impression of rolling her eyes even though those beautiful green lovelies never move a millimeter.

"I'm afraid there's nothing I can do for you." She slides a business card across the desk at the same time as she lowers her gaze back to her work. "Give us a call and make an appointment."

"Can't I make one now? It's kind of important."

She looks up, probably annoyed. Sighing, she says, "I'm sorry, it doesn't work that way. You have to call our appointment department. It's the 800 number on the card I just handed you."

The white linen card has a small DI logo and the word "Appointments," along with a phone number, just as she'd said. No names. No other information. There's an entire department just for making appointments?

"Please," I say, drawing her attention again. "There's no way you can just call him and ask if he'll see me?"

"Mr. Chen is a very important person. And he's in a meeting right now with other very important people."

Got it. I'm not important.

"And he gave explicit instructions not to be disturbed. The only person he would take a call from right now is Mr. Douglas."

Oh, the irony. The whole reason I'm here is that "Mr. Douglas" seems to have disappeared.

"I guess I'll give this number a call, then."

"You do that. Have a pleasant day." She immediately goes back to whatever she was doing before I'd walked in, and it's like I never existed.

I start the trek back to the elevators, feeling totally defeated, and press the 'down' button. Just as the doors open, I hear a voice from behind me. "Sawyer?"

I turn and see Mr. Chen exiting one of the conference rooms. In one hand—oh right... he has a bionic hand—he holds a tablet similar to the one my Mom ganked from me. I never asked what happened, but I'm pretty sure Frank met him in the service, so it might be an old war wound. And with all the crazy technology DI develops, I can guarantee that hand is state-of-the-art.

He passes the tablet to someone else and tells the rest of his people to go on without him.

Relief hits me like a wave, and I smile broadly while walking toward him. He does the same, then shakes my hand with his human one, a big smile on his face. "What brings you to our offices?"

"I was actually hoping to talk to you for a minute? Guess I should've called first." I look over at the receptionist, who now wears a shocked expression. I won't lie, it feels good.

"Nonsense. I always have time for you." Mr. Chen looks over at her as well, and her face turns redder than her hair. "Let's head back to my office."

He guides me down a long corridor, glass cubicles on both sides, little worker ants doing little worker ant things in each one. We go all the way down to the end, where a set of double doors have a brass plate saying, "Franklin Douglas III, President and Chief Executive Officer."

Instead of entering Frank's office, we turn to the one next to it, which indicates that Mr. Chen is the "Senior Vice President and Chief Operating Officer." Like I said, he's the one who really runs things around here.

It's funny, I've been working with Frank for almost three years, and I've never been here. Never seen anything beyond the receptionists' desk, and even then, it was only from the elevator doors.

Mr. Chen's office is gigantic, so I can't even imagine how big Frank's must be. Shelves full of boring-looking books and binders line two of the walls. Three TV sets with giant screens are mounted on the same wall as the office door, each showing a different news or financial channel. He has a fireplace on one of the walls with books, which seems like a fire hazard to me, but whatever. Above the mantle, a painting of Frank hangs, as if he's looking down upon everything that happens around here.

Mr. Chen sees me eyeing the painting and smiles. "That's sort of an inside joke. Frank and I know how ridiculous it is, but everyone who comes in here wonders about it. You know, did Frank make me put it up—or did I put it up to kiss up to him? That sort of thing. Keeps people distracted and off-balance when I'm making business deals."

"Uh, yeah. That's... pretty hilarious." The painting is so realistic, and the eyes look like they're staring into my soul. I see what he's talking about. I wish I was kidding when I say there are probably little cameras behind the eyes, so Frank really can watch what goes on from the Aerie.

Chen motions to a black leather chair in front of his desk, and I've never seen anything more comfortable-looking. He lowers himself into a plush captain's chair situated behind his giant mahogany desk and lets out a sigh. "Please, have a seat. You look parched. Let me get you something to drink."

"No, I'm actually—"

He holds up a finger to stop me while he presses a buzzer on his desk. "Pam, please have a beverage cart brought in."

"*Right away, sir.*"

"And please continue to hold all my calls."

"*Yes, sir.*"

So, while the rest of Douglas Tower looks crazy-modern and sleek, Mr. Chen's office is all dark wood and amber light. Behind his desk, on a credenza, is a picture of him with his wife and daughter, whom I've never met. There's also what looks like a graduation picture of his daughter, who's... wow... really cute.

I think he notices me staring, cos a second later he says, "That's Amy. She's starting college this year."

I just nod. What am I supposed to say, *Oh, she's really hot, sir?*

A young woman—another redhead... *Geez, Frank*—enters the office with a cart full of drinks and wheels it right over to me. There's everything: water, coffee, hot tea, iced tea, lemonade, soda... I don't know where to even begin. I grab an ice-cold water bottle and crack open the cap. The woman hands me a glass full of sphere-shaped ice, and I thank her.

"Thank you. That will be all, MJ." She nods in response to Mr. Chen's dismissal and quickly leaves the room. "So, to what do I owe the pleasure of your company today?"

"It's about Frank." His face betrays absolutely no emotion as he leans back and adjusts something on his bionic hand before flexing it once. When he says nothing, I continue. "I haven't seen him in a couple of weeks, and I was wondering if you could tell me where he is or what's going on."

"I'm afraid I can't do that, Sawyer."

"Because he told you not to tell me?" I think the question comes off sounding way more accusatory than I'd intended.

"No," he says, drawing the word out cautiously. "Because I don't know where he is."

Something I'm sure resembles panic comes bubbling from my lips. "What? Crap. Really? I don't know... Seriously? Then what—"

"Calm down, son. Frank has disappeared before. He always comes back. You know that."

"But for this long? And what about the company? And what about..." I lean forward even though nobody else is around and practically whisper, "...*you know what?*"

Mr. Chen drums his metal fingers on the desk, looks at me with a small smile, then stands, and heads to the drink cart. I'm pretty sure he's just trying to hide his face from me. It's a practiced action, for sure. I haven't spent so much time detecting with Frank to be so easily deceived.

"He doesn't really have much to do with the day-to-day operations of Douglas Industries," he says over the distinct sound of carbonation and crackling ice. "That's why he has me. As for his... *nocturnal extracurricular activities*, I believe there are others who can pick up the slack. Including yourself."

Yeah, if I wasn't grounded. I make a little noncommittal sound.

"How do you like the new cape?" he asks, almost as if trying to change the subject.

"It's amazing. Like flying."

"Good, good." He finishes pouring and leans against his desk, looking down at me. "I see you've recently made some modifications to Amber."

Shoot. I didn't know Mr. Chen would be able to see those adjustments.

He must notice the emotion wracking my features because he lets out a laugh and says, "Don't worry. I'm not upset."

"No?"

"Quite the opposite. I'm really damn impressed, Sawyer. As a matter of fact, if you ever decide you want a day job *in addition* to your nightly duties with the boss..." he nods his head to the big painting of Frank, "... I think we could use someone like you in R&D."

I won't make believe I'm not flattered and more than a little tempted. A job at DI could get Mom and me out of that crap-hole of an apartment and into a decent neighborhood. I hadn't even really thought about it. Now that I'm sixteen, there'll be a lot of new job opportunities open.

"Wow. Thanks, Mr. Chen. I... well... I don't—"

"You don't need to answer now. Just think about it, okay?"

I nod, then say, "You don't think we should be worried?"

He chuckles. "About Frank? Son, Frank Douglas is the last person I would ever worry about. If ever there was someone who could take care of himself, it's that man right there." Again he points to the painting.

I'm not convinced, but I still say, "I guess you're right."

"Is there anything else?" he asks.

"No, that's pretty much it. Thanks for seeing me."

"Thank you for coming to me with your concerns. But I'm sure everything will be just fine."

I shake his hand. But just as I'm turning away, I detect a flash of worry in his eyes. He's not as confident about Frank as he's letting on.

As I open the door to leave, I hear him behind me.

"And Sawyer..."

I turn back.

"Think about the job. It could be good for you and your family."

Back at home, Mom is making lunch for Aiden, who's running around in circles until he gets so dizzy that he falls on his face. Looks like he's feeling better. As soon as I walk in the door, she's on me.

"Where've you been? I don't think you're taking your grounding seriously enough."

"Relax. I went to talk to someone about doing the community service that I'm supposed to start." The "supposed to start" part is true, anyway. Another one of Mr. Blanchard's gifts to me for effectively dodging Logan's fist.

"Where did you go?" She looks at the skateboard hanging

from the backpack slung over my shoulder. "How do I know you weren't just out with your friends?"

I thought about this on the way home. I knew she'd have to be up by now, so I had everything planned out. "I figured you wouldn't believe me, so I grabbed a business card. I'm hoping to do some work for a charitable foundation."

Wow. Mom looks ashamed. That's a new look.

Then, I hand her the card I got from the receptionist. When she sees it, her expression morphs to surprised and lands somewhere in the neighborhood of angry. I have no idea why. "Douglas Industries? Why? Why them?"

"I don't know. I heard something about all the charity work they do, so I thought I'd check it out."

"No. You don't need to have anything to do with some big corporation. After church tomorrow, we'll talk to Father Pulliam about doing community service there." She tears the business card into little pieces and sprinkles it in the trash.

Well, that escalated quickly. So much for that job offer.

ELEVEN

MONDAY.

I jolt awake with a start. It takes me a bit to figure out where I am, even though it's my own room. I wanted to try to catch the late-night news on my laptop before sneaking out to patrol, but I must've nodded off. And, right away, I figure out why. Headache, chills, clogged sinuses, sore throat. That little germ-incubator got me sick.

After sneaking out Saturday morning, I decided to chill out last night so Mom wouldn't have any more reason to be suspicious.

I look at my clock, which is blurry from the sleep in my eyes, and see that it's after three a.m. Mom was kind enough to drape a blanket over me before calling it a night, but I listen at the door to make sure she's really asleep out on the couch. She's snoring. Not loud, but she's definitely out.

Then, I dip into the bathroom.

Uh, yeah... heroes have to pee, too.

It takes a lot of effort not to sneeze or cough, but I can't wake up Mom.

Back in my room, I put on my costume, which I'd retrieved from the roof earlier, and sneak out the window. It's not something I like to do because if someone spots me, they'll know precisely where Red Raptor lives—at least if they see me changing on the roof, they only know which building it is—but I can't sneak out the front door.

I scale the fire escape and stand on the edge of the roof. The cold, early morning air is fresh. Between that and being back in costume, I feel so good that I don't even mind when Amber greets me.

Bleep.

I take a deep breath—which is more labored than I care to admit—before plunging off into the darkness. My cape snaps out, and I glide down the street at about fifty feet up.

"Hey, Amber."

"I love the way you say my name."

"What's the scoop? Any news on the net about Harrier?"

"Just rumors and gossip streams." As if she senses my unease, she adds, *"I'm sure he's okay, Sawyer."*

Her tone is uncharacteristically... normal. Not trying to seduce me or anything. Just like... Mom... or something. I clear my throat.

"Yeah, thanks," I say. "What are you picking up? Anything close?"

"Traffic cams are picking up a mugging in front of Gentleman's Clearance House. Half a block south."

I flip mid-flight and let the swoop and dip pull me in the opposite direction. Most times, I'd have Amber make a call to the police, especially with how bad I'm feeling. However, with Harrier gone, someone has to remind these scumbags that there's still someone watching over the city.

Amber is never wrong. She's got eyes like the government —probably better. That's why it scares me that she has no idea where Harrier is.

I whip around the corner and see some dude, clearly heading to work, having his wallet taken away by a couple of guys with shaved heads and more metal in their faces than a scrapyard. Not much of a challenge, but my being sick will give them a little more of a chance. Should be fun.

I dive down and stomp the guy whose thumbing through the wallet with both my feet, sending him into a twenty-foot slide ending in a subway stairwell. I think he keeps tumbling down the stairs. I feel a little bad because that's an ER visit at best. Hopefully, it doesn't ki—

My thought is interrupted by a punch to my lower back.

I swear because now I actually have to do some work.

I assumed that after what I'd just done to his friend, the other assailants would have been hightailing toward the docks and into hiding. I turn to see another fist coming at my helmet. I don't understand that move. Who punches armor?

I duck, for no other reason but so the guy doesn't break his hand.

"What are you hoping to accomplish with that?" I say, my nose all stuffed up.

I dodge about three more attacks, each one lazy and unfocused. Then, I slam him into the metal lamp post and lower his unconscious body to the sidewalk.

I take a few steps and pick up the dude's wallet.

"Give it over, hero," the third guy says. He didn't run either? Geez. What's wrong with these guys?

I look up to see that he has the victim in a headlock, holding a knife up to his face. Suddenly, this isn't so fun anymore.

I start to reach for one of the throwing stars in my belt, but he's watching me carefully. He touches the blade to the man's face. "Move and I cut him."

I lift up my hands. "Okay, man. Stay calm."

"Give me the wallet." His hand shakes, which makes me nervous that he's gonna cut him whether he means to or not. "Slide it over here. Now!"

I toss the wallet over to him, and it lands next to his feet, credit cards and stuff spilling out. I can tell he wants to pick it up, but he's afraid I'll attack the second he no longer has the knife up to his victim.

He's right, but I try not to let him know that. "Just pick it up and let him go."

This is the point at which all criminals internally weigh the odds of escape. They know they've been caught, and that makes them a bit unpredictable. If he's got priors, he won't wanna go back. If he's a newb, he might not realize the consequences of his actions and do something rash. If he's a pro...

"How do I know you won't follow me?"

Yeah, he's somewhere in between. At least he's asking the right questions.

This isn't the first time I've dealt with someone like this. "You have my word," I say. "Just don't hurt him, and you can leave."

"Your word don't mean crap to me." He thinks for a

second. And it turns out this guy is smart. "Take off your mask."

"What?" It's so unexpected, it doesn't even register at first. There's a first time for everything. How did this go downhill so fast?

"Your mask. I wanna see your face."

"I can't really..."

"*I've alerted the police,*" Amber says into my ear. I can't answer her, but that's exactly what I needed to hear.

If I can keep him talking...

"Now." He pushes the point of the knife against his victim's face, and it draws a little blood. The dude whimpers like a beaten dog. I mean, I'm sure it's scary for him. But the thug has such a light grip, and if this guy had bothered to take even an introductory self-defense class, he'd be free, and the would-be-stabber would be on the ground clutching his nuts.

Instead, I have no idea how to handle this. Heroes and villains have an unwritten code where we don't do this type of thing. If everyone finds out our identities, it's all over. But this is just some low-level street thug.

"Okay, okay. Just stay calm." I retract my visor, and he just looks at me. "Happy?"

"Take off the damn mask, too, stupid."

My heart is racing. I have no idea what Harrier would do in this situation. I don't think I have any choice but to show the guy my face.

"I'm nobody," I say.

"Yeah. No crap. But that ain't the point. Mask. Off. Or..." he digs the knife in a little deeper, and the guy literally starts whining like a hurt puppy.

I lift my hand to my mask. I guess there's no real harm in it. He probably won't even remember what I look—*oh, no.*

The mugger pulls a cellphone from his pocket with his free hand. Another easy opportunity for the guy to escape. Anyone living in New York should really sign up for anti-mugging classes. The thug holds his camera phone up, waiting for me to lower my domino mask.

"Say cheese."

THWACK!

A boomerang flies out of the alley and knocks the phone out of his hand, followed immediately by a bola that binds his ankles together. He falls flat on his face, and I see a tooth bounce out of his mouth as his jaw hits the sidewalk.

I take my hand away from my mask, thankful that I hadn't had to remove it and run over to the victim to see if he's okay. The guy starts thanking me profusely, but I don't hear a word he's saying as I watch Osprey walk out of the alley and step on the mugger's neck. In my mind, it's like she's moving in slow motion.

"I hope you have insurance because you're going to need it."

Witty quips, judges? Six out of ten? Not bad. Not really good either. But she just saved my butt, so I certainly won't say anything.

She kicks him in the face, and he's unconscious. After picking up some things that fell out of the wallet, she walks over to return them. I don't hear anything as the guy thanks Osprey either, and I realize I must look pretty ridiculous standing there with my mouth hanging open. I just hope I'm not drooling.

I shake my head out and turn to the guy.

"Hey, take a self-defense class at the Y or something? We might not always be around."

"Y-yeah. I—thank you. Thank you."

He stands there, stumbling over more words to Osprey while I jog over to grab the thug's phone off the ground. Looking at the screen, I can see he hadn't taken any pictures, but I'm taking no chances. I pull off the back and yank out the memory card. I put it between my teeth and crack it in half. I toss it and the battery into the sewer drain, and stomp the crap out of the rest of the phone until it's tiny jagged pieces of glass and plastic.

"You good to go?" I ask the victim.

The dude tells us he's fine and that his work is only about a block away, so we watch to make sure he makes it okay.

I turn to Osprey, and I'm so happy to see her, but at the same time embarrassed about everything.

"So... I guess you saved me again."

She smiles that mind-melting smile, and for a second, I see something familiar there that I can't place, and I hadn't noticed before. Before I can think too hard on it, she's talking. "That's right. So we're no longer even. I guess I'll have to think of a way for you to pay me back."

"*I'm sure she'll think of something,*" Amber says.

I clear my throat. "I'm sure you'll think of something. How'd you find me? You stalking me again?"

"You wish. It came across on the police scanners."

Oh, right.

"Thanks, Amber," I whisper.

"You know... I've been coming by this neighborhood a

couple of times a night for the past few weeks, hoping to see you."

"That's the definition of stalking," I say with a little smile.

She gives me a playful shove, but I'm still processing things.

She's been looking for *me?* Of course she was. Why wouldn't she? I'm good looking. I'm badass. I'm...

"Yeah. About that..." What am I supposed to say? *My mommy grounded me from crimefighting?* "I've been working on an important assignment, and it's been keeping me really busy."

"You sure? Because I was afraid that maybe you didn't like me or something."

You could not be more wrong about that.

"Oh, no, no, no. That's definitely not it. Not it at all."

"Is this special assignment the same reason Harrier's been missing?"

Well, I certainly can't tell her I have no idea where my partner's been all month. "Uh, yeah. Kind of. In fact, I'm on my way to see him now."

She perks up when I say this. "How about I come along? Then we can call it even again."

And there it is. Is she using me again? This time to get to Harrier?

Stop being paranoid, Sawyer. She likes you.

"I really wish I could, but not tonight. This whole thing is really sensitive."

She looks deflated.

"I'll talk to him, though, and see if he'd be okay with you meeting him some time."

Sure. Like when hell freezes over.

"Promise?"

"Of course. Thanks again for your help." I go in for a hug, then immediately feel weird about it, and we do the awkward dance. I decide to shake her hand instead, and she gives me a weird look. So, I shoot my grappler across the street and get out of there as fast as possible.

Ugh. I'm such a freaking loser.

TWELVE

WORRIED.

I think about what I'm gonna do if I don't find Harrier. It's early morning; Mom will be awake soonish, and I don't exactly have a lot of time to go searching for him right now. Plus, I feel like absolute garbage. I wipe my nose with my cape, ignoring the fact that it immediately begins to drain again.

I could try to contact the Guild, but I'm not entirely sure how to do that. It's not like I have a number for them. Or an email address. Not even Amber is programmed to access the Guild Hall without Frank's passcode.

This kind of situation is precisely why the Guild was started, and I'm confused as to why no one seems to be more worried about Frank. Most of the time, they're just more adults making rules for no reason. But, I'll give them on thing... I used to think that if someone wants to fight crime, they should be able to fight crime without getting permission from anyone. However, Osprey's latest actions made me question that at least a little bit. Still...

I've met the Guild once. Well, most of the members anyway. It was when I first started working with Harrier, and he needed to introduce me to them. I'm sure it was just to get their approval, as if one of the head honchos needed their collective consent for his choice of partner.

He even put a blindfold on me so I wouldn't know where their headquarters was located—something about me not being able to reveal the location if I ever got captured and tortured or brainwashed. To be honest, the fact that they even consider that a possibility makes me kind of nervous. Anyway, I was excited about the opportunity to meet these people.

But like I said, some of the members weren't there. Cupid, the archer guy who flies, was pretty cool. His name would make you think he's a fat little baby, and you'd be right, minus the baby part... oh and he isn't little. And the super-speed guy, Fastlane—funniest guy I've ever met. Hands down. Bastet caught me looking through her boob window, and just smiled and winked at me. But most of them acted like they couldn't care less about meeting me. Firefly and Omar the Defenestrator were even hostile toward me. And Eaglestar, the guy I figure would have had the most say in it, didn't bother to show up.

In a way, it's like getting a bunch of movie stars together in a room. They act like they get along, but you can feel the tension because they all have such big egos, and they're trying to figure out who's more important. I guess it's hard for them when they're so used to being the most famous person anywhere. They all claim to be doing what they do because they want to help people, but I don't think anyone could do this without some level of self-importance and overconfidence.

Maybe even mental illness.

Some of them have their own partners, but most of them are labeled sidekicks, and I *know* Harrier doesn't care about *them*. So, I'm not sure how they'd react to me contacting them even if I could figure out how to do it.

Just another example of Harrier treating me like a kid. Because he doesn't give me access to information, I'm wandering around in the dark now that he's not around. How am I supposed to grow up if he never trusts me or gives me any responsibility?

Entering the Aerie, it feels cold and abandoned—lights are off, heat's off, totally silent. Scratch that... I do hear something coming from the control room.

Clackity, clack, clack, clack, clack...

My heart stutters a bit at the thought that Harrier's here and okay. I take a few quick steps, then think better of it. Although I assume it's Harrier, just to be on the safe side, I move in quietly. Good thing, too. There's someone standing at the main computer, but it's definitely not Harrier. With everything dark except for the computer screens, the figure is just a silhouette, and I can't tell much other than that it looks like a guy, and he seems to be in a costume. I can tell that he's smaller than Harrier but still bigger than me.

I silently climb onto the metal support beams above so I can literally get the drop on him. As I wait to make sure he hasn't noticed me, I can't see much more than I could before. Whoever it is had no problem getting into Harrier's system, so he must be really good at tech stuff. I go through a list of enemies who might have that capability, but none of them match the dark figure I see below. Either way, it's sort of a good sign, because most of the geeky villains who can handle that sort of thing aren't so good in the combat department.

I hop down, prepared to knock out the intruder, but I don't even come close. Before I can touch him—before I touch the ground, even—he casually grabs a staff that he has leaning against the terminal next to him and whacks me like Babe Ruth.

I barely feel it through my graphene armor, and I think he might've known that too.

Whoever this guy is, he's good.

I toss some throwing stars. It's more as a distraction than anything since I know he's gonna knock them down. I follow up with a flying kick at his head. He slaps me and the stars out of the air with almost no effort. Then, one of his heavy boots sends me sailing against the same terminal, stealing the wind from my lungs.

I can only hope he's not out to kill me because it looks like he'll be able to without breaking a sweat.

He approaches me, and now that my eyes have adjusted, I realize who he is. I've never met Redhawk—a name I really wanted, by the way. He lives in Boston—why would a hero from Boston break into Harrier's base?

"You ready to talk, or do you want to keep sparring?" It sounds like he finds the situation humorous.

"Redhawk?"

"And you're the new Kite, I presume?"

"It's Red Raptor now. And I'm not sure three years qualifies as 'new.'"

"Has it really been that long?" He smiles, and extends a hand to help me up, and I take it a little reluctantly. But like I said, if he wanted me dead, I'd probably already be.

Standing, I take a tentative step back, distancing myself from his staff.

"Red Raptor. Huh. Not bad. Aren't you worried people are gonna think you're supposed to be in Jurassic Park?"

"Maybe a little. But it's better than 'Kite.'"

"Tell me about it." He holds out his hand. "Name's Alex, the original Red Kite."

THIRTEEN

"Huh?" I say with all the intelligence of a baboon.

I've known about Redhawk for years. Sure, he lives and serves a few hundred miles away, but everyone knows Boston's guardian.

"You didn't know?" he says to me.

I feel like yelling at him. I feel like punching him. I feel like an idiot. Why hadn't Harrier told me? Was three years not long enough to earn his trust?

Instead, I just say, "No."

"Ah, well, you know Frank... you do know his name is Frank, right?" I open my mouth to respond, and he waves his hand. "Just kidding, man. Don't get your panties in a bunch."

"I'm not getting my panties in a bunch."

Bleep.

Amber can't let a comment like that go, and I know it. Too bad she won't get a chance to say anything.

"Well, I know all about you," he says and pulls a card

from his pocket—his Guild I.D. He's listed as a hero, not a protégé, like me, so he'll have the advantage of having seen my files. Me? I'd be lucky to get invited to the Christmas party. Oh, and if there is one, I don't know about it.

"That's great," I say.

"Come on, kid. Don't be like that. I'll tell you anything you wanna know. Even playing field, so to speak."

I sit in one of Harrier's leather rollie-chairs. "Was he always a dick?"

I mean it as a joke, and I think it came across that way, since Alex laughs, but I immediately feel the guilt, knowing that Harrier is missing.

"You know, when I met him, he wasn't much older than I am now. But what's crazy is I thought he was an old man. It was early on in his crime-fighting career. I think he realized he needed some help, but really didn't have anyone to trust—except maybe Luis Chen."

He practically spits Mr. Chen's name. There's something there, and I'm not about to ask. It also doesn't surprise me that Mr. Chen has known about Harrier for so long.

"I think Chen even tried his luck at the whole thing too. Successfully put away more than one supervillain."

Okay, that surprised me.

"Luis Chen?" I said. "I thought he'd always been a pencil-pusher or something."

"Yeah, more the 'or something' part. Ever heard of Yahtzee?"

"The game with the cup and dice?"

Alex chuckled. "No, back when I was a kid, Yahtzee was

one of the biggest supervillains in New York. Now, he's locked up in the Trench."

The Trench is an underwater, super-security prison where only the world's most vile villains get stored when no one knows what else to do with them. As far as I know, no one has ever escaped. They get penned in and forgotten.

"I'm surprised I haven't heard of him," I say.

Truth is, I'm in a sort of shocked state. I feel like there's an entire lifetime worth of information Harrier hasn't shared with me, and I won't make believe it doesn't hurt.

"I'm not. You were a kid... maybe not even born yet. I was barely a teenager, part of the police explorer's program. Wanted to be a cop. Part of me still does. I grew up around where you're from, actually. You know how rough that neighborhood can be. I learned everything I could—black belt in more than one martial art, as well as boxing and wrestling. I don't have your gift... took me years to learn to do what I do."

"Sorry," I say. I'm not sure why, it just feels wrong being able to pick up things so quickly while knowing the other Kites didn't.

"Not your fault. And I don't regret it either. I had more than enough reason."

I wait, hoping he'll continue without prodding, but he returns to the computer console and starts typing again. I'm patient. I don't know what he's doing, but as the first Kite, I think he's got more than enough right to do whatever it is. He punches the enter key, and a green progress bar starts inching across the screen.

He turns back to me, spinning in his chair. "So here it is. Even playing field. Just like I said." He leans forward. "One day, my whole family's out to dinner. You know that place in Bushwick—used to be a brewery, now it's some Italian joint? Pictures of tomatoes and vines all over the wall. A mural of a naked woman, leaves covering her good stuff. The servers all wearing bright white shirts, even though they're all shucking red sauce around. Classy joint. Mom even ordered wine.

"Anyway, we were just eating. I think I got veal parmesan because Dad just got a bonus check, and he said to get whatever we wanted. I didn't even know what veal was, just that it was expensive. I took my first bite when I heard it. Gunshots."

I lean forward, just like him. This guy can tell a story!

"Wasn't meant for us, but bullets don't care what names we put on them. Dead in an instant, both of them. I remember thinking how much their blood looked like the sauce. I was young... didn't get it, not really. My brother was even younger, though I almost think he knew more than me, cos he was crying in his highchair and wouldn't stop."

"That's awful," I say. I can't even imagine.

"There was a lot of screaming and people running. Someone took out a gun at the table next to us and started shooting back as they ran to the sidewalk. But it was too late for my parents."

"I never knew my dad." I have no idea why I said it. Seriously, like watching your parents get shot and growing up not knowing who your dad was are even remotely the same thing. It's just—what do you say to something like that?

"I know. And that's awful, too. Maybe a different kind of way, but still sucks."

"So, how'd you end up with Harrier?" I ask.

"After that, my brother and I ended up in the system. At Saint Barnabas Home for Boys. Not far from where you live. During a charity benefit for the orphanage, Frank, in his ten-thousand-dollar suit and shoes, sat down at the table with me and the other eight-year-olds. His knees practically touched his chest on that little chair, but he didn't seem to care. Even so many years ago, Frank always carried himself with an air of maturity. That was one of the most surreal moments of my young life."

I can't help but smile at the vision of that in my mind. Frank isn't a small guy, not by any definition.

"He just started talking to me, asking questions. Whatever. Then, it was my turn to perform. We all a special little thing we were supposed to do as a part of the evening's entertainment. I was supposed to perform some stunts as part of the benefit. I think he liked what I was able to do with my bo staff, but really, I don't know what it was. He never told me... Frank, right? Starting that night, Harrier began sponsoring me in competitions and training me in other forms that he knew."

"So, he adopted you? That's awesome."

Something like anger washes over Alex's features, but he hides it almost immediately. "I didn't say that," is all he says, and I let it stay that way.

I guess I hit a nerve because he doesn't really offer any more information, at least not freely. I ask a few more questions and find out that Harrier eventually let Alex in on his secret and allowed him to tag along on patrols.

"At first, I just wore a ski mask and body armor, but after a while, Harrier had the first Red Kite costume made for me."

"Why Kite?" I ask. It comes out as a groan.

"Why ask me? I hated it. Still do."

"What?" I've always assumed the first Kite had come up with the name himself.

"It was Harrier's idea. I wanted the name Red Hawk from the beginning, but Harrier thought it sounded too Native American or something."

"Wow," I say. Knowing Frank, he probably just didn't want the code name to sound as cool as his.

"Why are you back?" I ask. "I mean, why now? After so long, why now?"

I suspect I know the answer, but I want to hear him say it.

"Truth? I think something horrible might have happened to Frank."

Maybe I didn't want to hear him say it. My stomach does a flip and then crawls up into my throat. Between my own feelings and the news stations, I already felt like something was wrong, but I guess I'd let Mr. Chen's false confidence rub off on me a little. Now, every ounce of fear is back on me, and it's brought friends.

There's a ping on the computer behind Redhawk, and I see a familiar and horrifying face pop up.

"And this is gonna sound crazy," he says, spinning back toward the computer. "But I think Chef Maléfique is back."

"What? No way," I say. "He's dead."

"We don't know that. Not for sure. Chef Maléfique is nothing if not devious and resourceful. I have reason to believe he faked his death and has been biding his time."

"That's insane," I say.

"*He's* insane," Alex agrees. "And he's the only person I've ever seen Harrier come close to killing. And you know his one rule."

"No killing."

"Yeah, but you try being Frank and trying and failing to capture the same guy over and over again. It nearly drove him mad."

I may not know everything, but I know Chef Maléfique is the one villain Harrier could never ultimately defeat. Could never capture. It started to drive Harrier to the edge of what he would normally do as a hero. But I never thought he'd even come close to breaking his hard and fast "no killing" rule when it came to the "evil chef."

"They never discovered Chef Maléfique's true identity or his motivations," Alex continued. "He wasn't after money... in fact, most of his plans cost way more than he ever made from them. His purpose in life seemed to be to destroy Harrier—not kill him but destroy everything he stood for, and everything he did."

"Well, he didn't succeed back then, and if he is back, which I still don't buy, he won't succeed now."

"You know what happened to Toby?" Alex asks.

The second Red Kite, Toby, is an absolute enigma to me. I know less about him than I do about Alex. As a matter of fact, I didn't even realize they were separate people until I'd been with Harrier for almost a year—when I'd finally asked him about all the old Kite costumes.

"Hold on a sec..." Alex—Redhawk—click-clacks the controls of Harrier's supercomputer and works them like he's been using them for years... which he probably had.

"There's something I can show you if it's still here, but I have to warn you... it's pretty disturbing."

He taps a few more keys, and an image appears on the giant screen in front of us. A closeup of a terrifying face. Chef Maléfique. I can't see his body at this angle, but let's just say he's rotund. A sloppy, painted-on black domino mask and white makeup stain his face, and he has a thin handlebar moustache. Except for the actual chef hat he wears, he looks more like an old cartoon villain than anything else.

In the upper left corner of the video is a timer, and the demented villain appears to be filming himself while he talks directly into the camera.

I swallow hard. "Show it to me."

"Are you sure?"

I nod in silence, Alex hits the space bar, and the video begins to play...

FOURTEEN

MALÉFIQUEFOUNDFOOTAGE.MP4

10:00

What I really like best is the popping.

You know when you get that bubble wrap and squeeze those little cushion things? How good that feels? It's like that.

No, I'm not talking about *eyeballs*. Why would you think that? Those are more like grapes. Olives, maybe.

I'm talking about windpipes.

I'm sorry, is that a little too much? Maybe you better get off this ride here, then. It's only going to get juicier.

Must be this tall to ride.

No participation trophies here, folks. You have to be in it to win it.

Where was I? Oh, yes, the windpipe thing. It's always a difficult decision for me. It's my favorite way to do it—because, y'know, the *tingles*—but it's a little too quick for my taste. There are so many other ways to snuff out a candle that'll really last.

So, I try to be a good boy and not always go for the speedy, intense burst of joy. Let it sort of marinate, as it were.

That's how it is with my "friend." See what I did there? I put "friend" in air quotes because, if I'm being *frank*, we aren't all that friendly. I mean, I *am* always trying to kill him, after all.

Of course, I've had my chances to do it quickly. But where's the fun in that?

Torture? Sure. That's a given. When the time comes. But that's going to be the... the... what do you call it? *Amuse-bouche*.

No, no, no. That's not it, dadburnit.

Pre-dessert. Ha. How could I forget something that simple? Yes, the torture, when the time comes, will be like a brown sugar panna cotta with grapefruit *espuma* and cran-berry gel, topped off with some crunchy dark chocolate crumble.

Mmmmm. Yummy.

Then—and only then—will we move on to the best part. The actual dessert.

NO. Not some tiramisu, you hillbilly. I'm talking about roasted pears with espresso mascarpone cream. Or rhubarb and pistachio pavlova.

WAIT! Wait. Hold on. No, that's not it.

Strawberry, currant, and mint tart with mascarpone.

Yes, *that's the ticket.*

Remember that? I used to love that guy. Why doesn't he ever work anymore?

That's the ticket. Still makes me giggle.

.   .   .

7:57

But I'm getting way ahead of myself here. It'll be years before I'm ready for that. Right now, I'm somewhere in the middle, perhaps the removes or sorbet of my wicked menu. The kidnapping of a loved one. Yes, indeed.

One of the classics, to be sure. All the worry, the hand wringing, the popping of the acid-reducers that can be milked out of that one. It's just such a satisfying feeling to know the person you despise with every fiber of your being is going through the worst personal hell imaginable. It's even better when you're the one putting them through it.

The problem is, my friend has no loved ones. I'm not going to keep putting friend in air quotes, as I'm fully aware that will become tedious. You'll forgive. I'm sure of it.

Awww. No loved ones. Alone. All alone. Yes, it's all so very sad.

Mother died in childbirth. Father died—was *murdered*—sometime later by... oh no, I mustn't give that away. That would be so very spoilery of me.

No siblings. Nary an uncle, aunt, or cousin to his name. What to do, what to do?

Oh my, but the answer was quite simple, really. No, it couldn't be children, since he didn't have any—or *DID* he?—so it would have to be the next best thing.

A ward. Two words. Not like a trophy or plaque. A. Ward.

Ha! Now I have you thinking, "What the devil is he talking about? Does this story take place in the nineteen-aughts or some such? Chef Maléfique, that's so very Edwardian of you. Who has a ward nowadays?"

Don't worry, I'm going to answer that question, and you're bound to smack yourself silly when you realize it... A hero. A masked crimefighter. A person who runs around in a ridiculous costume.

Oh, giggle, giggle, tee-hee, but I'm one to talk, am I right?

But he gets his jollies by beating up people like... well, *moi*.

Yes, yes, now it's dawning on you, isn't it? They call them sidekicks. I'm not certain, but I believe the word comes from the ancient Greek word for "human meat shield."

What? You never realized it? They take some poor kid, dress him—or her, mustn't be a misogynist. Not in this sensitive political climate—up in spandex and bright, colorful tights, and train them to jump straight into the fray while spouting loud insults at the poor supervillain or bank robber. What's a criminal to do, just sit idly by and take it? Of course not.

So they send them into danger like a canary in a coal mine, scoping out what kinds of traps lie in wait, or how many henchmen may be hiding on the mezzanine above with machine guns, or what have you. Meanwhile, the "hero"... there I go using the air quotes again... skulks in the shadows in his—or her, yes, yes—dark-hued body armor, waiting for an opportune moment to strike.

No wonder they tend to go through them like a snack bar goes through fried butter sticks at a county fair.

Say what you will about those of us on the wrong side of the law. At least we hire minions of their own free will. And pay them, for Pete's sake. We don't bring in some poor orphan off the street and turn him into a little punchy-kicky machine.

They think they're the good guys, but I'm telling you, they're on the dark side of the game when it comes to that.

5:42

You were thinking that was a clock, weren't you? It's quite all right, no need to be embarrassed. But you're a smart one, and now you've figured it out. It's a timer. And it's counting down. And when it—Oh! There you go trying to get me to reveal spoilers again, you cad.

So, my friend's sidekick is a young man—let's call him Toby (because his name is Toby)—who dresses up in red, black, and white and uses the same code name as his predecessor, who left some time ago for personal reasons I don't have time to go into at the moment (you can see the time ticking away, after all). It is—get this—Red Kite. Kite. Isn't that a gas? And it had to be red. Because just plain Kite was taken, maybe? I don't know how these things work.

And you may wonder—because I sure as hell did—"Why would a hero name his human meat shield after a children's toy?" Or maybe it makes sense to you. I don't know, we've never met. I have no idea where your head is at.

See, the thing is, you're wrong whether you're asking the question, or whether you think you know the answer. Because a kite is not just a children's toy. It's also a fabulous bird. Go do a search on it, I'll wait.

Whoops. I just told you we didn't have time, and now I'm putting things on pause so you can type away on your typie-thingie and look at pictures. Shame on me.

But see? Fabulous, just as advertised. And, if you're really smart, you looked up "red kite," species name *Milvus milvus*, and were treated to something extra, extra fabulous after you sifted through all the nonsense about my boy, Toby. Because those little hawks are quite lovely indeed.

Sure, Toby is fabulous, too, I guess. By all accounts, the nicest young man you could ever meet. Of course, I've only met him when he was trying to shove his fist down my throat and his foot into my sensitive squishy parts. But even I am quite enamored of the boy.

I have, after all, been watching him for quite some time now. Not in a creepy way.

Well, okay, it's obviously creepy, but you know what I mean. It's not like I'm trying to do anything naughty to the tyke. Well, not like you might be thinking, anyway.

I've just been trying to figure out the best way and the best time to kidnap him so that I can tie him up and use him as bait.

3:31

Goodness, I just realized I'm almost out of time, and I haven't even told you who my friend is. He didn't just randomly choose the name Red Kite for his meat shield. He appears to have some sort of fetish for birds of prey.

He goes by Black Harrier. Or *The* Black Harrier. It's not very consistent, to be honest, and that bothers me quite a bit.

I'm not going to tell you to do a search to look up what a Black Harrier looks like because we're almost out of time, so you'll probably have to just wait until we're done here. But let me assure you, it's quite a beautiful and formidable creature.

I'm ignoring the fact that you may be, instead, thinking about a fighter plane, because the United States military decided to use that name for a jump jet. But I do want you to understand there's a reason they'd name a powerful fighter jet after such a bird. It really is magnificent.

(If instead, you're thinking about a yappy pup, then I can't *even* right now. Shame on you.)

Anyway, you may have already guessed that I have a somewhat complicated relationship with my friend. Perhaps even an unhealthy obsession with him. After all, the bird he's named after has the classification, *Circus maurus*. How funny is that? I love to put on makeup and put on a magnificent show, and... oh, you get it. Yes, I know circus has a different meaning here, but let's be honest: we both know I'm not all that concerned about that sort of thing.

To be fair, I feel like the preoccupation is mutual, but I suppose I've never really asked him. Maybe that's just wishful thinking on my part.

So we go round and round playing this game of hawk and mouse (because why would I say cat when this analogy makes so much more sense?) and having a great deal of fun. Okay, *I* have a great deal of fun, and he gets very angry and assaults me to within an inch of my life.

But my point is, we have this thing going on, and I'm trying to keep it interesting by upping the ante. Pushing the envelope.

2:20

Why use Toby as bait? Why, why, why, why, WHY!

Sigh... Because I know that it will drive my friend bonkers. He will be searching for him, and I will leave clues, and some of those clues will make no sense whatsoever. Why should I make it easy on the man? He's trying to put me away, after all.

Wait. Did I say will? I'm having trouble with my tenses here. Actually, I already did capture young Toby and tied him to a chair. I didn't just use rope, either. I've seen all those old films and television shows where the hero cuts through the rope, and so have you.

What do I look like, a silent movie villain, twirling my mustachios? Okay, so maybe my moustache threw you off a bit, I quite understand. No, I tied him up with rope, zip ties, titanium-alloy cable, and duct tape (you know, I used to think it was called "duck" tape, then only later realized you're not supposed to use it on waterfowl—but not until it was too late).

You may think this sounds like overkill, but believe me, this kid is resourceful, and if I didn't go to such great lengths, he'd find some way out. So, I made absolutely, positively, undoubtedly, unquestionably, undeniably... What was I saying? Nothing important, I guess.

So... I set the timer. Tick tock.

I know you want to ask me why I need a timer, but I'm sure you've already figured it out, and are just hoping that you're wrong about the answer. I assure you, you're not.

Most supervillains only have one reason for setting a timer, and it's not like I'm trying to be extra creative here. What's the best way to wound a superhero without physically harming him?

You already know.

. . .

1:06

At the risk of sounding foolish, I'm going to be candid with you and admit that I'm getting a bit worried here. You see, I didn't believe for a second that Harrier would be cutting it this close, and I did set quite the pile of explosives to detonate when the timer was done.

Perhaps I shouldn't have left such perplexing clues or so many red herrings. Now, it appears my entire plan, like chocolate, crumbles before my eyes. Dissolving. I may never get my dessert. Or my pre-dessert even.

I fortified this place so well to make it difficult for him to get in, and let my henchmen go home early so they wouldn't mess anything up, as they have a habit of doing.

I'm not sure this is going to work out at all.

Are you getting worried? You should be. There's a young boy here about to be turned into hamburger meat, and there's no way anyone is going to save him in time. Besides. That's not the main course I had in mind. Roast bird. Yum.

Me? Of course, I don't care if he goes splat. That was my plan. But Harrier was supposed to show up, and we were going to fight, and he'd realize it was too late to save Toby without everyone turning into bits and kabobs, and he'd have to say goodbye and be wracked by guilt forever.

Well, not *forever* forever. Just until I made him dessert. By which I mean, made him *into* dessert.

0:24

You see, unfortunately, he was supposed to find a way into this impenetrable room here, and then I would escape whilst he agonized over the fact that there was no way to get through the rope, the zip ties, the titanium-alloy cord, and the duct tape and then get out at the last second, as he is so famously wont to do.

Problem is, my henchmen aren't too bright, and they locked the door on the way out. But my copy of the key is out there. And, while I've been telling you this story, I've also been trying to open this—

The video glitches, and the screen goes black. It takes me a few moments to recover from seeing that.

Redhawk seems shell-shocked as well, even though it's obviously not his first time seeing the video. In fact, he appears to be pretty traumatized. When he finally speaks, he just keeps staring at the blank screen rather than look at me.

"Apparently, he was going to film it all and send it to the news. But he, ah, never got the chance. Harrier found it in a mini recorder buried in the wreckage before anyone else could get a hold of it. I'm pretty sure he showed it to me later to make me feel guilty for leaving. I don't know."

"Sounds like Frank."

I ask Redhawk what Chef Maléfique was like in person. He thinks for a second before answering. "You know the evil clown from *It?*"

"Yeah." I've seen him in the movie anyway. Never read the book.

"Imagine that clown, running away, screaming from something that terrifies him. That something would be Chef Maléfique."

I'm not sure I've ever shuddered before, but I do it now. "That bad, huh?"

"More evil than you can imagine. And the few pictures of him that were taken before he died don't do him justice. In those, he looks like a sad, fat cook, just like in that video. In-person, he was scary as hell to look at. Especially his eyes."

"What's with the whole chef thing?" I ask, now that I finally have the chance for answers.

Alex shakes his head. "Who the hell knows? I'm sure it has something to do with why he's a homicidal maniac, but your guess is as good as mine. There are rumors about him being some sort of... cannibal or something. But I've never seen any evidence to back them up."

Wow. That's a whole new level of scary.

"So, this is why you're here?" I ask.

"Frank couldn't stop Chef Maléfique from killing Toby, and I'm not going to let it happen again."

I swear. "You think it's that bad?"

Redhawk shrugs. "Can't be too cautious, I don't think. I'm going to hit the streets today and see if I can dig anything up. It's been a while since I did any patrolling around here, though. You think you might be able to go with me?"

Redhawk is known in Boston as a hero who is around when you need him. Night or day. Not like me and Harrier, who mainly patrol at night and let the police do their job during the day.

"I, uh, can go later on tonight," I answer. "But I kind of have school today, and I can't miss it."

"Then I'll do what I can on my own, and you can join me later on."

He turns, and so do I. Him for the gym and me for the window.

"Hey, Alex?"

He looks over his shoulder at me.

"If you're gonna train anyway, think you could show me a few moves on the staff?"

"It's not like one session—" He stops, and I think he realizes that it would only take one second with my particular talent. "Alright, yeah. Come on."

Once we're in the gym, he shows me some basic moves and, even with my cold slowing me down, I pick them up immediately. Impressed, he gets more complicated quickly, and I'm still able to keep up. Within an hour, he's shown me everything he knows, and I can duplicate it all perfectly.

I always wondered why Harrier never trained me with a staff, and I realize it's because it would remind him of Alex.

"That's it, man. That's all I got," he says.

"Awesome," I say, wiping my nose. "Thanks."

"Kinda makes me feel like I've just wasted my whole life learning stuff you picked up in one session." He laughs. "I'm kidding. Pretty cool gift you've got."

"Yeah," I say.

As we're about to leave, Alex suddenly has an idea, and we head back to the control center to try one more thing. He opens a compartment on the main computer panel that I've never noticed before and types in a code, then presses a red button.

"Ever met Eaglestar before?"

I'm puzzled by the question of whether I've ever met the most powerful being on Earth. It seems so random.

"No. He wasn't there the one time I was at a Guild meeting. Why?"

"Because you're about to." He looks at my slack-jawed expression and grins. "Don't get too excited, though."

"Why?"

"Cos he's kind of a douche-bag."

Just then, there's a sonic boom, and the Aerie rattles as if there's an earthquake. Redhawk opens the helipad doors, and I see the most amazing thing ever. Eaglestar, costume all red, white, and blue, floats down from the sky and hovers a couple of feet off the ground. His eyes glow, which creeps me out more than I would have thought.

Eaglestar was a World War II fighter pilot who shot down a lot of enemy planes and became a national treasure along with his squadron. They were sent on a secret mission to take down an airship the Nazis were using to transport some kind of artifacts—supposedly something of alien origin —and the rest of his squadron was killed during the fight. He managed to take down the other enemy planes escorting the airship singlehandedly but ran out of ammo in the process. So he did the only thing he could and rammed his plane into the ship, which erupted in a fiery explosion.

But instead of being killed in the crash, he was given extraordinary powers, including super-strength, invulnerability, flight, apparent immortality, and the ability to shoot some sort of energy out of his eyes. Yes. Laser-beam-eyeballs. Sometimes, the whole "I got powers from..." thing makes no sense at all, but it's happened enough that we all just have to accept it.

At first, the government used him as a secret weapon to help win the war—and hunt down the Nazis who also gained powers in that explosion—but it wasn't long before the word got out. Now, he's the world's greatest hero, and everyone loves him.

Then again, *everyone* hasn't met him in person.

"Where is he?" With his strange, hollow voice, it's hard to tell if he's angry or not, but it sure seems that way.

I look at Redhawk nervously, but he doesn't seem fazed by this. "He's not here. That's why I called you."

"*You* called me? That signal is for Harrier. And only Harrier." Redhawk was right. He does sound pretty douchey.

"Yeah, well, Harrier has been missing for a few weeks. I was hoping maybe you could—"

"Harrier goes missing frequently. Cases in other nations, undercover work, that monastery in Tibet... there are also missions with the Guild, even off-world on occasion." Eaglestar sounds more dismissive than anyone I've ever heard.

"Is there currently a Guild mission in progress?"

I can't believe Redhawk is talking to the guy this way. He scares the crap out of me.

"No."

"Then why bring it up?" Now he's even challenging him. Redhawk's got guts, I'll give him that.

"My point is that Harrier often disappears without warning, and he always returns. Why are you so concerned?" I wish he wouldn't keep floating that way. It's like he's too good to stand on the ground like the rest of us.

"Well, for one thing, his partner has no idea where he is."

Eaglestar turns his gaze on me as if he's noticing I'm there for the first time. I'm pretty sure I pee a little in my costume.

"Has he ever performed missions or left the country without informing you of his whereabouts?"

"Well—" I have to clear my throat because my voice is cracking from nervousness. "He's done it once or twice... for a few days. And there were a couple of times he took... um... women on trips. Like, vacation?"

"Is that a question or a statement?"

Confused and flustered, I look to Redhawk for some help. He speaks up. "We don't think any of those situations is currently the case. We're not even sure he's alive. As I was saying, I was hoping you—"

"Until you have some evidence of foul play, I suggest you stop worrying. Harrier can take care of himself." Eaglestar starts floating toward the helipad doors. "And don't use that signal again unless there's a major threat to this city or a planetary emergency. I'm not at your beck and call."

"Sorry to bother you then." Redhawk's tone is so sarcastic I feel like I could learn a thing or two.

Eaglestar stops his ascent for a moment and fixes his glowy, icy stare on Redhawk.

"In the time we've had this conversation, three-hundred seventy-two incidents occurred in which I could have prevented a crime or an accident. Nine lives have been lost. If you believe you were simply 'bothering me' then you are mistaken."

Eaglestar takes off so fast that he's nothing but a blur, and a sonic boom follows. Redhawk closes the helipad doors.

"Well, then. I guess we're on our own."

FIFTEEN

My head is pounding. It's like my sinuses are the Hoover Dam and the Snot-arado River is building up behind it.

I think about Eaglestar the entire way home. I never thought that meeting one of my heroes could freak me out so much. Meeting Harrier was definitely a rush the first time, and even though that feeling eventually faded, and he even started to annoy me sometimes, he's never treated me as badly as Eaglestar just had. I guess maybe I should give him more credit for the way he acts, considering who he is.

With Eaglestar, I felt like I didn't matter. Totally insignificant.

I like to think Harrier knew what a giant ass Eaglestar would be, and that's why he never introduced me to him.

I know they went on missions together and stuff, especially with the Guild. I kind of always assumed they were friends. But for him to not care at all that Harrier is missing and could even be dead... wow.

"Amber," I say, swooping down to my roof.

"*How can I please you tonight?*" she asks.

"Do you sit around thinking about the dirtiest way to say innocent things?"

"*Was I being… dirty?*"

I ignore her. "Still nothing on Harrier?"

"*I'm sorry. Nothing.*"

"Thanks. We're done for the night. Silent mode."

I manage to sneak through my window, strip off the suit, and climb under the covers just in time for Mom to come in to wake me up for school. I try the old "too sick to go to school" routine, and even though it's for real, she won't have any part of it. It's a good thing I got several hours of sleep before I left because this flu or whatever is starting to knock me on my butt.

As I ride my skateboard to school, my head continues to throb, and my throat starts to feel like it's on fire. *Great.* So I'm supposed to go out searching for Harrier with my predecessor, and I'm gonna look like an amateur because I feel like I've been run over by a truck. Redhawk's gonna wonder why Harrier ever chose me as his new partner.

It definitely doesn't get any better once I get to school, either. All the loud noise in the halls makes my head hurt even worse, and it seems like everything is closing in on me.

After first period, Javier runs to catch up to me in the hall as I'm opening up my locker. I wonder if he's gonna bring up the incident in the convenience store yesterday.

"Hey, are you okay? You don't look so good." He's acting normal. Maybe he won't.

"I'm coming down with something. That kid my mom babysits sneezed and coughed all over me."

"Oh, that stinks," he says, taking a baby-step backward.

"Yep."

"So…" He seems kind of nervous now. "Yesterday at that store…"

Think fast. What's my cover story? Why didn't I come up with a cover story?

"Yeah, that was crazy, right? I'd just finished an energy drink, and I've been taking these karate classes, and it's like I just went nuts with adrenaline or something."

You sound like an idiot. Shut up.

"Yeah, it was pretty cool. Can you… uh… teach me?"

That's not at all where I thought this would go, but I need to do whatever it takes to keep him quiet and on my side.

"Well, I don't really know what I did, but sure, I mean, we could train together sometime."

He looks like a kid on Christmas, or more accurately, like a kid on Christmas who just got every single thing he'd wished for *and* found out he was going to Disney World.

As I feel my nose tingle, I do the Dracula thing and sneeze into my sleeve in the crook of my arm.

So, of course, I have snot on my sleeve when Fabiola—that really hot cheerleader—decides to talk to me for the first time ever. She flips her hair over her shoulder and giggles at the girls she's with.

"Hey. So I hear you're on the wrestling team now."

Even though the words she's saying are obviously about me, I still find myself looking around to make sure she isn't talking to someone else. "Um. Yeah. I guess I am."

"Great," she says. "Wow. I mean, that came out of, like, nowhere. Does that mean you're coming to my party?"

"Party?" Of course I've heard about The Party, but I have to play it cool. Everyone is gonna be there. Suddenly, my invisibility doesn't seem to matter much anymore.

"Halloween, silly." She playfully slaps my arm, and I'm pretty sure she hit the boogers. "It's a costume party, and I'm gonna wear the skimpiest costume I can find. Trust me, you don't want to miss it."

She ain't lyin'...

"I don't? I mean, yeah, I don't."

"Follow me online for directions. 'Kay? 'Kay."

"Okay. Yeah. Sounds good."

As she's walking away, Fabiola grabs my arm for a second and raises an eyebrow when she feels my bicep. Her mouth curves into a half-smile, and she doesn't break eye contact until she's around the corner. I keep watching the spot where she disappeared as if I can still see her through the wall.

Javi picks his jaw up off the floor as he stares after her also. "That-that-that was—" He ends with an odd squeaky sound.

"I know."

"And she, like, *talked* to you. And touched you. And invited you *to her house.*"

"I know." I turn and close my locker, so I'm not late for class.

He finally looks at me instead of the empty space where Fabiola went around the corner. "Are you going?"

Let's see... Black Harrier is missing, Redhawk wants me to help search for him, and even if I don't end up dead, my mom has semi-permanently grounded me and won't let me out of her sight.

"Probably not." As I walk away, I can almost hear Javi's jaw hit the floor again.

Algebra 2 is a difficult enough class for me to stay awake in even under the best of circumstances. But when I'm sick, stayed up most of the night, and had the prettiest girl in school talk to me, my concentration is far from as good as it can get. My head feels like it's a blown-up balloon. Fire ants are crawling down my swollen throat, and I have chills.

Mr. Cross's voice sounds like it's coming from a TV in another room as he drones on about variables or whatever. I keep going back and forth in my head, thinking about Harrier and trying to figure out a way to go to Fabiola's party.

I start picturing Fabiola in Osprey's costume. Then I start to feel guilty. But why? It's not like we're dating or anything.

I have to stop letting my mind wander like this. I need to pay attention in class, or I'm gonna be in more trouble. Then I'll never be able to help figure out what happened to Harrier. That gets me thinking about Chef Maléfique. Even after having seen the video and pictures of him up close, I start imagining him like I used to, with glowing red eyes like Eaglestar's, and a tongue like a snake.

I go from feeling like I can't keep my eyes open any more to suddenly realizing I'm being woken up by the teacher, and the entire class is laughing at me. Worse, there's a puddle of mucus on my desk where I laid my head down, and a string of it stretching between the desktop and my face when I sit up.

When my teacher sees this, he quickly changes his attitude from annoyed to concerned. "Sawyer, maybe you should go see the school nurse."

"I think I'll be all right, sir." I sound like Rudolph when Santa made him wear the cap over his red nose.

"It's not a request. You look really sick, and I'm sure it's contagious. I don't want to spend my weekend in bed or worse, have my wife accuse me of getting my kids sick again. You need to go now."

"Yeah, okay."

I grab my backpack and head out the door, some of the other students still chuckling as I go. I'm so out of it I can hardly think straight, but I do start to worry about whether I'm gonna be able to help Redhawk out tonight at all. Then I hear a loud clanking sound coming from around the corner, like metal hitting on metal. I can't figure out what could possibly be making that noise.

Fear grips me when my imagination draws a picture of Chef Maléfique coming for me. It's a ridiculous thought, but I'm freaking delirious at this point.

As I turn toward the office, I see Logan out of class, running down the hall and slapping all the combination locks hanging from the lockers as he goes. I secretly smile, thinking Logan is finally gonna get busted for something, when I see Principal Blanchard come out of the teacher's lounge. But he completely ignores the racket Logan's making and makes a beeline to me.

He gets right up in my face like he's about to kick my

butt or something. His breath smells like old coffee, and long hairs are coming out of his nostrils and eyebrows in all directions. "Mr. Vincent, do you have a pass to be out of class?"

You've gotta be kidding me. I point after Logan, and the loud clanking still coming from his direction. "Seriously? But—"

"Do you have a pass or not?"

I try to think through all the snot clogging my head as I feel around in my pockets. I come up empty and realize I left the classroom in kind of a hurry. "Uh... I guess Mr. Cross forgot to give me one."

"We'll see about that." He starts writing out a referral slip. "Where are you going?"

"To see the nurse." I start to feel the tingling again, as well as an overwhelming pressure building in my sinuses.

"Are you really? You seem fine to me. Are you sure you're not—"

That's when it happens. The biggest, grossest sneeze I've ever had, and I can't get my hands out of my pockets in time to cover anything.

It explodes from my nasal cavity, all over Mr. Blanchard. Green slime is everywhere.

I try to hold back a smile as I apologize. "I'm really sorry—"

He pulls out a handkerchief and starts wiping himself off, beginning with his face. "Just go! Get out of here. Now!"

I know it's mean, especially for a supposed hero like me, but I feel so much better after doing that. When I get to the nurse's office, it turns out she isn't even here today. Due to budget cuts, she's only at our school twice a week, and today isn't one of those days.

The secretary tells me I look horrible, and to go lie down on the cot in the back of the nurse's office until she can get call my mom to come pick me up. Knowing full well that she's never gonna get ahold of her, I drift off for a nice, well-deserved nap.

Of course, once I'm asleep again, the dreams start up thanks to the cold meds I took this morning. Only this time, it's a dream about the past.

In fact, it's so much like a "life flashing before my eyes" dream that I should probably be worried that I'm sicker than I thought, and I'm actually dying.

It's like watching an edited recording of my adventures with the Black Harrier, only instead of from my own point of view, I see everything from a distance. The early months of my training, going up against ordinary thugs on the street. Then my first encounters with costumed villains like Music Master and Creeping Death. Then the more dangerous bad guys such as Med-Evil show up, and things get really hairy.

As it goes on, I can remember how I felt all along the way. How the whole thing went from being a constant thrill to just hard work, and finally, a job that I dreaded showing up to every night. But it wasn't Harrier who changed. It was me.

He was the same hero, with his drive to clean up the city and bring justice to criminals. He treated me the same way from the beginning to now. But I somehow lost that feeling I had when we began, and now I'm acting... what? Ungrateful? Like I took it all for granted? Like my life would be better if I went back to being just some lonely skater dude who tuned out life listening to heavy metal with my earbuds in and spent all my time after school practicing tricks on my board?

The school secretary wakes me up to tell me school's over and it's time to go home. It takes me a minute to shake out the cobwebs and get over the disorientation of having slept in a place I'm not used to. The cold meds and the sickness don't help, and the dream felt like it lasted for years.

An overwhelming feeling of loss hits me when I think about Harrier being missing. Just when I realize I should be happier with my situation as his partner, he might be gone forever—and it could all be over with.

SIXTEEN

CRAP.

That's the best way to describe what I feel like as I head for the Aerie. I had the unbelievable luck of Mom taking the brat to the theater to see some stupid 3-D kid movie, and because she could see how sick I really was, she left me in bed and trusted me to stay put.

Of course, when she gets home, she'll probably figure out right away that the lump under my covers is just a bunch of clothes and not really me, but I'll have to worry about that later. This is far too important.

As if being half-dead with the flu isn't enough, it starts pouring rain as I head out to meet Redhawk.

"Amber, anything new?" I ask as soon as my helmet's on.

"*Your girlfriend isn't far away,*" she says. "*And she's so wet.*"

"My... what? What is wrong with you?"

"*It's raining, Sawyer. Golly, you have such a gutter-brain. She's eight blocks east of here and moving north.*"

"Oh, my tracker is still on her?"

"Mission: Stalk Osprey is a complete success."

"I'm not stalking her!" I scream. Regret becomes tangible when the feeling of icepicks drags along my throat.

"Silent mode," I say. As much as I want to see Osprey, I can't get distracted. Not now.

By the time I reach the Aerie, I'm thoroughly drenched and hacking up a lung.

I get there even earlier than Redhawk was expecting. I enter through the hatch, and he gawks at me and the puddle that's quickly forming around my feet. I let out a big sneeze.

"You're not looking so good." Redhawk isn't just making an observation like everybody else. He seems genuinely concerned.

"Yeah, so everyone keeps telling me."

"Maybe you shouldn't go with me then."

Bullcrap. I'm going.

"I'll be okay. I took a really long nap this afternoon."

He doesn't look too sure, but I have a feeling he really needs the help, so he doesn't want to push the issue too much.

Redhawk grabs his equipment and starts to put on his mask. I happen to look over at the glass case with his and the second Kite's costumes. Now I know what happened to the other one, but Alex still hasn't told me why he left.

I decide this could be the only chance I have to ask him, considering how dangerous our mission is. "Hey, Alex."

"Yeah?"

"You don't have to tell me if you don't want to, but... I've always wondered why you stopped being the Red Kite."

Redhawk sighs and looks over at his old costume himself.

He considers for a long moment, then points to the same chairs where we sat when watching the Chef Maléfique video. I get some kind of PTSD flashback that sucks, and then I worry that he's gonna show me another one. However, I follow him anyway, and we each take a seat.

"I don't know what your situation is, but I get the impression you have a real life outside of... this. School, fun, friends. A girl... or boy?"

"Girl," I say quickly, then add, "Not that there's anything wrong with... you know, whatever. But girls, I like girls. Well, kind of one girl, but—"

Dude, shut up.

He laughs then gestures around the Aerie. "Yeah. Exactly. Well, that wasn't really the case with me."

"What do you mean?"

"Like I told you, I was an orphan when Frank met me, and all I wanted to do was to become a cop and bring criminals to justice. He took me under his wing and trained me until I was more effective than I'd ever be as a police officer."

So far, he hasn't told me anything I didn't already know.

"But what became even more important to me was for him to adopt me, since he was the closest thing I had to a parent in many years. He always made excuses about how a single guy couldn't adopt a teenage boy that way, but I know he just never really wanted the responsibility. Someone as rich as he is can hire lawyers to make pretty much anything happen, you know?"

I never really thought about any of this since I already had my mom. That must have been hard on him.

"So, even as Harrier trained me day in and day out, I

lived at Saint Barnabas until I turned eighteen, unlike my brother, who'd been adopted as a baby. Then I had to find someplace else to go. I kind of assumed I'd be able to move in here once that happened, but when I brought it up... well, you know how he can be."

"Definitely. But what was his excuse for not letting you move in?"

"He was worried about 'the appearance of impropriety.' I'm not sure whether he was more afraid of it scaring off the ladies or the implication that would result from a young guy moving in with a rich bachelor like that."

It takes me a second to register what he means, just because it isn't something I would have ever considered. "Seriously? But it's not like you're—" I cut myself off when I realize I don't actually know if what I was about to say is true. But it's none of my business and shouldn't matter anyway. What Harrier did was messed up. "I mean, it's not like you would interfere with his dating life or anything, right?"

Alex just smiles. He knows I'm uncomfortable, and for some reason, he has no desire to alleviate it by telling me anything one way or the other. Which is fine. Because, you know—like I said—none of my business.

"Didn't help that his advisors were such hard-asses either."

Advisors? I don't know of any advisors other than...

"Mr. Chen?" I ask.

Alex's nonresponse said all I need to hear.

"So when I packed up my stuff and left the orphanage, I just kept on going and left town. Never even said goodbye to him."

Wow. So, that's nothing like I was expecting to hear. I don't know what I *was* expecting to hear, I just know it wasn't that.

"Alex," a voice sounds from the hallway leading to the simulation room. "Who are you talking to?"

Mr. Chen rounds the corner, dressed in a black turtle-neck and black slacks. A far cry from his typical rich-man suits.

"Sawyer!" he says with enough excitement to share. Though upon second thought, it seems forced. Like he's caught off-guard by my presence.

What's he doing here in the Aerie? In all my years as Harrier's partner, I've never seen Luis Chen up here.

"Hi, Mr. Chen." I don't mean to, but I tag a little question mark on the end.

He gets closer, seems to compose himself, and gives me a once-over.

"You look like you got into a fight with death and barely won."

I laugh without much humor. "Yeah, well, at least I won, right?"

"What are you doing here?" we both say at the same time. Then, we both start to answer.

"You first," Mr. Chen says.

I don't think that's particularly fair, but I don't get the impression "age before beauty" is gonna work here.

"I'm here to help, uh, Redhawk with something."

"It's okay," Alex says. "Luis knows why I'm here."

"You do?" I ask. "I thought you weren't worried about Frank?"

"I wasn't... I'm not," he says. "But when a member of the Guild comes calling, I have an obligation to comply."

I snort mucous into the back of my throat. It's disgusting. "So, that's all this is? You *complying* with the Guild?"

"What's going on here?" Alex asks.

We both look at him, and I wait for Chen do answer, but he doesn't.

"I went to see Mr. Chen a couple days ago." Or was that yesterday? I'm so out of sorts I start to think maybe I should be at home sleeping. "And he told me there's nothing to worry about, and Frank can take care of himself."

Alex looks confused for a moment, but before he can speak, Mr. Chen chimes in.

"It doesn't matter anymore. We are all here now, and whether or not Frank needs saving, we've got the best there is working the case."

I almost roll my eyes at the attempt at flattery. Maybe it's the cold, but I'm pissed off. It's like every turn I take, someone isn't telling me something, or isn't being honest with me. I bet this is how Redhawk felt back in the day.

"Still sticking it to the Kites, are you, Chen?" Alex asks.

"That is unfair, Alexander."

"Is it? Things could have been completely different, had you not interfered." Resentment drips off his words.

"I was trying to protect you." Even though Chen's expression hasn't changed one bit, his tone has definitely softened.

"Right. And how did that work out?"

"You don't know Frank like I do," Mr. Chen says.

"I could have."

I realize I'm looking back and forth between them like I'm watching a tennis match.

"I don't know what you're complaining about," Mr. Chen says. "If I'd have advised him to let you stay, you wouldn't be your own hero. You'd still just be a Kite."

His words probably came out faster than he'd expected because his eyes went wide, and he looked at me.

"Yeah. Well. I guess that's that," Alex says. "Is that it?" He snatches something out of Chen's mechanical hand that I hadn't seen before.

"Sawyer, I'm sorry," Mr. Chen says.

I just stand there, swallowing against my scratchy, dry throat.

His eyes, pursed lips, tilted head—they all speak of some kind of sympathy or apology. To me, it doesn't matter. He said what he said. He'd meant it. It wasn't exactly untrue, either.

Redhawk hands me what he'd taken from Mr. Chen.

"Just push that button," he says.

I do, and what was a foot-long span of graphene extends into a full-length staff just like the one Osprey carries.

"Wow. Thanks."

"Anyway," Alex continues, "we have a lot to do, and that's all ancient history now. So, what do you say we go beat up some bad guys?"

I watch Mr. Chen, who just rubs his face.

"Yeah, sounds good," I say.

When I try to exit the Aerie in the usual way, Redhawk just crosses his arms and shakes his head. "I have a better idea."

"Be careful," I hear Mr. Chen yell at us, like he cares.

Redhawk takes me down a private elevator to a secret garage in a sub-basement under the building's regular parking levels. On top of everything else, I feel pretty angry and maybe a little jealous that Harrier's never shown me this area, but there's no reason to get into it now. For one thing, it's not Redhawk's fault Harrier never told me about it, plus Harrier's not around for me to discuss it with him.

"That guy's a prick," Alex says.

"Never thought so until now."

"But he sure knows his stuff." He points to my new staff.

"Oh, right. This was you?" I ask.

"Yeah, after seeing how awesome you did in training, I thought you should have one. I hope you like it."

He hopes I like it? It took Harrier three years to give me a gift. *Three years.* Here, I've known this guy for a day, and I've got a killer staff and entrance into a secret part of Douglas Tower I never knew about.

"I love it."

As the doors to the elevator open, the first thing I see is a giant black vehicle that looks like a cross between a Ferrari and a tank. How did I not know about this? Does Harrier not use it anymore, or does he just not use it when I'm around?

But what Redhawk really wants to show me is parked behind the big vehicle. A set of motorcycles, a big black one and a smaller red one.

I guess my expression at seeing these gives away the fact that I had no idea they existed.

"What's the matter?"

"I just... I never..."

I can tell from his expression that Redhawk didn't realize I had no idea about this stuff. "He was probably just waiting for you to get your license. But you're old enough now, right?"

"Yeah, probably," I say. Technically, maybe. I don't believe it, though.

He shows me how to start the bike, and then points out the other controls.

I turn the key, and the motor rumbles under me.

"Feels good, huh?" he asks.

"Hell, yeah," I say.

"Language."

I stutter over a response when he laughs. "I'm kidding. I used to hate him for that."

This guy... He's like the first person I feel like I can totally relate to. It's almost like he's been me.

He takes off, doing a little wheelie, and I follow, not doing a wheelie because at first, I have trouble just moving along on the thing. But then, like everything else, I get the hang of it from watching Redhawk. He's an expert rider, and it doesn't take long for me to replicate his ability.

Once I know what I'm doing, it's the most fantastic thing I've ever done. Even better than gliding around above the city. I thought skating on my board was cool, but this is about a billion times cooler.

Our helmets have mics and speakers in them, so we sync them up to communicate.

As we're riding, Redhawk tells me about the time after the second Red Kite was killed by Chef Maléfique. He and Harrier hadn't spoken much since their falling out, but he'd gone to visit Harrier after the funeral. Harrier had stopped putting on the suit and was spending all of his time sitting around his penthouse, drinking. That was when he showed Alex the video.

He wasn't sure what brought Harrier out of his depression a couple of months later, but he did see news stories about Harrier and me, the new Red Kite, together all of a sudden, so he always figured getting a new sidekick had something to do with it.

In other words, I somehow managed to drag Harrier out of his despair. Not something I would have ever considered.

Bleep.

"No way," Alex says.

"What?"

"He gave you Amber?"

"Oh, yeah. I guess she was his when you were with him?"

Redhawk switches lanes, and I follow.

"Dude, I used to fantasize about her growing up. In my mind, she looked like that chick from that one high school show in the 90s."

I have no idea what he's talking about.

"What are you waiting for?" he asks. "Answer her!"

I can't believe how excited he is about this, but I do what he says. "Hey, Amber."

"*OMG,*" she says. A phrase I've literally never heard from her virtual lips. "*Is that little Alex? Hmmm. Not so little anymore, are you?*"

As always, her words are laced with innuendo, and I can almost hear Redhawk blushing if that's possible.

"What can I do for you, Amber?" I ask.

"Ask not what you can do for me, but what I can do for you..."

"Enough," I say.

"Hey, let the lady talk," Alex argues.

"There's a disturbance two blocks over to the east," she says.

"What kind of disturbance?"

"Oh, you'll see."

Just like it had with Osprey, being out on patrol with Redhawk, it reminds me of the early days with Harrier. The main difference is that Redhawk actually has a sense of humor.

We roll up on the disturbance, and I'm not sure either of us knows how to respond. That is until I watch Redhawk leap off his bike and charge toward several men—I think they're all men?—dressed in Black Harrier masks. Some even have the whole outfit on.

"Wait up," I say, dismounting and doing my best to keep up. The cold is in my chest now, and I'm trying my hardest to not cough.

"What is this?" Alex growls. At first, he sounds like he's using a voice manipulator like Harrier, but he's not. That's just his anger roiling.

He slams one of them against the wall, and it's immediately evident that none of these people are fighters. A couple run. Some try to stop Redhawk, but very timidly, like someone trying to keep a lion away from their friend. You don't want to do nothing, but you know you have no chance.

Alex repeats himself with another slam. "What is this?"

"Wh-wh-what's wr-wrong with you?" the guy mumbles.

"Why are you dressed like that?"

I step in and try to keep the others away from Redhawk. He hasn't seen how they're acting. They're all terrified.

"It's Halloween, man!"

"It's *not* Halloween for a few days," Redhawk reminds them.

"Tis the season, dude."

"And what—all of you decided to dress the same?"

The guy pinned against the wall is still stumbling over his words, and one of the others by me says, "Someone paid us to do it, man. Even gave us the costumes. Let him go, dude. C'mon, let him go."

Redhawk punches the wall right beside the guy's head before dropping him the six inches to his feet.

Breathing heavily, Redhawk turns toward me and then the guy who'd spoken up.

"Who?"

"What?" the guy answers.

"Who paid you?"

"I... I don't know... just some guy."

"You didn't think it was weird that 'some guy' paid you money to dress up like Black Harrier?"

"This is New York, man! People act crazy all the time. We ain't gonna say no to free money."

"What did he look like?" Redhawk asks.

"We didn't see him. He told us to meet at Holy Mother Catholic Church. We talked in the confessional, I swear. Then, he said to wait five minutes, and everything we'd need would be in the priest's booth."

"What was in there?"

"The costumes... and a stack of these. He said to give them to anyone who commented on our costumes. I promise, man. We aren't doing anything wrong."

He hands Redhawk something...

A business card. But it's blank. Redhawk turns it over and moves his thumb. It's not blank.

"A handlebar moustache?"

Redhawk says a word my mom would probably kill me if she heard me say it.

"Get lost," he tells the Black Harrier wannabes.

They all fan out and run in different directions without looking back.

"Chef Maléfique?" I ask.

"Or someone who wants us to think it's him."

I tell Redhawk about the business card Harrier had on my birthday.

"What was on it?"

"I don't know. It was too far away. I couldn't see it. But then Harrier had it again in the Aerie on the same night he was researching Chef Maléfique. Can't be a coincidence, right?"

He shakes his head. "Let's go."

We get back on our bikes and zip around town, rounding up thugs and questioning everyone we can find who might know something. That wasn't the only group of Harrier cosplayers, either. They all had the business cards. Thankfully, Redhawk didn't beat the mess out of the other groups, but he did have some choice words for most of them.

Word must get around fast, because soon whenever we

catch sight of any criminal-types, they scurry away immediately like rats.

I'm a bit confused by Redhawk's behavior—like he's bipolar or something. He goes from pissed off and punching walls to cracking jokes and making quips. I tend to throw in some comments here and there, but he goes at it all the way. At first, I don't get why he would waste his time joking around so much with bad guys who obviously don't appreciate it. Then I realize it's a tactic. Not only do they not take him as seriously as they should, but I can tell they're really distracted and frustrated when he does it.

We hadn't been successful in capturing any of these lowlifes enough to question them, but one that we do is way too overconfident for his own good. As we approach and the rest of his gang runs away, he stands right in front of our bikes and flips us off with both hands and smiles. I toss him into an alley, my favorite place to take care of scum like him.

"I see you got a new boyfriend, Kite," he says. "Harrier getting too old for your taste?"

I hit him in the stomach. "What have you heard about Harrier?"

He has trouble talking with the wind knocked out of him. Guess I hit him a little too hard. "Nothing."

I bring my knee up and drive it into his face. Then I grab him by the shirt collar and yank him up. Blood drips from his probably-broken nose. He smiles, and I shove him hard against the dumpster. "I find it hard to believe someone in your line of work hasn't heard anything at all about this city's hero disappearing."

He wipes away the blood and sneers at me. "I don't care if you believe me or not."

"My new friend here is just as anxious to find out some information. I'm gonna let him ask a few questions now."

"Oh, I get it. The old 'good cop/bad cop' routine. It ain't gonna work, kid."

"I wouldn't be so sure about that. See, the thing is, *I'm* the 'good cop.'"

He looks nervous as Redhawk pops his knuckles and approaches him. Yeah, it's cheesy, but it's effective. I actually turn around because I'm feeling kind of nauseous, so I'm not really sure which bones Redhawk is breaking when I hear the screams and cracking sounds.

SEVENTEEN

NOTHING.

He didn't know anything.

How do I know?

There aren't many people outside of Black Ops who could have withstood Redhawk's interrogation. I kind of felt bad for the dude. Kind of.

Then we stumble across another gang who broke way easier. Finally, after hours of not being able to get any useful info, we have the name of a certain low-life snitch who supposedly knows something. Warren "Weasel" Wilson is never tough to find once you're looking for him. Every cop in town knows to go to Weasel if you can't get anything out of anyone else, and every criminal knows to stay away from him because he's under the cops' protection. And Harrier's as well.

He's not just called the Weasel... around the city, he's known as "the Net." Get it? His initials? W.W.W.?

We confront Weasel as he's pulling a con on some tourists

downtown. A bunch of people who don't know how dangerous it is to be in this neighborhood at night—or even in the daytime for that matter—stand around while he plays the cup game with the rubber ball on top of a cardboard box. A couple of the guys watching, who I'm sure he planted, win a few dollars, and the rest get confident and start throwing down fives, tens, even twenties.

I have to admit, Weasel's good. And from past experience, I know he's even better at lying than he is at getting people to willingly hand over their money. But with the right, ummm... motivation, I guess? He's definitely a pretty reliable informant.

Before we can even get close, Weasel has taken a couple hundred bucks from them.

"Oh, hey Weasel," I say, pushing through the crowd.

"Kite," he says in his nasal tone. "Come on, I'm workin' here."

"Oh, right... just trying to make an honest living."

Since I'm familiar with the game, I pull the ball out from his sleeve, and the crowd starts to get angry.

He licks his lips and his eye twitches. Man, he really looks like a weasel. The teeth, the snout, the beady eyes...

"Give the money back," I say. "Now."

He has both hands up, palms out while the crowd starts to close in.

"What kinda hero are you?" he says. "Pickin' on the little guys."

We make him give back the money as best he can, and most of the suckers are happy. Some of them probably even got back more than they'd put down.

Once everyone's gone, he says, "That was pretty messed up, Kite."

"Cry about it," I tell him. "And it's Red Raptor. And this is Redhawk."

"Like the color red, huh?"

"Shut up," Redhawk says, literally slapping him in the face. I almost laugh when Weasel turns back, flabbergasted that someone had just slapped him.

"Who slaps?" he argues.

"Would you rather I punch?"

"What the hell is wro—"

We grab Weasel and follow procedure, taking him into a nearby alley. For some reason, he's much less talkative than usual, so we decide to take him to a nearby rooftop to loosen him up some.

"How is this necessary?" he squeals.

Harrier found out years ago that Weasel is afraid of heights, so usually, as soon as he's uncooperative, we grab him and pull him up top, and he starts to sing. But even after I take him on a little ride with my grappler and we're on the edge of a high building, he's still tight-lipped. That's when Redhawk decides to pull one of Harrier's favorite moves and hang him upside-down from the ledge.

Weasel screams, and his voice comes back half a dozen times.

"Shut up, or you'll wake up the whole neighborhood," Redhawk says.

"Listen, stop. Come on. Please. You don't need to do this."

"We could have avoided it," Redhawk says. "But you had to be all... difficult."

From the smell, I can tell immediately that he's crapped his pants, but he's still afraid to talk. Redhawk and I both lean over him as he hangs there, looking straight down at the pavement ten stories below. Redhawk tries to get him to open up a little more, this time playing the "good cop" part.

"What are you so afraid of? You know you're untouchable in this town. Harrier's always had your back."

"Harrier ain't been seen in weeks. Who's gonna help me when—when—when... *someone* comes after me? C'mon. You seen it. The cops are afraid to leave their patrol cars lately."

"Well, maybe if you help us out, we can find him, and he can protect you."

Redhawk gives him a little shake, and some loose coins fall out of his pockets, clattering on the pavement.

"I-I-I-I don't think that's gonna happen."

"Why?" Redhawk asks.

"I can't tell you, man. Please."

That was my cue to be "bad cop."

"Let's just drop him, Hawk. If he won't talk anymore and he isn't any help finding Harrier, then what good is he?"

Redhawk looks like he's having too much fun with this. "I don't know, Raptor. It's a long way down."

I eye the alley again. "I know. I want to see what happens. Besides, once everyone he's ever snitched on realizes nobody's protecting him anymore, he's gonna be dead anyway."

Even with our lousy acting, Weasel is terrified.

"Wait! Maybe you guys can ensure my safety, huh? Like, keep me somewhere safe until things blow over."

Redhawk grins at me. "That sounds fair. Now, tell us what you know about Harrier's disappearance."

Weasel starts shaking, and at first, I think it's just because he's so scared of us dropping him. Then I realize he's sobbing uncontrollably, and it's because of what he's about to tell us. "The chef has him."

"Maléfique?"

"Y-you know another chef?" Weasel asks, but there's no bravado in his tone.

Redhawk couldn't have looked more shocked if he found out Santa Claus was holding Harrier at the North Pole. Between the business card and everything else, I think we both know this was a possibility, but to hear it from this guy's lips... Instead of expressing shock, it comes out as pure anger. "Maléfique's dead."

"Yeah, well... I guess he got better."

My turn again. "You better not be lying to us, or next time we hang you from the top of Douglas Tower."

"I swear, man. I swear. I seen him myself."

My mouth is so dry, I have trouble getting my next question out. "Is Harrier alive?"

"Last I heard. But word is, he won't be for long."

"Where is he holding him?"

"I don't know. Somewhere nearby, I think. But you better bring backup."

"Why?" Redhawk says.

"'Cause Maléfique's gathered everyone... all the big-time

crooks in town to work for him, and some from other places, too. In fact—"

BLAM!

Weasel's brain spatters all over the side of the building as a bullet plows through his forehead. I almost throw up right when it happens, but I don't need Redhawk and Osprey both thinking I can't stomach being a hero, so I manage to hold it down. I'm used to violence and a certain amount of blood. Bullets to the head, not so much.

Almost too far away to see, I catch a glimpse of the assassin repelling down the side of a building, sniper gun still in hand. It's hard to tell at this distance, but I'm pretty sure it's Deadeye. If it is, I'm not sure why Redhawk and I are still alive. He's such as good shot, and so fast, he could have taken down at least one of us before we even knew what was happening.

I guess we really couldn't protect Weasel. *Whoops.*

We glide down to the street as fast as we can, since the next shot could still be for Redhawk or me. We jump on our bikes and speed off in the direction of the shooter. Deadeye is on a bike also, so we're pretty far behind him thanks to his big head start.

I try to remember everything I know about the sharp-shooter. He's pretty unpopular, even with other criminals, because he uses guns. In many ways, the whole hero/villain thing is kind of a game, like with the mask thing. So using firearms is sort of cheating as far as most of us are concerned. It's fine for normal henchmen and minions, but it's definitely not cool when it comes to bosses. Either way, the truth is, if somebody wants someone else dead, he's the man to hire.

From what I know, he was special ops in the military, but I don't know what branch or anything more specific. The rumor is that he was part of some kind of experiment the government conducted on its own soldiers. It worked, but it also made him kind of crazy. On his first mission to clean out some village in the Middle East, he finished the job a little too well and then went after the guys on his own team.

With all the heroes and villains created by government experiments, you'd think it was all on purpose. Maybe they're all just trying to screw up in order to create the perfect super-soldier. Who knows? Either way, I think it's time to give it up. Even Eaglestar is a freaking psychopath.

I hear Deadeye's bike roar ahead. He's an expert at practically everything, and Redhawk's a good rider, but I'm sure Alex is holding back for my sake. So why is it that we're gaining on Deadeye?

As we start to catch up, I notice there seem to be a lot of cars around for this late at night. Then, all at once, twenty car engines turn over, and they start to move. Before we know it, vehicles of every kind pull up and surround us: cars, vans, trucks, more bikes. The hunters have become the prey.

Every side street we pass, more vehicles join the posse escorting us. It's no longer a chase. It's become a parade. All that's missing are the balloons.

Redhawk gives his bike more gas, and I follow close behind him, but our "escort" is quickly closing in. My rear tire gets a bump from what looks like a hearse, and the bike skids forward a bit.

At this point, I don't even see a way that we can get out of here, even if we wanted to. It's like we're at the center of a swarm of bees, and they're buzzing ever closer. So what's gonna happen?

"Amber."

"Yes, Sawyer?"

"You know, this is the kind of emergency you're supposed to warn me about."

"I'm sorry. The shooter was fully incognito, even to me."

That's a scary thought. Amber was supposed to see everything. Douglas Industries has satellites dedicated solely to Harrier's A.I. systems.

"Can you see anything up ahead?"

"Nothing. It's like a big black blotch over everything, including you."

"Well, that's fantastic," Redhawk says.

I can see a dozen ways this could go down, and none of them seem good. Are we gonna stop somewhere, or will they just try to shoot at us from all directions as we drive along? I assume not even these thugs are stupid enough to risk the crossfire, so I don't worry much about that option, yet.

Ahead, Deadeye's gunning for the big suspension bridge, and I notice there are no cars around other than the ones that are closing in on us. Something's happened to the typically heavy traffic crossing the river, and I'm guessing it isn't a welcome party for Harrier's favorite sidekicks—er, partners.

Not the good kind of welcome party, anyway.

After speeding up for most of our chase, Deadeye suddenly stops on the bridge and turns to face us on his bike. The dude is a serious badass. I mean, if I weren't worried he was gonna kill me right now, I'd probably be impressed. He's fully clad in leather. Not like a lame hair band from the

1980s, but awesome leather pants, a biker jacket with little silver spikes, and gloves to match. He climbs off and straightens his helmet, the full facemask painted like a skull, then slowly adjusts all of his weapons to make sure they're ready. I can clearly see a staff, a sword, and several sidearms. Plus lots and lots of ammunition. Like bandoliers across his chest, and magazines strung to his hips. I definitely can't see any way this is gonna end well.

We slow down as we approach him, and I notice there are now cars coming from behind Deadeye, driving the wrong way on this side of the bridge. On either side of us, the vehicles are pulled in close to each other, which fences us in. There must be somewhere between fifty and a hundred of them surrounding us now, each with at least a couple of guys getting out. It's hard to tell the precise number with so many stretching out into the dark in both directions.

We're good, but we're not that good.

As Redhawk slowly flips up the visor on his helmet, he doesn't seem too bothered by the whole situation. Which is in direct opposition to me, feeling like I'm about to pee my pants again. He climbs off his bike and starts walking toward Deadeye as the increasing number of criminals moves in on us.

Now that I have a chance to scope things out, I notice the variety of thugs in the group. Rival gang members who would usually kill each other on-sight are strolling side-by-side. Low-level costumed villains who I know were in prison very recently are scattered throughout the crowd as well. Right away, I spot Med-Evil in his doctor's getup and zombie makeup. At least I hope it's makeup. I wonder if the hearse is driven by Morty Mortician, but I don't dare turn to find out.

A lot of them are wearing costumes. Most of them aren't actual supervillains, but as we've been reminded time and time again, Halloween is coming up, so maybe they're just in the mood for dress-up.

I always hate this time of year. Not only is it hard to spot the actual costumed criminals among the partiers, but people seem to get crazier and braver. Just as some women feel like it's okay to dress up way more provocatively than they ever would any other time of year—as a "sexy schoolgirl" or whatever—so many jerks want to put on a mask and carry a weapon. Even guys who would generally cower in a situation where they'd have to fight, suddenly think they're invincible.

What I don't understand is why all these villains, who are normally willing to take on Harrier and me by themselves, are holding back when they have all this backup.

I follow Redhawk's lead and try not to look too scared. Redhawk keeps his collapsible staff in a sheath under his cape. He pulls it out and extends it, all in one smooth motion. It almost looks like it appears out of nowhere. I pull out the one he gave me, but it's not quite as smooth because I'm so nervous. I need to practice with this thing for sure. My brain may have learned how to do it immediately, but my muscles have some catching up to do.

Deadeye doesn't bother to unholster any of his many guns. Instead, he pulls out his own staff. His doesn't have the "push to extend" feature like ours, but something tells me that won't matter in a fight. Because his mask completely covers his face, I have no idea what expression he has. But I have a feeling it's a straight lip and furrowed brow.

He holds up his hand, and the mob of bad guys stops closing in on us, forming a circle that looks almost like a human arena.

Redhawk doesn't look at me, but he speaks just loud enough for me to hear him in our helmets. "I want you to hang back and let me take care of this. If you see a chance to escape, take it."

"But—"

"Just listen to me. Please. I don't need your death on my conscience." I step back as Redhawk lowers his visor and gets within striking range of Deadeye.

I said Deadeye is an expert... but really, he's the best assassin in the country. Maybe the world. He's a proficient marksman, and as dangerous as Harrier at hand-to-hand combat. Actually more, when you consider the weapons he uses and his lack of a "no killing" rule.

Redhawk is almost as good as Harrier. But somehow I don't think "almost" is gonna cut it. He shows off some of his fancy moves, spinning his staff around his body and over his head. Another one of his tactics to distract his enemies. Deadeye is a statue, watching like a cobra ready to strike.

In the middle of what looks like an ordinary spinning technique, Redhawk swings his staff directly at Deadeye with what should be a surprise move. Deadeye moves so fast to block it that it's almost too quick for me to follow. Then he strikes back immediately, hitting Redhawk's visor and cracking it.

Redhawk is obviously stunned, but he shakes it off right

away, and ducks before Deadeye's next swing can catch him on the side of the helmet. Then he jumps up as Deadeye's next swipe tries to take out his legs.

Instead of coming straight down, Redhawk uses his staff almost like a pole vault and lands his first blow, a kick to Deadeye's chest. This is the assassin's turn to be surprised, and he stumbles back a couple of steps but manages to stay on his feet. As Redhawk descends, he uses his body's momentum to swing his staff over his head and come down hard on the top of Deadeye's skull. It seems to ring his helmet but doesn't do much in the way of damage.

Deadeye returns with a jab to Redhawk's chest using the end of his staff, but Redhawk's Kevlar body armor takes the brunt of it. It turns out to be just a diversion anyway, as Deadeye's foot shoots out and lands a smack across Redhawk's face that shatters the already-cracked visor on his mask and knocks him back to the ground. He follows up with another swing of his staff, and this one makes contact with Redhawk's knee.

Redhawk manages to flip backward and up onto his feet just before Deadeye can land another blow. He pulls off the remnants of his cracked visor so it won't interfere with his vision and tries to catch his breath for a moment.

I start to move forward, but Redhawk holds up his hand immediately and gives me a warning look. He gets his second wind and goes on the attack, getting in several hits that Deadeye barely has time to block. He swings down hard from above, and when Deadeye blocks, the assassin's staff shatters.

Deadeye isn't the type of person you want to make look bad in front of all these people. He unsheathes his sword and goes after Redhawk mercilessly. Even though Redhawk is able to avoid any serious wounds, Deadeye does cut him a few times by connecting in the spaces between his armor, and the blood is starting to flow pretty heavily.

I hear movement behind me and spin to see a few brave henchmen are sauntering toward me. What? That's the only word I can think of to describe it. It's like they are hesitant still, but gaining confidence as they watch their fearless leader taking on Redhawk. They probably don't even consider how much better Deadeye is than them.

"You sure you wanna do this, fellas?" I ask. I'm more than sure that even with this cold or whatever, these guys'll be a cakewalk. But then a few more close in.

Behind me, Redhawk and Deadeye continue to dance around one another, but Deadeye continues to cut Redhawk more and more, while Redhawk lands fewer and fewer hits in return. It's evident that he won't be able to keep up much longer at this rate.

One of the thugs, let's call him Scraggly Beard, lunges for me, and I sidestep, grabbing his scraggly beard and thrusting him into the pavement. I don't bother to make sure he's gonna be down for a while. Two more come at me at the same time for a change. I use a set of moves I learned from watching Joe Lewis videos, blocking, and slapping down their attacks. Then, I combine those with a few one-inch kung fu punches, and both of them are flat on their backs in a matter of seconds.

The remaining would-be attackers back off.

At first, I think it's because of my expert display of

martial arts, but I turn to see something new transpiring behind me.

Redhawk knows he won't be able to beat Deadeye in this condition and uses his staff to vault up into the crowd of bad guys. Using their shoulders and heads, he jumps and flips parkour-style until he's on the railing at the edge of the bridge. He's holding his side, where there's a pretty deep gash in his costume between the armored pieces. That's the problem with Kevlar; if you want to be able to move, there's gotta be some unprotected areas.

Some thugs in the crowd start reaching for him, but he knows just what to say. "What's the matter, you don't think Deadeye can finish me off himself? He needs help from you losers?"

They respond immediately by stopping their advance, not wanting to incur Deadeye's wrath.

Redhawk turns and looks me in the eye, and I know precisely what his look is trying to tell me: *Don't let this be in vain.* I hear a shot ring out, and with a jerk, Redhawk goes over the edge of the bridge. I almost scream "No!" like they do in the movies, but then I realize how stupid that would be. I need to escape, and drawing any more attention to myself like that wouldn't make any sense.

I turn to see Deadeye holding his smoking pistol up, but he's shaking and breathing hard from his battle with Redhawk. He may not be severely wounded, but he's at least winded, which might give me just barely the edge I need.

The criminals are all either looking over the side to see Redhawk hit the water, or cheering and slapping each other on the back. Now's my chance.

I can't just get to the suspension part of the bridge up above—I'll still be surrounded, and Deadeye will have no trouble picking me off. I need to get as far away as possible, fast, while he's distracted. Unfortunately, we're almost to the middle of the bridge, so nothing else is close by.

I shoot my grappler away from the bridge, but I'm too far from any buildings, and it retracts without hitting anything. I run back toward the beginning of the bridge, but there are a bunch of guys in my way. I start fighting them one by one, thinking about how confident I just was. Now, with Redhawk gone, I feel like a lost little kid, separated from his mom at the store. How many could I take down if I had to? This time it's like an endless supply.

I determine the thinnest part of the blockade of minions in my way and start to plow through. Most of them go down with a punch or a kick, but with so many, some of them get in some good hits.

I need to try my grappler again because I won't be able to keep fighting like this, but I'm still not sure if I'm close enough. I try to calculate how many more steps I need to manage before I can successfully connect. Almost there...

I point my grappler and shoot. It extends as far as it can go, and I hear a satisfying *thunk* as the graphene hook buries itself into the brick, barely catching the closest building. I hit the button to be reeled in, and a bunch of thugs try to grab me as I soar over their heads.

Despite everything, I feel myself laugh a little as I zip up out of their reach and head away toward someplace safer. I must be more than a little feverish. I'm only about twenty feet off the ground, but that should be enough to get me to safety before—

CRACK!

I hear another shot ring out, and my line goes slack. I know immediately that Deadeye severed it with a bullet.

As I plummet toward the ground, everything feels like it's moving super slow. What a stupid way to die after everything I've been through.

The instant I feel my back hitting the ground, everything goes black.

EIGHTEEN

Bleep. Bleep. Bleep. Bleep.

"Amber?"

"And who might Amber be?" I hear the voice and am so confused. I'm in strange surroundings, including a bed that's way too comfortable to be my own.

My eyes open, and I see nothing but brilliant, blurry light. All I can hear is an annoying beeping sound and an even more annoying song being sung by the brat.

"Mom?"

And I have a stabbing pain in my... well, everything. But, hey, on the bright side, it looks like my cold is finally gone. Or everything else hurts too much for me to notice those symptoms. How long have I been out?

As my eyes focus, I see my mom staring at me with a worried look. She lets the whole Amber thing go, thankfully.

"Thank God you're awake. Father Pulliam was here praying with us just a bit ago. It's like a miracle! They were afraid that with such a serious head injury, you might be out for a long time."

"Head injury?" I look around at my hospital room. Yeah, about what I'd expect with the sorry government health insurance we have. At least nobody is in the other bed next to me.

"It's a good thing your friend was there to call the ambulance for you, or you might not have made it."

Did Alex survive?

"Friend? What frien—"

Mom moves aside, and I see an Asian girl standing behind her, giving me a small wave. She's cute, and sort of familiar-looking. With those glasses, she has kind of a sexy gamer vibe going on. The type of girl who can destroy you in *Call of Duty*, and you still want to make out with her later. She seems really shy, though.

Then something else hits me. Oh, hey. That's Mr. Chen's daughter, from the picture in his office. Does she know me? I don't know her. How did she find me? These questions and a million more cycle through my mind.

"Hey," she says, and I feel like Weasel, brains splattering on the wall behind me as my mind is blown.

Holy crap! That voice. I know it. Like, *know it* know it.

Osprey is Mr. Chen's daughter.

What was her name? Annie? Alli? Amy? Suddenly, a whole lot of things start to make sense.

"She's like your guardian angel." Mom smiles at her.

"Yep, that's me. I watch him like a *hawk*." That's definitely her voice. But it can't be. It is. Who else could it be?

"Thanks. I guess I owe you one." There's no way we can

talk about stuff now, but there's gonna be a whole lot to discuss later.

"Yeah. *Another* one, actually." She is not what I expected Osprey to be like in her civilian identity. But, then again, most people would probably say the same thing about me. It helps that she wears a wig with her costume. No wonder the blonde ponytail is so prominent. It's like she's saying, "Hey, look at me, I'm blonde." And those shiny, reflective eye covers in her mask...

I feel bad that I led her on about visiting the Aerie. Or maybe the reason she was watching me in the first place was to try to follow me there. Even so, I can't stay mad at her now.

Mom's look and voice change now that she's not so worried about me. "Then there's the matter of why you were out when you're sick *and* grounded. The first time I trust you in weeks, and you blow it. And what the h-e-l-l were you doing skateboarding without a helmet?" She literally whisper-spells the word, but I'm too confused to even snicker.

"Skateboarding?"

Mom starts to look suspicious at me, not knowing what she's talking about.

From behind her, Osprey gives me a warning look. "Must have lost your memory," she says. "You know... because of the head injury. The doctor said that might happen with a concussion. It's a good thing you wiped out into that pile of garbage, or it could have been even worse."

"Uh... yeah, I must have. I actually don't remember anything from before my accident." I squint at her. "In fact, I don't remember *you* being there at all. I do remember another friend being with me. Do you know what happened to him?"

Osprey gets a sad look. "Haven't heard anything. Sorry."

I don't know how Redhawk could've possibly survived that fall, especially with his injuries. But I can't worry about that right now.

Mom is looking at us like we're crazy, and then she gets kind of bitchy with me. "Anyway, when you get out, we're going to have a long talk about why you didn't follow the rules. And what kind of additional punishments we're going to have to add."

Osprey looks uncomfortable about the way my mom is talking to me. I'm not sure if she doesn't like it, or if she just thinks it's weird that Mom's acting that way in front of her.

Osprey starts moving toward the door. "Well, now that I know you're going to be okay, I think I'll get going." She seems pretty nervous for some reason. Something more than just not liking the way my mom is talking to me.

My mom grabs her arm. "I was just about to get a diet soda. I'll walk you out." She turns to the brat. "Aiden, you stay here with Sawyer for a minute and make sure he doesn't try to leave. Can you do that?"

He slumps in the vinyl chair.

"If you're good, I'll bring you back a candy bar."

Now the kid nods excitedly. Just what he needs, more sugar. My mom and Osprey leave the room, and Aiden stares at the beeping machines. I try to tune him out as he starts singing his song again.

"Do do do-do do do."

Guuh, so annoying.

So, Osprey was watching me again. She not only saved me, but she showed up in her civilian identity to check on me.

Despite my pain, I can't help a big smile. Maybe she isn't just using me to meet Harrier. Maybe she *is* a little bit interested in me for me.

And now, we know each others' names. Amy Chen.

The kid reaches up to one of my monitors like he's about to press a button or something. Leave it to that brat to ruin my moment.

"Don't touch that."

He gives me the side-eyed look he always wears when I reprimand him, then flops back down into his chair with his arms crossed. My mom pretty much gives him the run of the apartment, so I end up being the disciplinarian a lot of the time. Yet another reason why we don't like each other.

"Your mom was wheelly sad when you was sweepin'."

"Was she?"

"Yeah. She kept cwying and cwying and cwying."

"I didn't realize that."

For the first time, I wonder what she would do if I actually got killed, fighting criminals. It never seemed like I was important to her before, but things have changed a lot lately.

"It's a good fing the fat man was here with us to make her happy."

"Fat man?" I try to picture everyone my mom knows. Old boyfriends, neighbors... none of them were very fat. Even in my grogginess, I know something isn't right.

"You know. The chwef."

"Chwef? Who's a chwe—" I feel the blood rush out of my face. "There... there was a chef here?" I hear the beeping get faster on the machine.

Aiden nods emphatically. "He was super nice, too."

"What did he look like?"

"I don't know. A big, fat chwef wiv a curly moustache."

"Okay, okay. But—"

"He gave me this." The kid reaches under his chair and pulls out something that was apparently a gift from the fat "chwef" man.

A red kite.

I jolt upright in bed, and the vitals monitor starts going crazy. My heart rate speeds up so much it sets off the alarms. I pull the IVs out of my arms and try to stand up, knocking over the IV pole in the process.

My head is swimming, and I have tunnel vision as I hear doctors and nurses running down the hall outside. I slam against the doorjamb as I try to exit the room. Mom and Osprey turn around at the end of the hallway and are running back to me just as everything starts to spin.

Then I black out again.

NINETEEN

UHHHH.

My eyes crack a hair, and I can see blurry shapes at the foot of my bed. One is clearly Mom. Even through the fog, her fiery-red hair is unmistakable. The other, I assume, is a doctor. I can hear them, but it's like they're talking into a can at the end of a string like they used to back in the day.

In a strong but gentle voice, the other woman says, "Ms. Vincent, these injuries are just not in line with what one would expect from someone who 'fell on their skateboard.'"

I can tell she's using air quotes on that last line.

"His friend said he landed in a pile of garbage. That would explain the various cuts and bruises, no?"

"This looks more like he got into a very intense fight. Or worse..."

"Are you implying that I beat my son?"

"Gosh, no," the doctor says. "But do you know anyone who might have it in for him? A school bully or something?"

I want to hold on. I want to listen more, but I can't any longer, and I fall back into a dreamless sleep.

The next time I wake up, I'm in less pain, but I'm more heavily medicated. It's the middle of the night, and my room is so dark, I can't see anything until my eyes start to adjust in the dim light from the machines. I try to lift my arms and discover I'm strapped down to the bed like a criminal. They must not want me trying to leave again.

I nearly have a heart attack when I suddenly hear a voice in the darkness at the end of my bed.

"Sawyer William Vincent." I can just barely make out the outline of a figure who appears to be looking at my chart. A very large, very round figure. "You know what that sounds like to me? It sounds like a backwards name."

"Who are you?" I ask, but I'm sure the words come out mashed together. "What do you want?"

"Oh, I'm a trained professional. Don't mind me. I'm merely checking up on you."

Everything is blurry... really blurry, and the figure before me swirls around, and there's three of them.

"Are you my doctor?" I ask, noticing what looks like a white coat.

"Oh, no. Nothing like that. But I do have to make sure the doctors do a good job of patching you up for the big finale."

"The what?" With my question comes a sort of clarity. Not just in what I'm saying, and what he's saying, but literal clarity. I can see the big fat chef in front of me. The same one I'd seen in the video at the Aerie. He was alive. Very much alive.

I struggle against the restraints, but there's no way I'm getting loose all drugged up this way.

"The climax of the story. The big confrontation. The *dessert*." He lets that word linger on the air while he thumbs through my papers so quickly he couldn't possibly be reading anything. "It certainly won't be very enjoyable if you aren't in superb fighting condition."

"Maléfique."

"Oh, you *do* recognize me! And it's *Chef*, if you please. You see, it's more than just a name. It's a *title*."

"Do it," I say. "Kill me now."

"That wouldn't do. That wouldn't do at all." He's shaking his head vigorously, which brings back a bit of my confusion. "You see, I'm going to kill you in front of Harrier like I did his last little boy toy. And then I'm going to finally put him out of his considerable misery."

"You son of a bitch."

"Wow. Do you kiss that smoking hot mother with those lips?"

"Don't you even think about my mother," I warn. "What have you done with Harrier?"

"You'll see, child. You'll see. Once you're up and about, come to this address." He pulls out a small business card. This one, I can see writing on it, just like Harrier's. Then, he lifts up the end of my blankets. He starts to place the card between my toes, then makes a harsh slicing motion, and gives me a giant paper cut. "Oopsie."

He lets the card dig in between my toes, pushing it into the paper cut. I grit my teeth but refuse to give him the satisfaction of anything else.

"Oh, and do make sure you're by yourself, little birdie. I'd hate for something horrible to happen to that pretty mommy of yours. She's aged well. Like a fine wine." He covers my feet back up and then pats them a couple of times.

Chef Maléfique walks to the door, and when he opens it, I can see his broad back in the light from the hall. Then he turns. He's wearing a white coat, but it's not like the ones the doctors wear. His pulls tight across him, buttoned over his right breast. There's blood spattered all over it, smeared in large swathes.

"Although... if you wanted to bring your little girlfriend, I suppose I would allow that. I would very much enjoy seeing her again."

He slowly closes the door behind him. I struggle against the restraints, knowing full well I'll never get out of them in my condition. I spend the next few hours wondering how I'm ever gonna get through this until I can't fight the drugs in my system and drift off into some of the worst nightmares I've ever had.

It's night. Full moon. Foggy.

I'm an actual bird—some kind of hawk, probably a kite, I guess—and I'm flying around looking for something. Through the darkness, I spot an injured black harrier attempting to take flight from its nest on the ground next to a river. The white undersides of its wings bob up and down, but it's unable to stay in the air.

I swoop into a steep dive to help, but then a white osprey

catches my attention, and I fly off after her. Maybe it's mating season or something. I don't know, you know how dreams are.

When I remember the harrier, I turn and fly back toward it, but before I can get there, an alligator jumps out of the river and chomps it in half in its jaws. The alligator turns, and I see that it has a white face. It seems to grin at me, its teeth full of black feathers.

I wake up and try to figure out why I would have a dream that was so on-the-nose for my situation. It's like my brain is trying to tell me something, but all this medication is messing things up. Is Osprey a distraction, keeping me from finding Harrier? Or is she really someone who can help?

TWENTY

EXCRUCIATING.

That's how I would describe the next few days in the hospital. I'm either lying in bed by myself with my head spinning, trying to figure out my plan for saving Harrier and defeating Chef Maléfique, or I'm putting on a show for my mom, pretending everything is okay and I can't wait to go home. Even worse, the kid brings the red kite with him every time they visit, reminding me of my situation.

The upside is I can finally watch the news. The downside, I don't want to. The crime spree continues to worsen on the streets, and now that I know Chef Maléfique is behind it, the signs are everywhere. Gangs of criminals are now wandering the streets, dressed in Harrier costumes, doing whatever they want to, and ordinary people are hiding in their homes at night. The cops are either too overwhelmed or too scared to put a dent in the situation.

"The problem, hon," says a bald Englishman on the TV I

recognize as an ex-Guild member named Baron Steele, "is that no one wanted to listen to me a decade ago. This goodie two-shoes superheroing just ain't the way to stop crime."

"So what do you propose?" asks the anchorwoman in the other box, doing a pretty solid job not reacting to being called "hon."

"Same thing I did back then, right?" Baron Steele says. "Look, you ever meet a kid whose parents clearly never put a belt to their arse? They act out. Think they rule the roost. That's what we've got going on here in our beautiful city—a bunch of spoiled brats who've never been beaten within an inch of their lives. They need a firm hand."

The anchorwoman begins a retort but I decide I can't take any more and lower the volume. I think I might fall asleep for a bit, but otherwise, things are brutally boring.

I do have one break in my misery when Fabiola shows up to visit me. Not something I was expecting at all, but I'm definitely not gonna complain. I don't even know how she heard about me being in the hospital.

Despite the nippy October air, she walks in wearing a pair of ripped jeans and a white cotton tank top that perfectly contrasts her silky dark skin. She's so gorgeous it hurts to look at her.

"O-M-God... I heard your accident was bad, but holy crap." She touches the bruises on my face lightly and parts of me tingle.

"It's not as bad as it looks." I try to act tough, but just what little pressure she's applying hurts like hell.

She runs her fingers along the straps holding me down.

"What's this all about? Are they afraid you're going to fall out of bed?"

"I tried to walk out of here when I first woke up. You know, 'cause of all the drugs they have me on. So now they keep me strapped down to make sure I don't try it again."

For some reason, she really likes hearing this. "Oh, a bad boy, huh? That's intense."

I smile, which feels really stupid.

"So you... can't move at all?"

I make a demonstration of trying to pull on the restraints.

"Interesting," she says as she leans over me, and her hair brushes against me. She licks her lips. I swear. It's not the drugs. I'm pretty sober and become more sober by the second. She licks her lips again, and I'm fully aware that I'm naked under the thin dressing gown.

She speaks, and the scent of her strawberry lip gloss overwhelms me, makes me lightheaded. "I hope this doesn't mean you aren't coming to my Halloween party. Are you going to be out by then?"

"I..." My voice cracks, and I clear the frog out of my throat. "I'm not really sure when they're releasing me."

"Well, don't worry. I'm wearing a naughty nurse costume, so even if you're still hurt, I'll take care of you if you show up."

This is so bizarre that I start to think maybe I *am* just having another weird dream because of the medication. The thing is, I don't even like this girl. She's never even said 'hi' to me before I was on the wrestling team. I mean, yeah, she's really *really* hot, but her IQ is probably lower than her bra size. I fight the temptation to check to see if I can figure out what that might be.

"Well, I should let you get some rest. Get better quickly. I don't want you to miss out on the fun." I didn't think she could get closer, but then she leans in and kisses me on the lips. A real kiss.

My first real kiss. From the hottest girl in school.

Maybe things are gonna start getting better for me. Maybe.

Yeah, except for being in the hospital, having my mentor kidnapped by a homicidal maniac, and getting ready to confront that same maniac on what is probably the most dangerous mission of my life. Things are really looking up.

Fabiola turns to leave, and there's Osprey standing in the doorway. To say she looks surprised would be a major understatement. Fabiola looks at Osprey, then back at me. With a little wave in my direction, she opens the door and disappears around the corner.

Osprey finally shows up so we can talk, and it has to be right now. At the worst possible time.

"Who was that?" she asks coldly as she watches Fabiola leave the room.

That can't be jealousy, can it?

"No one." Real smooth, idiot.

"Sure, I always go around kissing no one."

"She kissed *me*," I say.

She looks me up and down. Her eyes linger on the "down" a bit longer than I would want. I quickly readjust myself as she smiles, and says, "Looks like you enjoyed it."

"What do you care, anyway?"

"I *don't* care," she says, shoving a lock of her black hair behind her ear.

As cute as she is, I still have a hard time imagining her as the same person I was fighting criminals with except for that little movement. I'd seen her do that enough as Osprey. She's a little bit skater-girl, maybe a little goth, but mostly kind of nerdy, and definitely not someone you'd think of as a costumed crimefighter.

Then I realize that must be how people see me. To most of the people at school who even notice me, I must seem like some quiet loser without any friends. Except maybe Javier.

As if I'd summoned the little pipsqueak with my thoughts, Javi leans in and knocks. Two short, succinct taps.

Does the whole world know I'm in here?

"H-hey, uh, Sawyer," he says.

"Javi, what are you doing here?" I'm afraid the question comes out like an accusation, but he smiles anyway and shuffles in. He's wearing a shirt with that dwarf from that one old fantasy movie. It says, "No one tosses a dwarf," in big gold letters. Poor kid is such a geek, but I can't help liking him.

"I heard you were here. Then I saw Fabiola..." He stops talking abruptly as if he saw Osprey... or Amy... or whatever, standing there for the first time. "Oh. Hey?"

Osprey smiles and introduces herself. "I'm Amy. Sawyer's told me all about you. Javi, right?"

That is a total lie. I've never mentioned him to her even once, but his face lights up like Times Square.

"Wow, really? Wow..."

He stares at his shoes for a moment.

"What's up, Javi?" I ask.

"Oh. Uh, yeah. My abuela is on the third floor. She's got something bad. I don't know. I can't pronounce it. But I'm pretty much here every day. Maybe... maybe when you're not so busy we could hang out? Maybe tomorrow?"

"I hopefully won't be here tomorrow," I say.

His face looks like a balloon that just got popped.

"But, I still owe you some karate lessons, remember?"

That perks him up, and he nods. "Right. Absolutely. Yeah. As soon as you're better?"

"You bet."

He starts backing away. "Cool. Well, I gotta go. Feel better."

"Thanks, Javi."

"Hope your grandma feels better too," Osprey says as Javi closes the door.

I should be nicer to him. He really is a good kid, and I can't blame him for wanting to be friends with the only person at school who's nice to him.

And if you add the fact that a lot of the other students blame me for sidelining the quarterback for a few weeks, they probably don't like me very much either.

But isn't that what I want? Isn't that exactly what someone like me or Osprey looks for in a secret identity? Then why do I feel so bummed about it right now?

Probably because, unlike with Fabiola, I can picture Osprey and me as normal teenagers who are boyfriend and girlfriend. Hanging out, playing video games, going out for burgers. Whatever "normal" teenagers do.

You know what? She doesn't even know that I know who she is, and she hasn't even offered to level the playing field.

"What was that all about?" I asked.

"What?"

"I told you all about him?"

"Look, believe it or not, when I was in high school, I was a total nerd."

I laugh. "Wasn't that like, last year?"

"So?"

"I just mean—"

She cuts me off. "You try being... like me... and being a Mathlete, concert violinist, and captain of the debate team."

"Whoa," I say.

"Yeah, pretty dorky, right?" she says.

"No... I mean, that's awesome. You play violin?"

She rolls her eyes, and I let it go.

"So, now that you know who I really am, are you gonna tell me your name?"

"No." She says it so matter-of-factly, as if she's answered the question a billion times.

"Why not?"

"You won't let me into your world. Why should I allow you into mine?"

Ouch. Good point. "Okay. I guess I deserve that."

"Let's be honest. The only reason you've been stringing me along is to get into my pants—tights, whatever. Until you're ready to introduce me to Harrier—or ask me to help you find him—it's going to be strictly professional."

I consider denying it all, but I'm afraid it will just make things worse. Because then I'd be lying to her, and she'd know it. For now, I'll have to pretend I don't know her true identity.

"I *would* like your help. Especially now that Redhawk is gone. He believed Harrier's disappearance was because he was investigating Maléfique, even though he's supposed to be dead."

"Chef Maléfique? Do you think someone is getting some sort of revenge for his death?"

I hesitate to tell her the truth. I still don't know her very well, and I really don't know how much I can trust her.

"We weren't able to find much out at all. From the computer or informants."

"You don't think Chef Maléfique could still be alive, do you?" she asks.

I calculate the risks of telling her versus the help she could provide and decide to let her know everything.

"From what I know about the explosion that he was supposedly killed in, I wouldn't have thought it was possible. But something really strange happened to me."

I told her about the night Chef Maléfique gave me the card. I also try to figure out when that was. Yesterday? Two days?

She then tells me about the day the chef showed up in my room when I was unconscious, and about the creepy way he kept staring at her.

"You didn't think it was weird that a chef came to visit me?" I asked.

"I don't know," she said. "People are chefs, right? Like... how would I know it was an evil supervillain and not just some guy who worked at the Olive Garden?"

"Yeah, that's fair. What day is it?"

"The thirtieth."

I show her the card he left. One side has the handlebar mustache logo. The other has an address scrawled on it, along with tomorrow's date and a time: Halloween, 9:00 p.m.

"I have to go there," I told her.

"Don't you think it's a trap?"

"Of course it's a trap. And Chef Maléfique knows I know it's a trap. But he also knows I'll go anyway."

"You can't." Wow. She genuinely looks worried about me.

"I have to. Harrier will die. If he isn't dead already."

"I'm going with you."

"No," I say, shaking my head. "No way. It's way too dangerous."

"So, it makes more sense for you to go alone?" I've never seen her this serious before. At least, not since she first beat me up.

"I can't put you in that kind of danger."

"Oh, the big strong man, huh? Gotta protect the little girls."

"You know that's not what I meant."

"You're not 'putting me' into anything. I'm making my own decision."

"But I can't—"

"Look, I don't want to embarrass you, but I'm actually older than you, and, unlike you, technically an adult. I'm going to go with you whether you like it or not, and I don't think there's a whole lot you can do about it."

I sigh. She's right. This is a woman who, without any assistance, became a crimefighter just by making her own costume and training herself to be a great martial artist and acrobat. Who am I to tell her what she can or can't do?

Besides, as I yank on the restraints, I don't think I can even get out of this bed without her help.

TWENTY-ONE

Osprey does a bit of recon work, going to check the address on the business card Maléfique gave me. Turns out, it's an old warehouse down at the docks. We devise a plan for me to sneak out of the hospital just after the nurse comes by during her rounds tonight. Now, we just have to figure out a way to get me there in time for my little meeting with the evil chef.

First, Osprey loosens the restraints that have been holding me down. I expect bells and whistles to go off, but nothing happens. I consider myself lucky for once this month. Then, she has to go back to my place and basically break in to get my spare costume because she'd dumped the one I'd been wearing somewhere along the way on our way to the hospital. I'm not sure what I had on when I got here, but I don't ask because I don't really want to know the answer. Chances are she got the clothes off of a homeless guy or out of a dumpster, not to mention that she had to undress and redress me while I was unconscious.

When—*if*—I ever get back to the Aerie, I'll be able to track Amber from Frank's computer and at least find my helmet... hopefully, my whole costume. But until then, I'm living in backup city.

It's almost as uncomfortable to think about her going in through my bedroom window—which I have rigged to be able to get into from the outside with a special trick and a screwdriver—and rifling through my stuff. It's not like I was expecting to have her over and cleaned up my room beforehand or anything. I just hope she doesn't do any snooping other than just looking for the costume and getting out. That could end up being really awkward. I have to force myself to stop going through the list of things she might come across that would make me want to die.

Oh, man. If she sees my browser history, I'm screwed.

All I can think of is her finding out I'd been net-stalking her.

"Okay, just breathe," I tell myself.

At least Mom didn't throw out the spare costume or give it away, even though she thinks I paid for it with money from "selling drugs." But it's is the old version, without the attached grappler, glider cape, and jets.

And no mints in the utility belt. Maybe I can stop by the hospital gift shop on the way out. Man, my priorities are seriously out of whack.

Probably the worst part is the helmet won't have Amber installed. Even though she'd missed a couple of emergency warnings, I'd much rather have her with me than without.

Nerves are really getting to me now. It's that anxious feeling you get right before boarding a rollercoaster.

The nurse rolls her little cart in and does some checks on me and then moves on to the equipment. As she checks on everything, I watch the news on the TV in the corner of my room like I'd been doing for days. In addition to the usual Halloween stories, they show the continuing rise in the crime throughout the city. I turn up the volume.

"In an unprecedented event, more than three dozen prisoners have escaped from Dellgate Prison, including several of the city's more deranged 'supervillains.' As of yet, there's no news on how, and Commissioner Mahlberg has declined media comment. I—"

She stops and touches her ear like she's listening to a voice lodged in there.

"This just in... we have a camera crew live at Times Square..."

A new feed pops up, taking over the whole screen. In the middle of Times Square is a massive gathering of people in costumes, jumping up and down to music playing from gigantic speakers.

When they show who's playing the music up on stage, I recognize him immediately. You can't mistake Music Master with his stupid colorful costume, a patchwork of post-grunge meets old lady quilt shop and bright orange hair. He reminds me a bit of that one comedian I used to watch with Mom when I was younger. He's playing a keytar, and whatever song it is, really seems to be riling up the crowd. His music can't exactly control someone's mind, but I know that he's able to cause people to feel different and intense emotions, and he's definitely pushing a hostile vibe with his spooky Halloween tunes.

The police surround the crowd as the dancers start moshing into one another, and some of them even break into rioting. The feed becomes smaller and shrinks into the top right corner of the TV, once again showing the news anchors.

"An impromptu concert in Times Square has really stirred some buzz," the female news anchor says. "Officials say there were no plans for this event, but after seeing and hearing a sample of the band's demo, they simply couldn't resist."

"I think I've seen this guy before," says the co-anchor, a guy who looks like he's had more than a little work done on his face. "I can't place him, though."

"Yeah, Dale, he *does* look familiar."

The song ends, and Music Master starts to talk. The camera zooms in. Up close, I can see his makeup. It's like some kind of drugged-out drag queen.

"Looks like he's saying something. Let's have a listen."

The full screen returns to Music Master. The volume of the audience gets louder, and I hear that sickly sweet voice. Everyone quiets immediately.

"Kite, Kite, protector of night, what will you do on this evening of fright? Danger, danger, I know you're no stranger to the man who will die if you don't find a game-changer. Scarier and scarier, can you break the barrier? So many of us between you and Black Harrier."

"Oooo," Dale says, smiling. "Freaky. Perfect for this Hallow—"

The screen goes black, and then a shaky black-and-white feed appears. In the corner of the screen, I can just make out an eyeball that's way too close to be clear.

"SWV. SWV. SWV." Finally, as if the cameraman figures out how to zoom out, Chef Maléfique appears. "SWV. SWV."

He keeps saying my initials over and over. Behind him, I can see what is probably the same warehouse Osprey checked out, but there's no sign of Harrier.

"Time is... ticking." He does a little dance. "Tick. Tock. Tick. Tock." But since the guy doesn't laugh or smile, it's super strange and makes me even more uncomfortable. "Didn't you know its rude to miss your reservation?"

Then, I consider what he just said. Tick tock? Crap. Is there another bomb? Is this Toby all over again?

"I hope you deciphered our little rhyme. Who am I kidding? Any idiot could have figured that out. Are you smarter than an idiot?"

I sit up a little in bed despite the restraints, but when the nurse glances over at me, I try to act natural.

"Our little bird must leave the nest to save daddy bird," Chef Maléfique continues. "But you know, if someone doesn't stop Music Master, the whole city will be moving-and-a-grooving to his particular tunes. Better hurry, I'm preparing the chef's special!"

You've gotta be kidding me. Did he just call me out on live television?

"What is this scary movie you're watching?" the nurse says. "A young man like you shouldn't be watching such filth."

"You're right," I say. Hoping to get rid of her, I turn off the TV.

She grumbles about "kids these days" and pushes her cart

out. After I know she's gone, I pull one hand loose from the restraints, then free myself completely.

I glance at the clock. Man, the nurse was late on her rounds. I've only got a few hours to stop Music Master from turning Manhattan into an angry murder zone, and get to the warehouse before Chef Maléfique does to Harrier whatever he's planning to do.

I make sure everything is unhooked from me. At least the IVs are out of my arms now. I hop out of bed and—whoa, that's not good. It's been too long since I've stood up, and I'm pretty shaky here. I'm sure the hospital food, with all that Jell-O and broth, isn't helping much either. I wonder if I have time to stop for a burger on my way to Times Square.

I have no idea what will happen if I don't make the meeting with Maléfique, but from what I've heard about him, I shouldn't take a chance on finding out.

My legs are so wobbly that I feel like I'm walking on noodles. How am I ever gonna do this?

Power through, Sawyer.

After the very short pep-talk, I crack open the door to my room and peek out to assess the situation. A couple of orderlies are talking down at one end of the hall, and a doctor is going through some paperwork at the other. When the doctor turns his back to me, I sneak out and head in that direction, then slip into the first non-patient room I come across. It's some kind of locker room. I thought it was empty at first, but then I notice a doctor asleep on a cot in the corner.

I'm gonna need to get out of this hospital gown if I plan to out of here without drawing attention to myself. I quietly check a couple of the lockers, but it looks like they're all locked. After searching for a minute, I find a couple of paper clips lying around and pick the lock on one of the lockers. There are scrubs inside, but they're pink. I need to try another one.

Damn, that doctor is waking up. No time to be picky about the color. I quickly pull on the pants and shirk the gown. Since Dr. Sleepyhead is sitting up now, I pull the scrub shirt over my head as I exit the room, hoping nobody is standing right outside to see me.

The pink scrubs are both too big and too short for me at the same time, and I look completely ridiculous. If anything, I'll probably draw more attention to myself than I would have by wearing the gown.

I manage to make it down to the end of the hallway, but just as I start to open the door to the stairwell, I see my nurse exit my room. Why was she back in there?

She peers down the hall in both directions and spots me just as I'm going through the door.

"Mr. Vincent! Wait there, young man!"

Great. Now security is gonna be after me. Why are they treating me like a criminal?

I head down the stairs as fast as my noodle-legs will carry me, which isn't very fast at all. Up above, I can hear handheld radios and a couple of security guys talking as they rush down the stairs, so I know I don't have a lot of time.

Just then, I see Osprey on her way up to meet me, still in her civilian clothes. She laughs. Which is fine. I look stupid. But before I can say anything, she rushes past me, dropping a duffel bag. A couple of flights up, the security guys shout in surprise, then make some unpleasant noises just before I hear what has to be their limp bodies hit the stairs and roll down.

Poor guys. They were just doing their jobs. But, better them injured than other people dead.

Osprey comes back down to join me and picks up the bag. I try to give her a stern look.

"I was hoping to avoid hurting anyone here at the hospital."

"Couldn't be helped," she says. "And you're welcome. What are you wearing?"

"It was this or my bare butt flapping in the wind."

She shrugs with a little smile as if to say, "That wouldn't be so bad." However, I'm sure that's just my hope speaking.

We exit the stairwell at the bottom near the lobby. A bunch of security guards have gathered there, knowing it's my only way out.

Osprey looks at the guards, then at me. "You ready for a fight?"

"No. And I said I don't want to hurt anyone."

She grabs me around the waist and pulls her grappling gun out of the bag. "Then I guess we'll have to improvise."

She shoots her grappler at the front doors of the hospital just as someone is walking in. The hook barely avoids taking the guy's head off and connects with a pole just outside the doors. When she hits the button to retract the line, we start to slide through the lobby fast. The guards try to grab us, but they end up running into each other like they're in an old-fashioned comedy film.

Just as we're about to go through the doorway, I notice a

kid standing by the door holding a Happy Meal. I grab it out of his hand. "Sorry!"

I immediately feel guilty about taking the kid's food, but it had to be done. Sometimes stuff happens when you're working for the greater good.

As soon as we're through the door, Osprey disconnects the grappler again and shoots it up to a nearby rooftop. Before anyone can even follow us out, we're gone.

Once we're safely on a nearby rooftop, I open up the box. "Dammit!"

Osprey looks worried. "What is it? What's wrong?"

"Nuggets. I was so craving a burger. Even a crappy one. And look at this! Apple slices! I don't even get fries."

"You poor baby. Maybe we can stop—"

"No. There's no time. Did you see the news?"

"What? News? No, how the heck did you expect me to see the news while I was sneaking into your bedroom. Your mom was home, by the way. Almost caught me."

"None of that matters," I say, tossing a McNugget into my mouth. Chewing, I tell her about Music Master and Chef Maléfique.

"Holy crap. How are we supposed to get to Times Square and stop a mad man *and* get to Maléfique in time?"

"Dunno."

It's the most genuine answer I can come up with. I know what Harrier would want, even though it might not be my first instinct. If it comes down to him dying or dozens or even hundreds of citizens... he'd gladly sacrifice himself. That's what being a hero is all about.

"I'm not even sure we're going to get there in time as it is," she says.

I scarf down the food—even the apples—and get my costume on as quickly as I can. It fits kind of snug since it was made a couple of years ago, and the design is a little bit different from the newer one. It also doesn't offer as much protection because it's Kevlar instead of graphene. Plus, it doesn't have some of the newer pieces of armor attached to my new one. But there's an old grappler in the bag. One of Osprey's, I assume. As well as some other random equipment that might come in handy.

It's also missing the glider cape, which means traversing the city will be extra tricky.

I try not to gawk as Osprey changes into her own costume, but it's really difficult. I'm probably gonna be dead within the next couple of hours anyway, what do I have to lose? I sneak a peek, and she immediately busts me.

"Eyes forward, soldier."

"Sorry. It's... you know." My face must be redder than my costume right now.

She smiles. "It's okay. I know how irresistible I am." She finishes pulling on her costume and her wig and walks over to me. "Don't worry about it. I had to strip you down before I took you to the hospital, so now we're even."

She's standing so close to me that I can feel her breath. I should try to kiss her. What difference will it make? I'm going on a suicide mission. I start to lean forward.

But what if she doesn't want me to? Is she giving me a signal right now? How do I know? Why am I such a geek? I think she wants me to. I'm gonna go for it. But what if she doesn't?

She leans in and gives me a small kiss. On the lips. The *lips*! But then she pulls away. What does that mean? Was that a real kiss? Or a "hope you don't die" kiss? Or an "okay, I feel sorry for you" kiss? Maybe her seeing Fabiola kissing me wasn't so bad after all.

I don't have time for this!

"We better get going."

She isn't happy taking orders. "Yes, *sir*."

"I'm sorry. You didn't see that crowd at Times Square. And I've seen what that guy's music can do to people. I hope I'm wrong, but there's a good chance people are already dying. And, if Chef Maléfique is as insane as I've heard, I'm not interested in finding out what happens if I'm late."

"Alright, alright. I get it. Let's go."

She thinks I don't realize that she just turned the tables and gave the orders, but I do. And I don't care. We just need to go, and egos be damned.

We take off across the rooftops in the direction of Times Square, but Osprey still wants to talk. "You don't really think he'd kill him, would he? I mean, he's had him for weeks. Why would he all of a sudden kill him now?"

"Maybe you missed the part where I said he's insane." That came out harsher than it should have. I should be happy about the kiss. Why does it seem like I'm upset about it?

"Just seems like he went through a lot of trouble to capture Harrier and lure you there... even keeping you alive when he could have easily had you killed, or even killed you himself."

"I don't know about easily," I say under my breath. But again, this is no time for egos.

"Even for a crazy person, that doesn't make any sense."

"He's punishing Harrier, and I'm somehow part of that plan. I just don't know what part."

Actually, I do, assuming he was telling me the truth. He wants to kill me in front of Harrier to torture him. He knows Harrier will blame himself for getting another kid involved after what happened to the last one.

But I can't let Osprey know any of that.

As we run across the roof of one of the nicer buildings in the neighborhood, I hear loud music, and at first, I think it might be Music Master. Then, I look and see that a bunch of teenagers are out front and talking really loudly. It sounds like there's some kind of fight going on. If only that was it.

Even though I tell myself to stay out of it and focus, I still glance down to check out what's happening. In a coincidence I wouldn't believe if I saw it in a movie or TV show, it turns out to be Fabiola's party. The biggest event of the school year. And I'm missing it.

But the noise isn't because of a simple fight like I thought it was. Someone dressed in a Black Harrier costume is shoving someone dressed like... me? And the Red Raptor guy isn't fighting back. A group of teenagers in other costumes starts to surround the smaller kid.

I know I'm repeating myself when I say I don't have time for this. But something tells me I'd better *make* time.

My old helmet may not have Amber, but it still has the onboard microphone and amplifiers, as well as sound dampeners. I turn up the volume and listen in. I immediately recognize "Harrier's" voice. Of course, it's Logan. Who else? But what really surprises me is the voice of "Raptor."

It's Javier.

"I'm sorry. I'll leave," Javi says.

"Not until I'm done with you, loser. The only reason we invited you was to get your idiot friend to come."

It's not like I can see Javi's face under that mask, but there's no doubt in my mind he's terrified.

"He's in the hospital," he says.

"I know, you stupid moron. So why did you bother to show up?"

From my utility belt, I fish out a… well, fishing line. It's hyper-durable and strong, made for situations just like this. I attach it to a drainpipe and rappel down the side of the building just as Osprey notices I'm not keeping up with her. She glides down after me. "What are you doing?"

"I have to."

"There's no time!" Osprey shouts.

"I have no choice."

I get closer and see Fabiola come out with her naughty nurse outfit on. Even in the middle of all this. *Yowza.*

I shake the impure thoughts away and watch as she stomps toward the altercation. It's a major relief, her being there, since I'm sure she'll put a stop to it and I won't have to step in. I almost turn to head back to the rooftops when she grabs Logan's arm.

"Just hit him and get it over with. I can't believe he had the nerve to come to my house."

Wow, was I ever wrong.

Just as Logan cocks his fist back, I squeeze between them. He gives me a strange look. "Who the hell are you?"

"I'm the *real* Red Raptor."

"He's called 'Red Kite,' you freakin' 'tard."

I look at Osprey, and she smiles as she says, "You're right. We had no choice."

I haul off and pop Logan square in the face. Even in my weakened state, it's plenty hard enough to knock him unconscious. There are a hundred other ways I could have taken him down, some of them without hurting him. But that just wouldn't have felt right.

Fabiola rushes to his side and lifts up his head. "Logan! Logan?" She stands up and shoves me as hard as she can and then gets in my face.

"What did you do to him? How did you—?" She stops and tilts her head. She squints, and I can tell that a hint of recognition is starting to form.

POW! Osprey knocks her on her ass with one punch, then turns to me, wearing a crooked grin. "Well, I knew *you* weren't going to do it."

The rest of the crowd backs away, afraid to mess with us.

We turn to leave, and Javier calls after us. "Hey!" I turn around for a second to give him a chance to thank me.

"That's Kite's old costume, you know. You really should update it."

I can't even catch a break after saving someone.

But his comment does remind me that I'd transferred most of my tools and weapons to my new utility belt when I got it, which means I only have basic stuff with me on my most dangerous mission ever. I look down at my old, slightly faded backup threads, then turn to Osprey. "Are you sure you don't remember where you dumped my good costume?"

TWENTY-TWO

CRAZINESS.

As we head toward Times Square, I start to see that the news stations don't begin to do justice when explaining the situation on the streets. That's pretty odd since networks live to stir up fear and exaggerate everything. But there's more crime going on in the city than I've ever seen. I'm not talking about typical Halloween pranks. There's serious looting, brawling, and rioting all over. Osprey and I try to do what we can along the way, but it's a drop in the bucket. Scratch that— it's a bucket in the ocean. And as much as I want to stop every little thing from happening, say it with me... we don't have time.

Sadly, the police aren't even coming close to getting a handle on the situation, either. They're all pretty much wandering around trying not to get shot.

Harrier isn't the only hero in the city, but he's definitely the most famous. I start to wonder where everyone else is when I realize they must already be at Times Square. I don't think any of them will be a match for Music Master, though. Then the thought strikes me... *Will I?*

A short while later, we are standing on the precipice of the busiest tourist trap in America. Just close enough that we can hear the beginnings of Music Master's music. I've been debating when would be the right time to do this, and I admit, I'm still not sure. But there's a good chance we're gonna die, and I might as well just get it out of the way.

I inhale deeply. "Did your dad make that helmet?"

"Yeah, but I made some modi—" Osprey answers before she realizes the implications. Then, even through her lowered visor, I can see her mouth part, and words start to form.

I smile.

"You're joking. How long have you known?" she asks.

"Since the hospital."

"But how?"

"I visited your dad a few weeks ago. He has a picture of you on his desk."

"And what—you just remembered my face?" she asks, skeptical.

I probably blush a little, but my mask is down, too. "Kinda hard to forget."

For the first time since changing, I'm so glad Amber isn't installed on my old helmet.

I don't think she knows what to say either.

I decide to break that awkward tension. "Okay. So if your helmet is like mine, you have dampeners?"

"Yeah," she says. "I've never used them, though."

"We should be able to sync up our microphones." I reach

for her visor, and we make eye contact. "I..." I clear my throat. "There we go."

I adjust mine and say, "Can you hear me?"

"Loud and clear."

"Can you hear anything else?"

"No. Creepy."

"Yeah, but you'll be happy when you're not being controlled by that loser's hippie music. Now or never, you ready?"

"Nope."

"Good. Let's go," I say.

This time, she doesn't argue, and we take off together.

The closer we get, the more we're slowed down by crowds, and the more I worry about not getting to my "reservation" before it's too late. This is all just part of Chef Maléfique's plan. Music Master is working for him, just like all of the other criminals in town seem to be now.

It continues to worsen until I feel like we're wading through a horde of zombies. Most of them are ordinary people, which makes it both easier and more difficult at the same time. It's easier to take down a normal person than an experienced criminal, but it's more difficult because we really don't want to hurt them.

"Make way!" I scream.

"Does that ever work?" Osprey asks.

I shove people aside as gently as I can, but they keep attacking me, full of rage. I can't hear Music Master's music, but these people are clearly being affected by it. How long does its effect last? I don't have any of the information I desperately need. That's always been Harrier's job.

"No."

I am not prepared for what I see when we arrive in Times Square. Yeah, there're the typical glowing signs and billboards, larger-than-life Victoria Secret models, and, of course, that seafood place from that one movie. But there's also absolute mayhem, and even the police are involved. Except, they aren't helping. They're just as crazed as everyone else, throwing stuff, screaming, punching, kicking. Then, as if that's not enough, my heart plummets into my nether regions.

In the middle of it all, Gargantuan Grey and Royal Rampage, both Guild-affiliated heroes, a bipedal werewolf and fully-sentient great ape who, for some reason, wears a giant gold crown, are tearing through the crowd with abandon.

"You seeing this?" Osprey asks through our linked-up helmets.

"Yeah, unfortunately."

A bright green blur appears out of thin air about a hundred yards in front of us, then disappears in a crackle of dark energy.

"Was that..."

"Stygian," I finish for her.

Stygian is a hero too. No one knows for sure since he doesn't speak any known language, but we all think he's from another dimension. He looks human enough, but he's green and covered in scales. Oh, and he can teleport.

"Are they all possessed or whatever?" Osprey asks.

"That's what it looks like. We've gotta do something."

"Riiiight... but what?"

Before I have a chance to answer, I'm grabbed from behind and pulled. I spin, ready to clobber whoever it is and stop, my fist an inch away from beating a woman. A pregnant one at that.

"Don't hurt anyone," I say to Osprey, my eyes fixated on the twenty-something-year-old who'd just attacked me.

I peel the woman's fingers off my arm and back up.

"You don't want to do this," I say.

She screams something, pointing at her bloated belly, but I can't hear it through my dampener. The look on her face is just pure rage.

Music Master is definitely drawing out their anger. I mean, we all have it, buried deep inside. Memories of our dads who beat us, or weren't there at all, teachers who told us we'd never amount to anything, bullies like Logan. Whatever it is that causes it, the anger is there. Now Music Master is taking advantage of it.

There are thousands of people, a lot of them tourists, clearly on family vacations and checking out the most famous spot in the city.

Imagine?

"Hey, honey, let's take the kids to New York to see Gulliver's Gate. Maybe we'll even get possessed by a supervillain and watch our children gut-punch homeless people."

"We have one advantage here," I tell Osprey while I continue to fend off Violent-Femme. "Music Master is expecting *me*. Not you."

"How is that an advantage? There are literally dozens of

supers out there who could probably kill either of us just by stomping hard enough."

"I don't know. I'm still trying to figure that out."

How do we use that to our advantage? How... how? I've literally got nothing. I don't even think Harrier has seen anything of this magnitude.

"We've gotta get closer. We're running out of time."

"Not without a plan," I say.

"You and your plans."

With that, Osprey whips into action. She goes for the Canadian Shield, who is easily twice her size. But she has surprise and sanity on her side. Even so, he still bats her away with his massive shield. She uses the momentum and falls into a roll, coming up in a perfect Brazilian jujitsu stance. Who is this girl?

The Canadian Shield rushes her, and she snatches his wrist, then lets her body roll along his arm. Her other elbow connects with his jaw, and the big man goes down.

I'm sure he'll recover quickly enough, but I don't watch the rest of it. Instead, I parkour through and over people, using them as objects, I make it to the throng of the concert in a matter of minutes. I have to dodge punches, and I get caught in more than one mosh pit—why is anyone moshing to this crap? I'm just glad I can't hear it.

I feel my ribs crack, and I'm flying through the air. Cool. I'm out there for four seconds, and I'm dead. Awesome.

I land hard on my back and slide, slamming into several citizens along the way. Not being able to hear anything is disorienting at best. I stand and see my attacker, Royal Rampage, well, rampaging toward me. So, that crown... I'm

guessing the film studio that owns the name *King Kong*
wanted to charge too much for him to use it.

At one time, he was an ordinary gorilla being transferred
from the Central Park Zoo when the driver of his truck
collided with a GenLabs hauler. GenLabs is a shady tech
company out of Jersey. Yeah, I know... anything from Jersey,
right?

Turns out, their hauler, which was supposed to be
carrying "harmless chemicals" across the harbor, was actually
carrying some sludge. It killed the drivers of both vehicles on
contact, but it left Barry the Gorilla with the intelligence of a
ten-year-old and the strength of a god.

Oh, and they were transporting him because he broke the
record for the largest gorilla ever. So I guess, not exactly ordinary. He's a thick mass of muscle and bone. Six feet two
inches and over nine hundred pounds, and all of that is
hurtling toward little hundred-and-thirty-pound me.

Both of his fists pound the pavement, cracking it and
sending spiderwebs out. They're like freaking bowling balls.
He roars when he nears me. I can't hear it because of the
dampeners, but oh, my, God can I feel it. It literally shakes
my chest, and I think I feel spittle. He lowers his head and
goes for another spear.

I dive to the side, avoiding him but crashing into a group
of pedestrians who turn on me. Now, I'm blocking punches
and kicks from all sides while hoping Royal Rampage doesn't
eat me. I could really use Amber's warning system
about now.

One of the teenage girls—purple hair, *My Little Pony*
shirt—starts swinging her metal-studded purse at me. It

clearly doesn't hurt, but it's a perfect example of just how chaotic this place is. I'd have a better chance of catching every raindrop in a thunderstorm than quelling this crowd without first stopping Music Master.

I "feel" Rampage's roar again and turn to see him barreling toward me. His fist hits my chest with the force of a pickup truck on a straightaway. I fly back fifteen feet and smash into a stack of speakers. It topples, and out of the corner of my eye, I see Osprey swoop in to knock two men aside before the weight of it crushes them to death.

I stand and turn just in time to see Gargantuan Grey, long fangs, sharp talons, and yellow eyes coming at me.

Still recovering from that last hit, I have no choice but to brace myself and prepare for impact. That's what I do, but there is no amount of preparation I could have done. Every ounce of air evacuates my lungs, and I'm gasping even as I land.

Music Master's crappy song assaults my ears, and I feel a fire inside of me. My helmet must've come off. I start to look for it, but it's no use. Everything around me goes red. Logan's dumbass, pudgy face... I see it on everyone around me. I lash out, hitting things, people, anything within striking distance.

Then, Frank fills the forefront of my mind. Everything he ever did to piss me off—not trusting me enough to tell me what happened to my predecessors, not telling me about the garage below Douglas Industries, his stupid voice-changer. I hate him.

He didn't even trust me enough to tell me about the business card he clearly got from Chef Maléfique. Am I his partner or not?

Chef Maléfique. Frank. The warehouse.

I blink and focus, recalling every YouTube video I'd ever watched about centering my chi. I calm just long enough to see my helmet on the floor and make a leap for it.

When it's in my hands, I stare at it. I hate this helmet. I hate this costume. Red Kite. What a stupid name, and it was Frank's idea. I hate him.

A scream rings out, and I think it might be mine. Though, it sounds more like a howl. It *is* a howl.

I recognize the battle going on inside of me, but it's just so difficult to fight. I almost don't want to fight it. I like the anger. It's like an old friend.

I feel my helmet slip over my head, but it's not me doing it. When silence comes, I see Osprey standing in front of me, and Gargantuan Grey laid out on his face a few yards away.

"Are you okay?" she says.

"Did you do that?" I ask, pointing at the werewolf.

"Couldn't let him kill you now, could I?"

I can't see her eyes with those reflective covers, but I imagine she's winking at me.

"Look out!" I shout as a see Gargantuan Grey rise, head tilted to the sky and howling.

We leap out of the way as he lunges. He continues until he smashes into the iron fence surrounding the stage where Music Master continues to pound away on his stupid keytar. I glance up at him, but he's just as distracted as everyone else, lost in the music, like I'm not even there.

While Grey recovers, I turn to see Osprey is gone. I look out over the crowd, hoping to see her somewhere, but I have no luck. There's just too many people.

"Where are you?" I say into my microphone.

"A little busy," she says, sounding winded. "You'd better stop this guy, quick."

"Me?"

Her response is a series of shouts and moans as she fights whoever she's fighting.

I turn back and see Rampage and Grey beating on each other now. Better that than focusing their super-strength on helpless people.

I rush the stage and leap up there. No one even tries to stop me. Music Master stands several yards away, playing his instrument. His head snaps toward me, but again, barely even seems to care about me, just a few strides away. His music isn't the only thing loud about him. His stupid, colorful costume and bright orange hair hurt my eyes just looking at them.

Obviously, he's controlling the sound, so if I can take him out, it should stop. I look around the stage, expecting to find a full band, but it's empty except for the speakers. I try to walk, but a sudden, sharp pain in my side drives me to my knees. Had Rampage actually broken something? Jumping onto the stage must have aggravated it. I also feel nauseous. Great... puking is gonna end up becoming my signature move.

Through the pain, I can't concentrate enough to hit him or his keytar with my throwing stars. If only there was some way of reaching him from here. I can't even crawl over to him.

Then, remembering Osprey's solution to reaching the door at the hospital, I pull the old grappler off my belt. It's a piece of junk compared to my new one, but it'll do for what I have planned. Music Master's expression goes from passive to curious. Then it changes to realization a second too late as I shoot the hook at him, and it attaches to his keytar, which is strapped around him. His playing stops immediately.

I brace myself and retract the cable, and because he wasn't ready for it, he's pulled toward me extremely fast. Just as he's about to reach me, I muster all my strength and do a flying kick, allowing the grappler to launch me toward Music Master as he continues moving in my direction. I grit through the pain in my side, and my kick nearly takes his head off. He drops to the ground like a sack of potatoes. I check to make sure I didn't kill him, but he seems to just be unconscious.

I unhook the keytar from its strap and smash it against the stage as hard as I can, even though I know he has many of them, and this won't stop him the next time he gets out of jail. It takes everything I have not to bash him over the head.

Everyone is still going crazy in the crowd. Why? Why didn't it stop? I look at the soundboard, next to where Music Master had been standing. Lights are still moving up and down on the board's indicators. He was just playing along to some music he'd pre-recorded. I swear and start turning down all the knobs and flipping switches, but it doesn't seem to do anything. How can I stop this thing?

Then I remember another hero I'd caught a glimpse of in the crowd. Darkstryke...

He controls electricity. If I can spot him...

As I search the chaos, a couple of guys from the mob climb up onstage and attack me. I do my best to take them down as gently as possible, but I don't have time to be too careful. Then I spot what looks like a small lightning storm nearby.

I climb up on one of the giant speakers so I can see Darkstryke among the rest of the rioters. There he is, purple and silver leotard, V-shaped headband-thing, and long blond hair. He kind of looks like a wrestler from the 80s or something.

I try shouting to him, but he can't hear me over the music and the yelling. So I pull out my boomerang and toss it at him as gently as possible, just to get his attention without injuring him too badly. The last thing I need is to knock him unconscious and ruin my plan.

The boomerang hits him on his back, and he flinches in pain, but he doesn't go down or anything. Turning around, he spots me waving my arms at him. "Hey, Dorkstryke! I'm over here!" I taunt, grimacing as the movement makes my side burn.

He throws a ball of electricity at me, and I leap out of the way. It fries the one speaker and leaves scorch marks, but the rest of the speakers are still functioning.

I move directly in front of the soundboard and flip him off with both hands, which I can see enrages him even more. His eyes narrow, and he points both fists at me as they start to glow and crackle. I'm not that familiar with his powers... how long do I wait before I jump out of the way without him moving his aim? I guess if I wait too long, at least I'll have gone out saving thousands of people. I decide to just count down and hope for the best. "Three, two, one..."

I spring from the stage just as Darkstryke unloads with everything he's got. The lightning blast temporarily blinds me and, I assume, everyone else. The soundboard, the PA system, the speakers—they all blow, sending sparks and smoke all over the stage.

Aaaarrrrgh. I lie in agony, but everyone around me starts to settle down, looking around in confusion as their eyes recover from the brightness of the blast.

"Amy," I say. It's the first time I actually use her name. I like the way it feels, saying it.

"You okay?"

I groan. "I'm hurt. This... dumb... armor..."

I look down and see that there's a piece of the Kevlar cracked and sticking into my ribcage. I yank it off, and the pain immediately subsides.

"What happened?" Osprey asks.

"I think I stopped him... but it was too—"

I was gonna say "too easy" when Osprey swears and shouts, "Look at the screens!"

I do as she says, and I see the giant visage of Chef Maléfique, bigger than anyone would ever want to see him. I chance switching off my dampeners and hear him.

"Tick, tock, tick, tock, tick, tock. So much time you're wasting." He points to an imaginary watch on his arm. "Better hurry up. Don't be late."

The camera pans to a fuzzy figure in the background, but it's only up there for a blink before it's gone.

"Was that Harrier?" Osprey asks from wherever she is.

"I couldn't tell. I hope so. He was moving, at least."

We both meet up and take the least amount of time possible to make sure Music Master is tied up, and everyone else is okay. We leave things in the capable hands of the other supers—who, by the way, are very apologetic and thankful—and the NYPD before grappling up to the rooftops and starting toward what I hope isn't our final destination.

TWENTY-THREE

ISOLATED.

We finally arrive at the address. Talk about the shady part of town. I think I saw a dead body in the gutter a couple of blocks back. This is the kind of place the mafia owns to store their guns and lie low while the fuzz searches for them.

A bit of false hope comes. I start thinking I'm actually gonna be on time for my "reservation." But reality is a bitch, and it slaps me hard.

"There's no way this is opening," I say, tugging on the massive roll-up door. There doesn't appear to be any other way in, either.

"You didn't mention the place looks like something out of a Marilyn Manson music video."

"I'm sorry," Osprey says. "I didn't really think that was pertinent information."

The place is huge—like an airplane hangar. It's covered in graffiti. Giant spiderwebs, creepy dolls with red eyes and bloody noses, black and white skulls, amongst other stuff like gang tags and symbols indicative of this neighborhood. Right in the center are two giant butcher knives, crossed... and a handlebar moustache.

It's scary as hell on the outside. I figure most of it is Chef Maléfique's work, though, trying his best to elicit fear.

We circle the perimeter, pushing our way through waist-high weeds. It must have rained here recently because I'm ankle-deep in mud, and it's starting to get cold. I'd forgotten that this suit didn't have built-in heat.

Sure enough, aside from the massive garage door, there are no other entries, and all of the windows are covered with sheets of metal and welded shut.

"Well, now what?" I say.

"The roof?" Osprey suggests.

"It's either that or dig. The roof sounds like a better first option."

We grapple up to the roof and, honestly? I start to panic about what's gonna happen as Maléfique's deadline passes.

I remember my dream about the black harrier getting eaten by the alligator while I was distracted by the white osprey. I'm sure it was just a dream, but I can't help but worry that Frank is being devoured, even now.

Bye-bye, hope.

On the roof, there's nothing there. Same problem. No doors, no skylights, no way in at all. The entire area is covered in junk and stupid horror stuff, as if someone put up Halloween decorations years ago and never bothered to take them down.

Just as I'm about to give up, Osprey whisper-shouts, "Over here!"

I run to see that she's found a small hatch buried in the far corner, hidden in some debris. She also figures out how to open it, since it's not obvious just from looking at it.

As it cracks, smoke pours out. But... it's not smoke... it's a chemical smell... like a fog machine.

We start the climb down into who knows what. I go first, looking up at Osprey, wondering if I'd have made it here without her help. She's been anything but a distraction.

TWENTY-FOUR

EXPLOSIONS.

Really cool and fun in an action movie. Not so much up close in real life.

You know what you never consider when thinking about explosions? First of all, we all realize you can be blown to pieces, or struck with shrapnel. But the heat... The fire is so hot without my climate-controlled suit, I can feel sweat pouring down my spine. Explosions are just one of the traps Chef Maléfique has waiting for us when we get inside. If he wanted me dead, he could have killed me a bunch of times by now. He could have sliced my throat in the hospital. Deadeye could have shot me instead of killing Weasel. The entire mob of bad guys could have converged on me on the bridge and taken me down with the sheer force of numbers.

It's the same with all the explosions. None of them are big enough or close enough to kill me, but they do make me dizzy and knock out my hearing for a while. I consider switching the sound dampeners on again, but the last thing I need is to be caught unawares in this hell-house.

There's fog machine smoke everywhere, and every now and then, one of the things hisses and expels more. I'm a little embarrassed when one goes off to my left, and I jump. Truth is, I'm completely on edge. I know the explosions aren't deadly, though. Probably not even loud enough to bring the cops, if he has as much soundproofing as I imagine he does. So I go in knowing that he doesn't want me dead—yet—but I still have to worry about what kind of shape I'll be in by the time I reach him.

It feels like a thousand years ago when I saved that woman in the alley from that group of a dozen thugs. But somehow, this reminds me of that. Like when the biggest, toughest gang member hangs back while the others soften me up. All this nonsense is meant to just make me weak, break my will.

Unlike that night, now I have to worry about Osprey's safety. I'm sure Maléfique probably knows that Harrier doesn't give a damn about her, so the only reason for him to allow her to come with me would be to hurt or kill her in front of me. Demoralize me further. Just one on a long list of reasons why I should have figured out a way to prevent her from joining me.

Like a carnival funhouse, albeit one with deadly traps, Chef Maléfique has the entire warehouse set up in some sort of maze, with everything in it meant to disorient me. The "walls" are made of kitchen stoves, each one's timer going off, beeping incessantly. Hallways shrink and then widen, then turn back on themselves.

The hallway opens into a small room with walk-in freezers wide open, pouring out freezing-cold air. Thick cuts of meat hang... like animal legs or... human torsos. No, I'm gonna go with cow legs. In addition to the explosions, loud French-style music blares from hidden speakers like we're in some bistro in Paris. It's absurd. He isn't even French. Doesn't sound French. But there's this whole stupid schtick.

Every fifty yards or so, there's a big flatscreen TV with the sound blasting over the music. Right now, they're playing recorded news stories about how Harrier hasn't been seen in so long. Another tactic to throw me off, I guess.

I turn to Osprey. "Stay close. The last thing we need is to get separated in this madhouse."

She shakes her head. "Oh, you don't have to worry about that. I have to admit, I'm pretty much terrified."

"Right."

We continue forward through a wall of hanging streamers. When I shove them aside, a blast of liquid hits us. Immediately, I begin to worry that it's acid or some chemical, but I'm soon convinced it's... wine?

"This guy is insane," I say.

At one point, the hallway narrows until it's nothing more than a crawlspace. In fact, he probably just led us up into the actual crawlspace of the building now that I think about it. It's really dark except for the TV screen up ahead, suddenly filled with Chef Maléfique's face.

"Welcome to my kitchen, wee little birdies. Or is it dinosaur now? Raaahr. None of it makes *SENSE*."

He really emphasizes that last word, and I catalog it for later, in case it means something more than just the ramblings of a madman. However, he did say birdies, plural. That means he knows Osprey is with me.

He continues. "We're going to have *so*. Much. Fun. But first, I suppose you'll be wanting to see how Harrier's doing at some point. Well, no time like the present." Maléfique steps back from the camera, and now, that fuzzy figure is clear as a bell.

It's horrible.

Harrier and I have been in bad shape after some really intense fights, but nothing like this. His uniform, except for his mask, is almost completely gone, and what's left of it is hanging in tatters from his bruised, bloody body. He, himself, is suspended from chains that are cuffed around his wrists, and he's covered in cuts from head to toe. He's obviously been tortured.

I must have let out some kind of sound when I first saw him, but I can't tell you what it was. This time, I don't need Music Master's keytar tones to feel the anger well up inside of me after the shock wears off. I can't wait to get my hands on that evil bastard. He won't know what hit him.

"Oh, and by the way—this is for you being late." He reaches for something off-screen, and suddenly an electric jolt zaps Osprey and me. It starts at our feet and zips through us. Now I know what the wine was for. It wasn't too bad. I've been hit with a Taser before, and it was along those lines.

I whisper to Osprey. "Glad you came along?"

"I'll be fine," she says through gritted teeth. "We need to save him."

She looks back at the screen again. I'm gonna have to force myself not to think about the torture Harrier's been through while he's been here. I mean, Maléfique has a thing for butcher's knives. If I dwell on it too much, it's gonna throw me off my game and put all of us in even more danger.

While Osprey and I are focused on Harrier, a hidden trap door opens beneath her, and then immediately closes again, even as I dive after her. I'm met with nothing but steel. I hear her start to scream, but it cuts off as soon as it shuts. I have no idea how far she fell, or what she landed on at the bottom of the drop. It could be spikes for all I know. I may have just watched her die.

What if she *is* dead? What in the world would I tell Mr. Chen? How could I explain bringing his daughter on what I knew would be the most dangerous date of her life?

I try to pry open the trap door with my fingers, but I can't get a grip around the edges. I grab one of my throwing stars to see if I can force it open, but I don't have any luck with that either. In desperation, I start pounding on it, but I realize it's not gonna help anything.

"I'm gonna kill you!" I shout.

Snow fuzzes on the TV screen. "No killing," Chef Maléfique says in what I'm guessing to be his Black Harrier impression.

I whip my throwing star, and it smashes into the display, sending out shards of glass and puffs of smoke.

"Oh, so childish," he says, voice echoing over the speakers even without the TV. "That was expensive."

Once I calm down, I continue to crawl, determined to get through the maze as quickly as possible so I can save Harrier, and hopefully now Osprey also.

The crawlspace ends by opening up into a dark room that

appears empty from what I can tell. I can't see the bottom, so I drop another star, waiting for it to ping. From what I can figure, the floor is only about a twelve-foot drop. I lower myself, then feel around with my foot, allowing my eyes to adjust to the darkness. Normally, I'd use my light, but I don't want to give away my position to anyone—or anything—that might be lurking in here.

Just as I start to be able to make out where I'm going, and I reach the center of the room, bright lights suddenly come on from all directions, blinding me now that my pupils have fully dilated.

I shut my eyes and fall to my knees. Why is Maléfique doing this? Why not either kill me now or let me get to where he's keeping Harrier so he can kill me then? Is he somehow making Harrier watch this, assuming it'll torture him? From what I saw on that video screen, it's hard to imagine Harrier being able to focus on anything right now.

This is apparently the stage portion of the "restaurant." Even with my eyes shut, the light is so bright that I can't think straight. They flash on and off, getting faster and faster until they produce a strobe effect.

"Hello, sweetie."

I turn around, and Sinsation is already behind me. There must be a hidden doorway somewhere in here.

No matter how many times I see her, I can never get over how hot she is. I've never been to a strip club, but I imagine this must be how the women look before they take their clothes off. Most heroes and villains don't actually have costumes like the ones in the comics. They wear some combination of lightweight body armor, Kevlar, and other microfibers. But Sinsation is a major exception, all in spandex and glitter, like she was drawn by a pinup artist.

So, idiot that I am around attractive women, I stand there with my mouth open instead of reacting immediately. That gives her plenty of time to roundhouse kick me in the helmet, knocking me to the floor, and again my helmet comes off and lands ten feet away. What a piece of—

She kicks me again while I'm down, and I flop over. Now my head's throbbing on top of everything else, and I think I strained my neck.

I'm not sure what kind of technology she uses, but she's able to do a lot of things with her light shows. Right now, I feel myself not being able to move very well or to track her with the strobe light flashing. I don't know whether it's a trick of the lights or if I somehow end up with gaps in my perception, but like the lights themselves, she appears to flash in and out of places. On top of that, she's an Olympic-level acrobat, cartwheeling and flipping all over the place.

The next thing I know, she's behind me again, this time using a flying kick to my back, which slams me into the wall, breaking the light fixture there. I can feel where the glass cuts into my face, and even through parts of my old costume that aren't armored.

I forgot what an excellent hand-to-hand fighter she is on top of the light show. Her stiletto boot slices across my face, and I feel the warmth as my blood trickles down. I can't see her. Then I realize what Chef Maléfique is doing.

Sense. That's what he'd said.

Music Master was the sound. Sinsation, the sight… he's toying with my senses.

Harrier taught me what I should do the next time we fought her. I close my eyes, listening for her footsteps. If I can't trust my sense of sight, I'd have to focus on the others. She's so quiet, I almost don't pick it up, but then I hear an almost imperceptible crunch as she steps on a piece of shattered glass.

I hate hitting a woman—my mom would kill me if she ever found out—but I kind of think Sinsation deserves it. Oh, man, I hope that doesn't make me sound like some kind of a-hole who makes excuses for abusing his wife or something. I mean, she is helping a homicidal maniac who's trying to kill a teenager, isn't she?

And right now, she's doing a pretty good job of it.

I swing out my leg, and it connects with her stomach. From the sound she makes, I can tell I got her pretty good. I continue my momentum forward and punch for where her face should be, and I'm successful there as well. My next move is to sweep her legs out from under her, and I hear her fall to the ground.

I leap onto her chest and hold my forearm against her windpipe. "Turn it off."

She tries to wriggle out from under me, grunting with effort. Her voice sounds almost like a cartoon duck because of the pressure on her throat. "Get away from me, you little—"

"I said turn it off!"

Finally, she gives in and presses the buttons in her glove or whatever it is that controls her light shows. Now I have to figure out what to do with her. I can't have her showing up when I'm in the middle of my showdown with Maléfique. It's gonna be nearly impossible to defeat him as it is.

"Roll over," I say. Then I realize I'm subconsciously bracing for Amber to make a smartass comment before I remember she's not here and relax a little.

I pull a zip tie out of my utility belt. She does what I ask, but as I start to bind her hands behind her back, she flips over and gets me into a headlock with her legs.

I can't breathe at all, and I feel myself losing consciousness fast. Things start to go dark with little stars flying around as I feel around for something to hit her with. My fingers close in on something... my helmet, lying on the floor just a foot away. I grab hold of it, and just as I feel like it's gonna be lights out, I get both hands around it and smash her in that smokin' hot face of hers as hard as I can.

Her leg-lock goes slack as she collapses to the ground. So much for going easy on her. I zip tie her legs together so she can't follow me even if she comes to. I wipe the blood off my face with her pink and grey half-cape, and it comes away really saturated. That boot was more than just a little scratch, I think, but it's too dark to make any real assessment.

All I can think about is resting right now, but I have to keep moving. Harrier may not have much time left, even if Chef Maléfique doesn't directly kill him, and I don't even want to think about what that wannabe-French-freak and his men could be doing to Osprey right now.

TWENTY-FIVE

My question is answered in the next room. It's set up like a sort of a makeshift bar. Dark wood countertop, a mirrored wall with bottles of various liquors. I'll give Maléfique one thing, when he picks a theme, he really leans into it hard. There's even a mannequin wearing a black shirt and jeans, frozen in the act of wiping down the bar. Above the bar, situated a few feet apart from each other, are another half-dozen flatscreens. Each one shows me the same room from different angles. Osprey, in a giant cage. It's hard to even worry about her; the relief that she's alive is so strong.

"Lookie, lookie, little birdie," Chef Maléfique says over the speaker system. "Have you ever seen an Osprey in a cage? It's like your own little private zoo. Maybe she'll perform for us? Oh, and who is this—is that the zookeeper?"

A chain-link door opens on the side of the cage opposite where Osprey is standing and in walks a dark figure. Despite being newer-looking televisions, the live feed is absolute crap.

It isn't until he steps into the center of the cage that I can tell who it is.

Deadeye.

He wears his trademark skull helmet, which I figure he'd want to take off since he's not on his motorcycle, but I guess that's his way of shielding his identity. Now, there are no bandoliers full of ammo, and I can't see a single gun on him. For that matter, he doesn't even have a weapon. No blade. No staff. He cracks his gloved knuckles.

Osprey drops into a fighting stance. Thank God. She looks okay. My best guess is that the trap door led right into the room on these screens.

They circle each other for a second, and Deadeye looks like he's playing a game while Osprey seems prepared to fight for her life. She cartwheels in, and Deadeye is ready for it. He kicks straight out and catches her full-on. Still upside down, her body looks like a rag doll as it's launched across the cage.

Deadeye stalks toward her, no urgency to his movements at all. When he gets close, she does a whirlwind like she's breakdancing. Both feet catch him in rapid succession.

That's a badass move I'll have to remember. She winds up in a handstand that she uses to catapult herself to her feet. Two quick steps and she's on him, unwilling to give him the chance to recover. She gets a few really good hits in before he brings an elbow around, and she crumples.

The feed is cut the moment she hits the floor.

"No!" I shout.

"That's enough entertainment," Chef Maléfique says.

"You may want a drink. I know, I know... underage, but I won't tell. We have so much more fun to be had firsthand!"

The mirrored wall shatters, and all the bottles of alcohol come toppling down toward me. I leap out of the way but still get hit by a few. They don't hurt, but it does distract me to the fact that more fog starts rolling in through the vents, but then I smell it, and it absolutely isn't fog.

This is typical of supervillains in this town. They come up with some hokey plan and think it's clever. First, they assault my hearing, then my sight. Now? Smell. Music Master, Sinsation, and... there's only one baddie who smells this bad. Creeping Death.

Who is Creeping Death? Imagine someone who smells like a fart and looks like a massive tarantula. It's just a ratty old costume, worse than one you'd pick up at a Halloween store, but that's part of what makes it so scary.

So who am I gonna face when I get to "touch," assuming I live that long?

I can't think about it right now. I just have to focus on the moment and worry about that if and when it comes up.

I follow the room toward a dark hallway I feel a... stickiness on the bottom of my boots. Soon, I notice webbing hanging down from the ceiling also. It doesn't get bad enough that I can't move, and I know from past experience with Creeping Death that it won't do any good to try to cut it. It'll just stick to the blade and keep pulling like the cheese on a good slice of pizza.

I can see up ahead that there's a dim light coming from an opening and more of his noxious gas. My helmet, even this old one, has an air filter built-in, but after having gone through so much with Gargantuan Grey, Royal Rampage, and Sinsation, the thing is cracked to hell and won't seal no matter what I do. I have to make a decision to either go through quietly and assess the situation, or rush in and try to take him by surprise. Again, these are the kinds of calls Harrier makes, and, again, I realize I'm not very good at it, having not had a lot of practice.

I decide to go in headfirst and fists blazing.

It's hard to get a running start with the stickiness, but I'm going at a pretty good speed when I burst through the opening and roll forward. I get up into a crouch and look around, but I don't see the Creepster anywhere. It does become immediately apparent that this is supposed to be the dumpster area behind a restaurant. Two large blue dumpsters take up half the room, adding to the stink. There's a thick, yellow haze, making it so I can't see more than a few feet in any direction. The smell is already beginning to burn my nostrils and my lungs.

I cough. A bunch. It almost makes me wish I still had a cold, maybe then I'd be too stuffed up to smell it.

I turn in circles as quickly as I can without making myself dizzy, hoping to catch him before he can get to me from any direction. Somehow, I didn't think about him coming from above like a spider, so when he lands on my shoulders, it's a complete surprise. He's bulbous with that stupid costume on, and I find myself off balance. Sharp fingernails dig into the sides of my head. He's surprisingly strong for a bony old man.

If you've ever seen Beetlejuice, turn him into a spider, and you can get a good visual for this guy. He's so disgusting.

Luckily, it doesn't take much for me to figure out how to get him off. I bend as if I'm gonna do a backflip, which ends up slamming his head into the floor. As soon as I hear the crack, I feel his hands loosen, and I jump away to get my bearings. But then he drops another one of his gas bombs, and it feels like napalm in my lungs. He uses the distraction to disappear again into the haze. These villains absolutely have the advantage on me. They've probably seen the hangar with the lights on. All part of screwing with my senses.

Okay, think, Sawyer. These crazies always do things according to their theme. What's he gonna do next?

Attack from below. I think of it a split second too late as I feel something clamp around both of my ankles. I can't move my feet. They're in some kind of cuffs that are attached to the floor.

I hear Creeping Death's cackling laugh. I don't know if this guys' been smoking two packs a day for fifty years, or if he's just breathed in too much of his own creations, but he sounds like he's gonna hack up a lung. Just like I can never tell whether his old, faded costume is part of his theme, or if he's just too cheap to get a new costume. It looks like it hasn't been washed in my lifetime.

Some kind of whip snaps at me from behind and wraps around me, pinning my arms to my side so I can't move them. The old man dances around me in circles, wrapping his long whip, like a spiderweb, tighter around me. Between the dancing and the cackling, I'm almost sure he's completely lost it.

There's one idea I had a couple of years ago that Harrier gave me a lot of praise for. After continually being locked up by these costumed villains and not being able to get to our lock picks in our utility belts, I convinced him that we needed to come up with a way to hide them in our gauntlets. Because we wear bracers over our forearms, it wasn't too difficult to hide the tools up there. I squat down before he can get the whip around my legs, and my hands are able to reach the cuffs around my feet. In less than ten seconds, I'm able to unlock both cuffs without him noticing a thing.

I don't know what Creeping Death's plan is, or if he even has one, but it ends now. As soon as he gets to the point where he's directly in front of me, I launch myself forward, and the crown of my head smashes into his nose. He was not ready for that at all.

He drops his whip, and I roll in the opposite direction that it's wrapped around me. I'm free, but I still can't see him through the haze. Eyes shut, I hear him whimper from the ground where he's lying. I'm sure I broke his nose, but the old fart probably broke a hip or something, too, when he fell.

What? I'm supposed to feel sorry for this guy?

The whip starts to move, so he must be picking it back up. No way I'm letting him have another crack at me. I grab the end closest to me and yank on it as hard as I can. I think he's afraid to let go because he'll fall down again, so he's hanging on tight as I see his nasty old spider costume coming at me. I prepare to kick him hard, but at the last second, I sort of feel bad. I mean, he looks like someone's grandpa.

Instead, I step out of the way, and he runs into the nearest wall headfirst. He spins on me, hissing? What the crap?

He lurches forward and bites me on the neck. Actually bites me.

"You crazy old bastard!" I shout. All concern for his elderly ass flees me, and I punch him as hard as I can in the side of his wrinkled face. I stared down at his unconscious form. I reach up and touch my neck. It's hard to tell because there's still blood dripping from where Sinsation's stiletto got me, but it doesn't seem like he broke the skin.

Wrapping him up in his own whip to make sure he can't come after me, I decide I better check his pulse to make sure he didn't croak. It's weak, but still there. And, dude, his breath smells worse than his stink bombs.

I scour the room, and it turns out the only way out is an opening in the ceiling. I use the junky old grappler and shoot it up into the opening. It attaches to something solid. Rising up above the room, I notice tiny cameras in each corner of the ceiling. I didn't see any in the other spaces, but I didn't get up this high, so I'm sure they were there.

Apparently, all of this is part of a show for Chef Maléfique's entertainment.

I climb through the opening in the ceiling and crawl through what feels like a duct, thin metal bouncing under my movements. In the darkness, I start to notice a slight downward incline, and then it suddenly gets steeper. Too late, I realize it's actually moving, and the surface has gone from ordinary metal to something really slick. I start to move faster, and just when I'm about to put my hands out to the sides and stop myself, razor-sharp blades spring out.

Maléfique's voice booms from unseen speakers. "Anyone in the mood for Sawyer Allumette?"

I pull my limbs in as close to my body as I can so I don't

get cut, but that makes me like a bobsledder hurtling down the slide.

As I spot a light up ahead, I prepare myself to be launched into whatever's at the end of this ride.

TWENTY-SIX

The slide dumps me out in a cavernous room filled with tables and chairs, all nicely decorated with white table-cloths and candles. I gotta hand it to him; it's really nice. Like someplace Frank would send me to get food to bring back to the Aerie. And I go crashing through all of it at very high speed.

My guess? It's time for the "taste" portion of the program. I have no time to even catch my breath before a giant hand grabs me by the cape and lifts me into the air like a doll. Perhaps we're skipping taste and going straight to touch.

La Cucaracha pulls me in close. I should have known.

"*Hola, mi amigo.*"

Looks like he's back in fighting shape. And, with his body odor, he could have easily been the "smell" portion of their plan instead.

He doesn't realize it, but knowing what he did to Osprey gives me extra ammo to want to pound this oversized bug into the ground.

Who am I kidding? I'm exhausted, and I'm not sure how I'm even gonna make it through a fight with another boss, much less inflict any pain on them.

"*Ay, Papi,*" he says, then chuckles as he flips me over, grabs one of my ankles, and lifts me completely above his head.

There's no way I'm defeating this monster in my condition. I might as well just give up now. He throws me at a thin metal sign that says, "Please seat yourself," but it might as well be a concrete wall. Groaning, I roll into another part of the gigantic room. When I come to a stop, I want to lie there and just let him kill me. I'm ready for it to be over with.

But then I see them. Chef Maléfique. A couple regular Joe henchmen dressed like servers. Harrier. On the other side of the room. I'm so close to the end. I can't give up now.

La Cucaracha is gonna be on top of me any second now. I can hear him grunting as he walks toward me, his exo-suit making a whirring sound with each step. I feel around in my utility belt, trying to figure out what I might still have in there.

Most of the compartments are empty. Just a few throwing stars, but I know they're worthless against him.

My hand closes around a small metal tube. Pepper spray? I shrug internally. Why the hell not? Last-ditch effort. Go down fighting. He grabs me again. I spray it directly into his face, and he screams in rage. I'm not sure how much actually got into his eyes, though, because the eyeholes in his mask are pretty small. Either way, I can't believe that with all the high-tech weapons I usually have at my disposal, I took him down with something I can get at a convenience store for a couple of bucks.

I mean, I didn't actually take him down, but I slowed him long enough to gain a desperately needed advantage.

I pull out a throwing star and try cutting the cables again like last time, but it's useless. The new ones are made of some really strong material. I guess he—or, more likely, Chef Maléfique—wanted to make sure he couldn't be defeated as easily as he had been last time.

He starts spinning, metal appendages sticking out. He becomes a violent tornado, and I do my best to avoid him, but my luck has absolutely run out along with my energy. One hits me, and I'm sent staggering, and eventually, I'm on the floor again.

I lie there, trying not to just die, trying to will myself to move because if I don't, this guy is gonna recover and kill me. After a few failures where I topple into some of the dinner tables, I manage to stand weakly, and I grab something. I don't even know what it is. A chair leg? A signpost? It doesn't even matter what it is. Maybe I can use it to break the batteries in that power the suit. I know from past experience that when the suit's not working, La Cucaracha can barely move. Plus, he doesn't really know how to fight, so I'd be able to take him down quickly.

I swing directly at the batteries, but they're also made of something too strong to be affected by it. If I hadn't lost my new graphene staff on the bridge, I might have a shot, but now, I'm just desperately kicking and punching a couple of his more vulnerable areas. He barely notices as he spins and claws at his eyes.

Then, without warning, he stops and looks directly at me. His eyes bulge like an old cartoon, bright red, and full of hate. Two catcher's mitts grab me by my shoulders. His hands are absolutely massive. They lift me above his head again and tosses me across the room in Chef Maléfique's direction.

I allow myself to go limp, so I don't break anything as I hit the floor and roll once again to a stop. For a second, I feel like I can't move, and I'm worried I'm gonna be paralyzed. I wiggle my fingers and toes just to make sure I still can.

I look over at Harrier. He's seated—strapped to one of the chairs—at a table. The white tablecloth is stained red and pink from his blood. He tries to lift his head long enough to see if I'm okay and manages to get it up for a second, and in that second, I manage to squeak out an "I'm sorry."

La Cucaracha makes it over to me before I can even think about moving yet, and he's still in a rage. Looking at the bright side, if I live through this night, I don't think even Harrier could say he's gone head to head with this many rage-infected heroes and violent villains in one day.

La Cucaracha stands above me and, with a roar, lifts his foot for the killing blow. It's sort of funny in a morbid kind of way, him being a bug, doing what he's about to do. He's gonna literally stomp on my head, and I can just see every time I've ever killed a pest that way. Squish. Like a melon. There's no way I'm surviving this.

BLAM!

A shot rings out, and La Cucaracha slumps down, collapsing on top of me. He's so heavy, especially with the exo-suit, that it's only slightly better than having my head caved in under his boot. I keep thinking that the uber adrenaline people say moms get when their kids are in danger will kick in, but really, I might as well be trapped under a train or something.

Behind him stands Deadeye, once again holding an actual smoking gun in his hand. Chef Maléfique shoves him to the side as he throws a tantrum about La Cucaracha almost killing me.

"I warned him to stick to the plan. Why is it so difficult for everyone to stick to the plan?" He runs over and kicks La Cucaracha's lifeless body over and over, screaming like a little girl who had her ponytail pulled on the playground.

This is the first chance I have to get a good look at Chef Maléfique in person. So much different than in the pictures, video, and even while I was drugged up in the hospital. So much scarier. Who'd have thought a chef could be so terrifying? His face is painted like a mime... I guess more of the French influence. All black and white. His chef jacket is also stained with blood. And he's wearing one of those big floppy hats. He's way too overweight to be exerting himself this way, and he starts breathing heavily as the sweat smudges his makeup.

This is not what I was expecting at all. It's kind of... sad.

I try again to push La Cucaracha off of me, but he's far too heavy, or I'm way too weak. Probably both. Chef Maléfique finally stops and tries to calm himself, breathing heavily as if he'd just run a race.

"I never did like him anyway," Maléfique says. "Couldn't be even a bit original." He brushes his jacket off, smoothing out wrinkles. He snaps his fingers, and his two regular henchmen come over and—with a lot of effort—drag La

Cucaracha off of me. Then they roughly help me get to my feet.

I thank them both by using my last bit of energy to knock them unconscious with roundhouse kicks to the head.

Chef Maléfique makes a tsk-ing sound. "Now, what did you go and do that for? Do you have any idea how hard it is to find good henchmen these days? And let me tell you, their union is a real problem. I can barely afford the overtime anymore."

I'm starting to see why criminals get so annoyed with the witty banter. It's no fun when you're on the other end of it.

Deadeye pulls his bo staff from its sheath on his back and faces me. I can barely stand, and my legs are shaking hard, but I try not to show it. He can probably kill me with one blow—what am I saying? He can *definitely kill me with one blow*. I've been going on fumes for too long now, and I don't think there's anything left in me. I've been ignoring my injuries because I'm afraid of what I'll find when I start to check them out. It's like I'm already defeated, and I haven't even gotten to my main enemy yet. I just have to go through the deadliest assassin on Earth to get to him.

"Where's Osprey?" I demand, but it comes out weak, just like me.

Deadeye shakes his skull-helmeted head.

No.

She's dead? She can't be dead. But if Deadeye is here, that means she lost.

"You bastard," I say. He pops me right in the mouth with the end of his staff and I taste blood. Really? After everything else, is that all there's going to be for the "taste" course of this meal?

I know if I let the emotion get to me, I'm a dead man walking.

So now, the only question left is whether Chef Maléfique had Deadeye shoot La Cucaracha to save me for himself, or if he wanted to give the assassin the honor of killing me. Thankfully, I get the answer right away.

"Mr. Deadeye," Maléfique says, huffing. "I believe I have this young man right where I need him at this point. Thank you for all your assistance with my grand plan—you were absolutely brilliant. Now go take the rest of the evening off."

Deadeye doesn't care about killing people. He's not one of those emotional thugs like Music Master or La Cucaracha. He's all about the money, and I'm guessing Maléfique paid him enough for his services already.

He just shrugs and puts his staff away. People always talk about letting out a breath they didn't know they were holding, and until now, I've always thought that was stupid. How could you not know you were holding your breath? But then, I notice I'm starting to breathe again. As Deadeye leaves the warehouse, I feel like I've been pardoned from a death sentence. Except the reality is that Chef Maléfique is far more dangerous than even Deadeye.

And now it's down to Chef Maléfique and me.

"Release Harrier. Now." With Deadeye gone, I get a little bit of confidence back, but I'm mostly faking it because I have nothing else to lose. I can't believe Osprey is dead.

"Oh... I see. You think you can just waltz into *my* restaurant and start barking orders. What in the world gave you that idea?"

I move toward him and make it clear with my body language that my intention is to beat him senseless.

"No. Nyet. Non. Nein. Don't step any closer, little bird. Or the girl gets it."

I look around. "What girl?"

Is she still alive?

Hope floods my chest as he walks over to a wine rack and swings one of the lower doors open. Osprey tumbles out to the floor, her hands bound with rope in front of her. She doesn't look too good.

Chef Maléfique holds Osprey by her hair—her real, black hair. Her costume is torn, and her cape is missing. She looks like she's nearly unconscious.

"I'm so glad you listened and brought your girlfriend, little birdie. She's oh-so-delicious. Once I'm done with you and Hack Derrière over there, I'm going to have *so* much fun with her." He sticks out his slimy tongue and licks her neck from her collarbone to her ear. She recoils enough to spit on his face, and he sticks out his tongue again to lick it off his own cheek.

I take a step toward him, but that causes him to yank her head back hard, so I stop. "Let her go. She isn't part of this."

"Isn't part of this? Of *course* she is. She was always part of the plan. You can't possibly think you met by accident, can you? Think about it. She was there when you needed her. To save you. To push you along. To make sure you got here. Did you think it was all a coincidence? Everyone works for the Chef."

What? *No.* He can't be telling the truth. What does he mean? That Osprey was working for him? For Harrier? What?

I go through everything in my mind. She showed up when I was falling, so she was watching me then. She was there when that punk tried to take my picture. And she somehow, she was there on the bridge, saved me from that criminal mob—Chef Maléfique's criminal mob—and took me to the hospital. Was she a spy for Chef Maléfique that whole time? Moving me toward coming here all along? Or is he just trying to get to me some more and make sure I don't trust anyone?

My features must give away what I'm thinking, because Osprey speaks even though it seems like it's a huge effort for her. "Not... true."

Chef Maléfique sneers. "Oh, don't be so modest, girl. You were wonderful. Don't denigrate your fantastic performance by pretending it was all real. I'm sure he knows deep down that someone like you would never want anything to do with someone like..." He turns and looks at me in disgust. "... *him.*"

"You're lying."

"Oh, and her father..." Chef Maléfique says.

My heart drops further, if that's possible. He knows who she is? He knows Luis Chen is her father?

"Yes, yes. Luis Chen. I think he deserves the Academy Award for Longest Performance."

Chef Maléfique turns slightly toward Harrier.

"Played this sucker for the fool he is for... how many years?"

I just can't believe it could be true. The Chens working

for Chef Maléfique? I've had my problems with Mr. Chen these past weeks, but he and Harrier go way back.

Osprey somehow gets up the strength to lift up her knee and then slam her foot back into his crotch. Maléfique snarls with rage and throws her down to the ground.

I run to her while the chef doubles over in pain, holding his junk. He makes a strange groaning noise that is gonna keep me awake at night if I ever get a chance to go to bed again after this.

Osprey looks up at me, her eyes pleading. She can barely get her words out through her sobbing. "Please. He's lying. Please don't..."

She passes out. She seems to be okay when I check her pulse and everything. I look back at Harrier to make sure he's still breathing. I'm done with this game. I have to get them both to a hospital right away.

At this point, I don't care who's telling the truth. Chef Maléfique's gonna pay for this. All of it.

I wipe blood from my face with my forearm—or it could be tears. Standing, I face Chef Maléfique, who is also trying to get up. The rage continues to build inside of me, and I can feel the adrenaline pumping again. I'm in bad shape myself. The injuries from my fight on the bridge hadn't healed yet, and now I have brand new ones that might even be worse, but I'm gonna finish this fight. And I'm gonna win.

Chef Maléfique holds up his hands. "Hold on. Before you get all punchie-hittie with me, there are some other things I think you're going to be very interested in hearing."

"This better be good."

Why am I even letting him talk? As long as he's talking, I can get some of my energy back.

"Oh, it's good. Very good. Much better than you can even imagine." He strolls over to Harrier and slaps him in the face. "You still awake, bird-brain? I'd hate for you to miss the most exciting part after three years of careful planning and moving everything into place."

Chef Maléfique grabs Harrier by the chin and lifts his head up. Harrier winces.

"Hands off him, or I kill you now," I say.

"You think he's trying to clean up the city because criminals killed his father? That *is* what he told you, yes?" He lets go of Harrier's chin, and Harrier grits his teeth as he tries to hold his head up. After a second, his neck gives out again. Silverware rattles as his head hits the table.

"Oh, no, no, no," Chef Maléfique continues. "You've got it all wrong, boy. The Black Harrier is just trying to clean up the mess his daddy left behind. As this city's top criminal. You see, his papa's death left quite a vacuum at the top of the underworld. And we've all been trying to fill it ever since."

I look at Harrier to see if there's any reaction to help me figure out if Maléfique is telling the truth, but he still can't lift his head.

I make a dismissive sound with my lips. "I don't care. Why should it matter to me *why* he does it? He's cleaning up the streets; getting rid of garbage like you."

"Why should it matter? Hmmm. Why *should* it matter?" He taps his index finger on his lip as if he's in deep thought, and turns back to Harrier. "What do you think, Frankie-boy? Should I tell him, or do you want to do the honors?"

With a considerable effort, Harrier raises his head and looks Chef Maléfique in the eye. His voice comes out as a rasp, but not like his voice-changer, not the kind I usually make fun of. It almost sounds like a death rattle. "... no..."

"Fine. Fine. Fine. I'll do it then." Maléfique waddles over to me and gets right up in my face, and I have to do everything in my power not to punch him as hard as I can.

"The first reason you should care, young man, is that your mentor here was the one who killed him."

No. It can't be. That's our number one rule. Our only rule. *No killing.* How could Harrier have started his career by killing his own father? I don't believe it. He's lying just like he's lying about the Chens.

"I know. Shocking, isn't it? But this squeaky-clean do-gooder just couldn't handle the idea that his father was such a notorious blaggard, and it simply drove him over the edge. But wait... there's more! It gets better."

It makes me sick to see Chef Maléfique relishing this so much. I'm not sure how much of my shaking is adrenaline, how much is due to my injuries and weakness, and how much is just from me wanting to thrash this evil bastard.

"The second reason—the most important reason—is that Franklin Douglas Jr., kingpin of crime for many years, and responsible for more death, destruction, and misery than anyone else in this city's long history... Oh... wait for it... This is so good. Is there someone to give me a drumroll?"

He looks around at the dead and unconscious men around the room. Then he does a little drumroll with his tongue.

"Was your granddaddy!"

As my head tries to wrap itself around what Chef Malé-fique just said, I see a look of satisfaction stream across his face like I've never witnessed from another person. It takes a second for me to register exactly what he means, but when it hits me, it hits me hard—like getting the wind knocked out of me.

And then Maléfique literally knocks the wind out of me. I hadn't even noticed how close he'd gotten, and he punches me in the stomach, and I feel my diaphragm push all of the air out of my lungs. I lean forward and gasp for breath, and he hits me with an uppercut so hard that I feel myself standing up straight before falling back and hitting the ground.

Then he kicks me. First, in the ribcage, then again in the kidneys. That's when it becomes glaringly apparent that he's wearing steel-toed shoes. I cough, and blood comes up.

All fight is gone. I just want to lay here. To let him finish me off. It can't be true. But what if it is?

Chef Maléfique looks down at me, and I imagine that he's gonna start laughing, but then I remember what Redhawk said about him being deadpan. In fact, I don't remember him laughing at all during the two times we've interacted or on video. He could kill me now, right in front of Harrier, but he's making sure what he revealed to me is sinking in.

My brain is trying to calculate how Harrier's dad could be my grandfather without it being the obvious answer. I met my mom's dad when I was little, before he died, so that can't be it. Could my dad have been Harrier's brother? No—he was definitely an only child.

That only leaves one other option. But it feels so wrong that my mind rebels against it. Pushes it out as if it's poison.

I force myself to my hands and knees, blood dripping from me like drool. I turn to Harrier. "Is it true?"

No response.

"He's just saying it to get to me, right? To mess with my head." Harrier continues to just sit there, his head pressed against the table, arms bound behind the chair. I crawl over to him and get up close. Close enough that he can see me without lifting his head. I can hear Chef Maléfique following slowly behind me. He wants this. He wants me to experience every second of it.

"Is. It. *True?*" I ask again.

His response is barely a whisper. If it wasn't so quiet in here, I wouldn't have been able to hear it. "Yes."

Flames well up inside of me. Ones that I have to release. But I can't take it out on Harrier. Not right now. I spring from my position on the floor like a wild animal and land on Maléfique's rotund chest, knocking him to the ground. He wasn't ready for it one bit, and his head smacks against the floor.

I start pounding on his face with my fists. One after another and then again. Even with all the violence I've witnessed and participated in, I've never seen anyone beaten as savagely as what I'm dishing out myself right now. It's like it's not even me—I feel like I'm watching everything happen on a TV show or in a video game. I don't even know how long it goes on for. My fists are stained with blood, and the makeup on Chef Maléfique's face is now just a black and white smear.

Through the rage and the hitting, I somehow hear it. I don't know how many times he said it before I noticed, but it barely registers in my ears. Harrier's raspy, almost inaudible voice.

"Stop."

I freeze, crouched on Chef Maléfique's chest, my right fist raised high, ready to piston down. I'm breathing heavily, and I can feel my heartbeat throbbing in my head. I look down at Maléfique's beaten, bloody face, barely clinging on to life. I watch as a drop of blood falls from my fist into the middle of his forehead and mixes with the swath of the stuff already there.

I look back at Harrier and see tears streaming down his face... the first time I've ever seen him cry.

Then Chef Maléfique spits out some teeth and talks to me, his speech distorted by his broken nose and busted lips. "Do it."

And he laughs. For the first time, I hear the bastard laugh, and it's more frightening than anything else he's done. Sick, twisted... evil.

And I suddenly realize why I'm really here. The truth about what's going on. Chef Maléfique didn't lure me down here to kill me in front of Harrier. He'd already done that before with another Red Kite, and Harrier came back stronger than ever. He wanted me to kill *him* in front of Harrier. To break me. To get me to become the one thing Harrier and I could never live with: a murderer.

And it almost worked.

I roll off of him and look at his plump, broken face as he continues to laugh. At the very least, he has a concussion, a broken nose, and a dislocated jaw. Probably a detached retina. But he'll live if we get an ambulance here soon.

I manage to get myself up and stagger over to Harrier. Pulling my lock picks out again, I unlock the chains holding him and try to help him to prevent him from dropping to the ground and injuring himself even more. I lower him to the floor, and he lies there momentarily, near unconsciousness. I need to call for an ambulance now that the building is secured. There's no way I can handle this myself at the Aerie.

Somewhere in my periphery, I notice Osprey stirring.

Then, Black Harrier does something more superhuman than anything I've ever known even Eaglestar to pull off, and pushes himself up to his hands and knees.

"You should relax, Harrier, we'll have help on the way soon." But he ignores me completely. "Frank, it's over."

Harrier starts to crawl over to Maléfique, who continues his insane fit of laughter. He reaches his nemesis and leans over him, barely able to hold himself up. If anything, Chef Maléfique is laughing even harder now, gasping for breath. Maniacal.

Harrier grabs both sides of his mortal enemy's head. "Shut. Up." He twists Chef Maléfique's head quickly, and there's a sickening crunch.

And the laughter stops.

TWENTY-SEVEN

Dad.

Not a word I'm all too familiar with, especially when it comes to addressing someone. It's too weird for me to call Harrier that. At least for now. Plus, I don't think that's what he wants anyway.

Mr. Chen—who absolutely wasn't working for Chef Maléfique, by the way—helped create a story about how Franklin Douglas III had been kidnapped and held for ransom by some Middle Eastern regime that he'd fought against in the war. It explains his condition, as well as why Frank hasn't appeared in public for so long.

At first, I didn't want to see him because I was so angry. I'd gone to the hospital, but only to visit Osprey—Amy Chen. She was in a wheelchair for a couple of weeks after the fight with Deadeye, but she was healing quickly and back on her feet in no time.

Turns out, her dad doesn't even know she's Osprey. She

begged me not to tell him, and I agreed. How could I not? I keep it from my mom.

About a year ago, she was borrowing one of her dad's computers without him knowing and came across some information on Harrier and all the tech he uses. Because she's so good with all of that, she was able to not only access a lot more, but get a hold of some of the spare stuff at Douglas Industries. When I think about how much she did on her own, plus the fact that she's been able to hide it all from someone like Chen, I'm even more impressed with her than ever.

One day, I show up to see her, and she's gone. So, already there, I figure I'll swallow my pride, and wander down the hall to the private rooms where Frank is recovering.

I don't knock. He's just staring at the wall, sitting upright in a bed that is a million steps above the one I'd been given after my battle on the bridge.

"I guess I owe you an explanation," he says without looking at me.

"You think?"

I'd planned to go easy on him at first, with how bad off he is physically and after all the psychological torture he must have endured. But you know what? He's a big boy, and he's gotta own up to this. It's time for him to give me some answers.

I start with the most important part.

"Why the hell didn't you tell me I was your son? And what about Mom? Seriously? You live in a damn Manhattan penthouse while we eat crap in a dump of an apartment in

Brooklyn? Please, try to spin it, but no matter how you slice it, Frank... it's bullshit."

I expect him to tell me to watch my language or my tone, but instead, he just says, "You're right."

I wait for him to say more, but he doesn't.

"Nope. Nu-uh. You don't get your five syllables or less answer. Not this time."

"All right." He takes a breath. "I didn't know you existed until just before I showed up in that alley. Your mom and I met when we were young. I had no idea she was still in high school. She got into a club I own with a fake I.D. I never saw her again after our one night together, and she never contacted me about being pregnant. I get the impression she wasn't sur—"

He cuts himself off, but I know what he's gonna say. She wasn't sure who the father was, because he wasn't the only guy she'd been with around that time. Knowing my mom, this isn't a surprise to me, and I'm long past it bothering me.

I'm still pissed at him for a lot, but I figure I'll let him continue. "So what changed?"

"A few years ago, I was contacted by a sleazy lawyer who claimed I had a child out there I wasn't aware of. Apparently, your mom had been dating him, and mentioned that she had, uh, been 'seeing' me shortly before you were born."

He pauses and takes a long drink from a hospital water bottle. Now that I think of it, I'm actually shocked they don't have him recuperating somewhere else. I mean, the private suite here is nice, but this is one of the richest men alive. And his next statement confirms that.

"A man of my considerable means and... reputation is always slapped with paternity suits, most of which turn out to be false. The few that aren't, I... well, I make sure they're taken care of."

I can only hope he means financially, but now isn't the time to ask him to be more specific about that.

"This guy was different. He was ready to go to the papers, the news channels, the entire internet. He didn't give a damn about me helping you or your mom; he was more interested in how much money he could squeeze out of me if he kept quiet about it. As you can imagine, I don't appreciate being blackmailed."

Derek—I vaguely remember my mom being with him for a month or so. He was a douche. Couldn't stand him. Frank hasn't even told me what happened next, and I already feel sorry for this guy. Not really...

"I'd been on a... break from crime-fighting, but it got me motivated again." I figure this must have been the time after the second Kite was killed. That would go along with what Redhawk told me.

"So, Harrier paid him a visit. It didn't take much for me to uncover several things that would not only get him disbarred but sent to prison, including jury tampering."

He smiles, and it kind of scares me because it isn't the fake Frank Douglas smile he uses in public. It's the smile Black Harrier gets on the rare occasion when he enjoys his job.

"I also maybe... roughed him up a bit. Just enough to make sure he left Frank Douglas alone, as well as anyone else he was thinking about extorting. I also found out that your mom had no idea what he was doing."

That's a relief. My mom isn't perfect, but I'd hate to think she's capable of such heinous things.

Derek... what was his last name?

I guess it doesn't matter, but I always wondered what happened to that guy. Not that my mom doesn't break up with guys often, but I do remember that relationship ending so abruptly that it puzzled her.

"Didn't it matter to you that you might actually have a kid out there?" I ask.

I notice the blip of his heart rate increasing a bit before he answers.

"Of course it did. Just because I wouldn't allow that ambulance-chaser to blackmail me doesn't mean I didn't want to make things right."

He's so vehement about this that I have no doubt he's being honest.

"I immediately started investigating the situation. You, your mom, everything I could find. My plan was to get ahold of some of your DNA and test it against my own. But I didn't need to."

"Why?"

"Because that day you were attacked while I was observing you... I saw you fight. You copied my moves exactly, and took out those thugs without much effort."

I think back to that first day we met. It's strange to hear about it from his point of view. This is also the most I've ever heard him talk at one time.

"Your ability is rare. Very few others have it, but I'm one of them. And I knew immediately you'd inherited it from me. That's why I took you on as a protégé and began training you. So you could use it properly and stay out of danger."

"But... how could you let me keep living in those crappy conditions when you knew I was your son?"

"Because I couldn't take you away from your mom, but I couldn't give her access to a lot of money either. I had Chen send a few checks from Douglas Industries at first—not much, but nothing to sneeze at, either—under the ruse that she was part of some class-action lawsuit against the company. I had to know how she would react." He takes another long drink.

"And...?"

"And she immediately blew it all on herself and her vices. From what I could tell, she didn't spend a red cent on you or make any attempt to make your life better."

The look on my face must be pretty bad, because he looks like he doesn't want to go on.

"I'm sorry, I shouldn't—"

"No." I shake my head. "I want to know the truth. All of it."

No matter how much it hurts.

"I was afraid that if she had even more money, she'd end up overdosing or drinking herself to death. So instead, I tried to help you out directly. Buying good food, electronic devices, letting you hang around the Aerie as often as possible."

So many things make more sense now, including why it seemed Alex got shafted out of things I didn't... like Amber. Shudder.

You know, I don't know what pisses me off more, the fact that he lied to me, or that I'm not even mad about it anymore.

"Well, I'm glad I know now. When will you be able to return to crimefighting?" I ask.

Just as he's about to respond, a doctor enters and starts talking about discharging Frank, finally.

"Look, Sawyer," Frank says. "I've got to handle this. Why don't you come by my place tomorrow night? We can talk more. I'll order in some *Le Meilleur Plat*."

I cringe, and he adds, "Maybe something less... French."

We both laugh.

I wave and leave Frank alone with the doctor to discuss things.

The next morning, I'm up early, hoping to leave for school before Mom can stop me. I'd been more or less avoiding her since the whole "escaping the hospital" incident. Except she's already made me a Pop-Tart and is waiting with her purse by the front door.

"Oh, hey, Mom," I say, snatch the pastry from the counter. It's still hot, and I juggle it in my hand while doing my best to skirt by her.

"Not so fast, Mister," she says.

Groan.

I hate it when she calls me that.

"I'm taking you today."

"Wait... What? Why? You don't have to do that." I push by her again, and she grabs my arm, spinning me to face her.

"Actually, I do. You've been absent for so long that Mr. Blanchard called to say I needed to sign you back in. Besides, you haven't exactly been forthcoming with me lately, and I'm going to make sure you get to class. God, that still looks really bad." She pushes her thumb against my cheek, where Sinsation kicked me. Only moms do that. Touch the place where they know you're hurt, like somehow it's helping. I wince and pull away.

"So, what—you don't trust me now?" She'd be an idiot if she did. I don't let her answer. "You know how embarrassing it is for my mom to walk me to school?"

"Oh, you want to talk about embarrassing? How about having a son who *escapes* a hospital room in the middle of the night?"

She won't let it go... keeps harping on it day in and day out. Apparently, it's time for round thirty-two.

"I told you I was sorry. It was the drugs. I was freaked out and paranoid, and I just... I don't know? Snapped."

"So you've said."

She leaves it at that, then shoves me out the door. Not hard, but enough for me to know any argument will be moot.

We walk in silence all the way to my school. When we get there, I do my best to avert my gaze from everyone pointing and grinning at the loser walking through the front doors with his mommy.

First stop, the school office. Mr. Blanchard's secretary stares at me. It takes a moment for me to realize there's something like sympathy in her eyes.

"Mr. Blanchard should be expecting us," Mom says. "I'm Ms.—"

"Vincent," the secretary says. "Yes, yes. Sawyer, you look... Are you sure you're ready to come back to school?"

I turn to my mom whose face seems to say, "Yes, you are."

"Yeah. I... it looks worse than it is."

Mr. Blanchard comes out a few seconds later and gives my mom the same look his secretary gave me. Like he's apologizing to her for having to deal with me, or something.

"Mr. Vincent, why don't you go ahead and get to class? Your mother and I will get things squared away here."

Again, I eye my mom, and she nods me along.

"Yeah. Okay." I readjust my backpack, trying to keep my face straight as my textbooks poke into my bruised ribs.

I hear them talking in hushed voices as I leave, but I'm so beyond caring what they say or think. If they only knew I'd saved the Black Harrier and stopped the city from descending into absolute mayhem...

I round a corner toward my locker and see Javi standing there. He rushes to meet me midway.

"I heard you were coming back today. What happened? Are you okay? I—"

"I'm fine," I say. "Just a few bruises still healing."

"Looks worse than that," he says.

"Looks worse than it is," I say for the second time in as many minutes.

"That's good. I... so..." He starts a few sentences but I'm distracted.

Over his shoulder, I see Logan strutting toward us. His shiner from where I'd decked him at Fabiola's party was healed up, but I wouldn't mind giving him another one.

"You know what, Javi? I think it's time for your first karate lesson."

"What? Now? Here?"

"Sup, loser?" Logan says, literally shoving Javi aside. "The hell happened to you?"

I glance at Javi and smile.

"Oh, you didn't hear?" I reply.

Logan just stares at me like a gorilla in a cage. I wouldn't be surprised if he starts scratching his ass.

"I was down in Times Square when that concert was going on, and everyone went nuts."

"That right?"

"Yeah, I don't remember much of it. Police just said I cracked. Nearly killed a guy." I get a crazy look in my eye and step so close to him, I can smell his gross breath. "Now, I'm on all kinds of meds just to keep me from doing it again."

Logan backs away. Tries to make it look like he's just shuffling his feet, but I know when someone is scared. I follow him.

"They don't even know what caused it... neither do I. One minute I'm fine and then the next, WHAM!" I crack my hands together, and he stumbles back into the lockers behind him.

After a nervous titter, he steps aside. "Yeah, well... whatever. We didn't miss you, dork."

He doesn't stick around for me to respond and definitely walks away faster than normal.

I smile again, then turn back to Javi, who looks just as terrified as Logan.

"Whoa," he whispers. "That really happen?"

I shake my head. "Not a word..." That's not entirely true. I *was* in Times Square...

"So why—"

"Lesson number one: it's better to intimidate your foe into backing out of a fight than engaging in combat. Come on." I throw my arm around Javi's shoulder. "Let's get to class."

My mom thinks I'm going to Douglas Industries for my community service, so she doesn't give me crap when I don't come home after school.

I enter the Aerie through the hatch. It's dark and cold, but that's normal.

"Kite... Sawyer, right here," Frank says. No voice box, but still only five syllables.

I cross the room and find him standing by the display cases containing the Red Kite costumes. A new one is erected next to them, and in it, the black and gray "uniform" I've become so familiar with over the years.

"What are you doing?" I ask.

"I've been through too much," he says, adjusting the cape on the invisible mannequin. "I'm getting too old. And I broke the rule we're never allowed to break."

"What are you saying?"

He turns to face me. "I'm done."

"Don't be crazy." I laugh, but it's definitely just awkwardness. "This city needs you."

He grunts. "It's time for someone else to take over as the Black Harrier."

The shock is so much, I almost feel the blow physically.

"Me?"

He shakes his head and turns back to his uniform. "You're not ready yet."

As if on cue, the swishy door that leads to the training rooms opens, and someone comes through, dressed in a new Harrier costume. He's still pulling on the gloves as he approaches us. He's not wearing a mask yet, and I recognize him immediately.

"Alex!" I run over to him, full bore, without even thinking about it. "How did you—I thought you were—"

"Hey, kid. Yeah, so did I. Glad to see you're okay."

"What happened?" I ask.

"Don't know. Not really. I'm not sure how long I was in the river, but I woke up on a fishing boat after some guys pulled me out of the water. I wasn't in as bad of shape as I should've been, but it still took me a little while to recover. Not nearly as long as this guy though, right?"

He points to Frank.

I didn't see it before, but as Frank struggles, I notice the cane he uses to limp over to Alex. "How's it fit? Chen worked hard on it."

"Great."

"Wow," I say under my breath. His new suit is badass. So much cooler than Frank's ever was.

Alex—Harrier, I guess?—turns to me. "Well? Are you going to be my sidekick or what?"

"Whoa," I say. "We don't use the 's' word around here."

He laughs and stretches his hand out. Before I shake it, I turn to Frank. He nods, and I extend my hand, but this time, Alex pulls back and looks to Frank.

"You sure you're ready to do this? No turning back?"

"You're the Black Harrier now."

"Good. Because I've made my first big decision already. I figure I'm going to need some extra help out there until I get up to your level, so I invited someone else to come along."

Osprey steps through the entrance and takes in the posh surroundings of the penthouse lair. "Nice crib."

Frank gets his old look back. "I thought I said—"

"Ah-ah-ah. I'm the Black Harrier now, and I get to choose my own sidekicks."

Osprey and I both respond at the exact same time. "*Partners.*"

"Oh. Right. Sorry."

"My dad doesn't know. I'd appreciate it if everyone would just let me tell him my own way," she tells Frank.

"You're an adult. You make your own decisions," he responds. Then, he turns to Alex. "She gets approved by the Guild before she even talks about crime-fighting. That understood? I may not be the Black Harrier anymore..."

He lets his words linger on the air.

"Yes, sir," Alex says, saluting Frank. "I'll make sure of it."

Frank grunts again.

Alex shakes his head, laughing a little as Frank turns back to the display cases.

"Well, then," he says, heading toward the door. "Let's go, *partners.*"

I follow him, and he stops.

"One more thing," he says, looking at me directly.

"Yeah?"

"I hope you don't mind... I took Amber." He smiles, and so do I, more than a little relieved if I'm being honest. "Let's go kick some ass?"

I'm definitely in the mood to beat up some bad guys.

EPILOGUE
BATTLEGEAR

Idiots.

That's what they are. Every last one of them. We had a whole team together, ready to finally take on the Guild. I had a perfect plan in place this time. It would have been big. The biggest. The greatest heist in the history of humankind.

We all could have been rich beyond our wildest dreams if they had just listened to me. But they have no self-control. The attention span of goldfish, the lot of them. That rotund chef threw a few silver coins in their direction, and they all abandoned our plan in an instant, said they'd get back to it.

"Just hold on, Battlegear, and when this is done we'll do your thing," they promised.

"Plus, we won't have Black Harrier in our way anymore. One less hero to worry about..." they surmised.

Yeah? How'd *that* work out for you, morons?

"Don't do it!" I said.

"The guy's insane. Literally!" I warned.

"There's no way this works out in our favor," I predicted.

Hey, but why listen to me? I only have one of the greatest intellects in the country. Plus a preternatural skill with technology. You think I became Eaglestar's archnemesis because I'm a pushover? Because I don't know what I'm doing?

What was it Maléfique had going for him again? Oh, yeah—he was batcrap crazy and liked to kill everything in sight, including his own henchmen and teammates. He liked to taunt heroes until they were so angry they went overboard and caused traumatic injuries to everyone they were fighting. That's beneficial! Oh, wait, I can see now why they went with him instead. It makes perfect sense, right?

They're all in prison now. Or worse. Look at the Cockroach. Bullet to the forehead—by his own employer, even! All except for Deadeye, anyway. But that guy was already a loose cannon. I think I'll pass.

You want to get rich living a life of crime? Don't work with the evil ones. Stay away from the crazy ones. Work with guys like me who are in it for the cash. Who can think straight. Who don't get off on blowing up sidekicks just because they want attention.

Oh well, back to square one. I was tired of working with those imbeciles all those years anyway. Time for some new blood. Some clay I can mold into what I need, rather than broken-down old has-beens like Creeping Death and Med-Evil.

I already have my new plan. I don't need people with powers. I'll provide the powers. I don't need pros with "experience" who are going to contradict me at every turn. All they need is a few practice heists, and we'll be ready for the big time.

And those feeble-minded fools—the ones who are still alive, anyway—can watch my new team execute our plan on the tiny television screens in their prison rec rooms and cry in their prison lunches and rock themselves to sleep in their prison bunks as they think about how it could have been them.

Now all I need is to find some young, naive people who are real lowlifes to set things in motion...

ALSO IN SERIES

SIDEKICK
SUPERTEAM
SCIONS

GET 3 BOOKS FREE!

...as a thank you for reading *Sidekick,* book one in Raptors.

We hope you enjoyed it! Please take a moment to encourage you to review the book on Amazon and Goodreads. Every review helps further the author's reach and, ultimately, helps them continue writing fantastic books like this one.

Check out the rest of our catalogue at www.aethonbooks.com.

To sign up to receive a FREE collection from some of our best authors as well as updates regarding all new releases, visit www.subscribepage.com/AethonReadersGroup.

JOIN THE STREET TEAM! Get advanced copies of all our books, plus other free stuff and help us put out hit after hit.

SEARCH ON FACEBOOK:
AETHON STREET TEAM

JAIME CASTLE HAILS FROM THE GREAT NATION OF TEXAS where he lives with his wife and two children and enjoys anything creative. A self-proclaimed comic book nerd and artist, he spends what little free time he can muster with his art tablet.

Jaime is a #1 Audible Bestseller, Audible Originals author (The Luna Missile Crisis) and co-created and coauthored The Buried Goddess Saga, which includes the IPPY award-winning Web of Eyes.

The Buried Goddess Saga (Epic Fantasy)

Web of Eyes
Winds of War
Will of Fire
Way of Gods
War of Men
Word of Truth

(Science Fiction)

The Luna Missile Crisis

Raptors (Superheroes)

SIDEKICK

SUPERTEAM

SCIONS

Baron Steele

JEFF THE GAME MASTER (LitRPG)

Manufacturing Magic
Manipulating Magic
Mastering Magic

Find out more at www.jaimecastle.com

CJ Valin is a writer and artist living in Los Angeles. His award-winning work has included novels, short stories, comic books, screenplays, and non-fiction books and articles. A life-long science fiction and comic book fan, he created the "Raptorverse" as an homage to his favorite superheroes from childhood.